GONE ROGUE SERIES

Rogue DEFENDER

PATRICIA D. EDDY

If you love steamy romantic suspense, I'd love to send you an exclusive short story set in Dublin, Ireland. Castles & Kings is ONLY available for my newsletter subscribers. Visit my website and let me know where to send your free short story! http://patriciadeddy.com.

For everyone who's done the right thing, even when it's hard. And for all of us who are "beautifully broken."

A NOTE FROM PATRICIA

Rogue Defender takes place in Panama.

Domina is Panamanian. She went to college in the United States, so she speaks English very well, but her native language is Spanish, as is the native language of her colleagues.

To be authentic to her story, much of her dialogue and all of her inner thoughts should be written in Spanish. But for ease of reading, I've used English.

Her speech is slightly more formal than Leo's, simply because English is her second language, though she is fluent in all but perhaps some of English's more *colorful* idioms.

Representation matters, and I have attempted to honor Domina and her culture in other ways: food, traditions, her love for her country, and the various locations used in this book.

The Panamanian people have a beautiful, rich history, and I hope you will enjoy learning a little about it in Rogue Defender. Thank you.

CHAPTER ONE

Leo

THE SOLE of my shoe catches on the polished tile floor. With an *oof*, I slam into the fridge. Its meager contents rattle, something inside topples over, and I curse my failing body. And the lack of carpeting in most of the apartments in Panama City.

Carefully, I open the door. An upended bottle of hot sauce drips all over the carton of eggs on the shelf below. Great. After I set it to rights, I grab a can of club soda. Cleaning up the mess can wait. I need to get off my feet.

My right leg aches with each shuffling step toward the patio. Nerve damage, deteriorating cartilage in my knee, and three missing toes don't do shit for my balance on my best day, and this is nowhere *near* one of those.

Four hours of surveillance, and all I have to show for it is a mild sunburn. I'm starting to wonder if my client's deadbeat husband might actually *be* dead. Working as a private investigator was supposed to be the easy life. Especially in Panama. The cost of living in this neighborhood is cheap enough I only need to work three or four cases a month. Assuming I can solve even *one* of them.

In the distance, the sun filters through the palm trees along Panama Bay. Five stories up, the sounds of the city fall away. If I were the kind of guy who believed in "inner peace" and all that bullshit, this would be the place I'd find it. Too bad I gave up on that dream a long time ago.

The scent of gardenias wafts up from the courtyard, and I pop the top on the can. Damn if I don't still crave something a hell of a lot stronger. But that's a dangerous road with nothing but darkness at the end of it.

My phone buzzes. I don't have to look at the screen to know who's texting me. Only one person has this number.

Trevor: How's the weather? Clear skies after the storm the other day?

Seven years retired, and the man still talks in code.

Leo: You haven't used an unencrypted mobile in a decade. Neither have I. You have something to say, just say it.

Trevor: Fine. I made some calls. The Chief of Station in Panama City is Moses Ferrier. Part Boy Scout, part pitbull. Stay on his good side. If I have to call in another favor with Pritchard, he'll never let me hear the end of it.

Leo: Give me a little credit after twenty-two years on the job. I know how to fly under the radar. How's Dani? Read her latest on the corruption in the Chilean Health Ministry. Riveting stuff.

Trevor: She's good. Thank fuck she didn't have to travel for this one.

Leo: What about you? Clear skies?

It's a loaded question—one I don't expect him to answer.

Trevor: Found a new therapist. I think he's helping. Dani's almost home. I'll check in next week.

I cough, choking on a healthy swig of soda water. The damn stuff isn't supposed to come out my nose. But the idea of Trevor Moana—who used to be one of the CIA's most lethal assassins—*voluntarily* going to therapy isn't one I was prepared for.

The man spent three days in the worst prison in the world —*La Crypta* in Venezuela—being tortured every fucking minute. When his team destroyed the facility and freed everyone the government had locked away deep underground, Trevor was a shell of the man he'd been only seventy-two hours before.

Sinking back into the chair and propping my good leg on the railing, I stare up at the faded blue sky. The club soda's almost gone, but I can't go back inside yet. Too many memories hitting me from all sides.

I stayed in the van while the rest of Hidden Agenda—a K&R firm out of Seattle—Dani, and the former head of the Joint Special Operations Command, Austin Pritchard, pulled Trevor out of that prison. But what I heard over comms brought back parts of my past I'd buried under too much rum and tequila.

And now that I'm sober, all those memories are here to stay. Trapped in the dark. Bound to a chair. Suspended from a beam. Beaten within an inch of my life.

Eight days as the Loma Collectivo's prisoner. They used every enhanced interrogation tactic in the book—and a few no one had dared write about. I didn't give them what they wanted. But I'd accepted my death. Hell, I begged for it.

They took my eye, most of the dexterity in my right hand, and left me with nerve damage so severe, half my face might as well be paralyzed. So what does it say about me that I blew through my mandatory shrink sessions and was back at work as soon as I got the medical all clear?

Something flutters in my peripheral vision. What little I have of it. The prosthetic eye *looks* real, but everything to the right of my nose is a void. Turning, I catch a pair of birds on the patio railing very *clearly* mating.

I'm about to give them some privacy when my neighbor opens her sliding glass door and steps outside. The lovebirds squawk and fly away. Her whispered, *"Dios mio,"* is followed by a soft laugh, and I stare at her through the whorls in the wrought iron divider. I haven't lived here long—only a couple of months. We've yet to meet.

The few times we've passed in the halls though...I've cataloged everything about her. Her curves. Her dark brown hair. Her full lips. It's training. Know your surroundings. Always.

At least that's what I tell myself.

Something startles her, and she tenses. Sparing me only the briefest of glances, she rushes back inside while I polish off the last of the club soda.

Muffled—but tense—words make the hair on the back of my neck prickle.

None of your business. You're a civilian, remember?

The phone call from Ferrier's office the other day—the one that had me contacting Trevor for intel—warned me the Chief of Station wasn't happy with an ex-CIA officer starting up P.I. work in his territory.

My neighbor's angry voice carries through the open patio door, but before I figure out what she's saying, the entire wall shakes.

A man with a rough, local accent says something in Spanish I can't make out, then adds, "Shut up! Or you will be sorry!"

"Let me go!" my neighbor cries.

"Quiet, bitch!" Something crashes—close to the balcony. Whoever's in her apartment made it past the front door.

Shit. Ferrier's warning be damned. She's in trouble. The soda can tumbles from my hand, landing on the small table with a hollow *plink.* Staring between her balcony and my kitchen table—where my chest harness hangs from one of the chairs—a dozen scenarios race through my mind.

Until her choked cry clears them all away and training takes over.

I lunge for the strap. Precious seconds pass as I struggle to get my right arm through the damn thing.

The sound of a fist hitting flesh sends my heart rate spiking.

Move it. Now.

Nerve pain arcs across my shoulder as the harness settles into place. I race back out to the patio. This is a bad fucking idea. But I want the element of surprise. Wrapping my hands around the railing on my neighbor's side of the divider, I grit my teeth, bracing for the pain.

I vault around the wall and land in a crouch on the concrete. Pure adrenaline and the sight in front me are the only things that keep me from collapsing in agony.

The man's at least six-three, wearing a rumpled suit, complete with wingtip shoes. But then I zero in on his hand around the woman's throat. She claws at his arm. "You're hurting me!"

"Back away, shithead," I growl and cock the hammer of my Glock. My neighbor's brown eyes widen. As the man focuses on me, she screams at the top of her lungs.

For all of a second until he squeezes her neck so hard, he cuts off her air.

"Let the lady go or you'll find out how hard it is to piss when you're missing half your dick."

"Listen, *American*," he growls as he shoves my neighbor to the ground and advances on me, "you shoot, and you'll spend the rest of your life rotting in jail."

He's not wrong. I may have a license for this gun, but that doesn't mean the National Police won't send my ass to prison and throw away the key for killing a Panamanian citizen. If the Chief of Station doesn't murder me first.

With a shrug, I holster the weapon. "Have it your way. Less blood to clean up."

The man rushes me, and I duck my shoulder to catch him in the solar plexus. But my right leg wobbles, and we fly back, landing next to a low coffee table with him on top of me. His fist connects with the side of my face. Pain sings along my jaw. The edges of my vision shimmer.

"Fuuuck," I groan.

A flash of dark hair moves behind him. I roll away just as something shatters. Dirt scatters over the polished tile floor.

"Stupid bitch!" he roars. A cactus tumbles off his back, all spindly leaves and silvery barbs. Before I can grab his legs, he throws a lamp, catching the woman in the side of the head. She crumples to the ground with a tiny moan.

This is bullshit. I'd rather take my chances with Ferrier than let this fuckwit go free. Lucky for me, nerve damage stole most of the sensation from my right hand. Tightening my fingers around the cactus stalk, I push to my feet. "Hey, asshole."

He turns, and I hit him square in the face with the plant. "My eyes!" he cries.

Dropping the cactus, I let loose with an uppercut to his chin. He staggers back, then lands on his ass.

Slamming one of my shitkickers down on his family jewels, I relish the way his face twists in pain. "You picked the wrong apartment to break into." A swift kick to the head, and he's out.

Panting, I turn in a circle, scanning the rest of the living room. Along the back of the couch, a plain, dark blue throw blanket is folded neatly. I make quick work of ripping three long strips from it, flip the guy onto his stomach, and hogtie him. He won't be going anywhere for a while.

"Wh-who...are you?" Pushing up on an elbow, my

neighbor winces. Her eyes don't quite focus on me. Shock? A concussion?

"I'm Leo. I live next door. Don't move, okay? You could be injured." I shuffle toward her, but she scrambles back.

"Stop." She blinks hard, her gaze dropping to the gun holstered under my right arm. "Is he...dead?"

"No. He'll live. Unless you'd prefer otherwise." The joke fails, miserably, if her wide eyes are any indication. "He'll be out for at least a few minutes. What's your name?" I frown, suddenly aware that she's staring at my scarred face. Does she notice that the right side of my mouth doesn't move like the left? That my right eye doesn't track her as quickly or as completely?

"Domina. Domina Sanchez." She tries to get to her feet but collapses with a muttered curse.

I'm at her side in two steps, holding out my hand. "Domina, we need to call the police. Come next door with me. I don't want you alone with him. And I should lock up my gun."

She lets me help her up, but once she's standing mostly under her own power, Domina shakes her head. "He...he broke in. My doorknob was rattling, and when I went to check on it, he snapped the chain and forced his way in. I don't think he knew I was here."

"What the hell does that have to do with anything? He *hurt* you." I still have a gentle hold on her elbow, and I can feel her shaking.

"You tied him up. I can call the police. They'll take him away. Go back to your apartment, Leo. I will keep your name out of this."

Keep my name *out of this*? "I hit him in the face with your cactus. He's going to remember that. And me."

She straightens her shoulders with a wince and steps back. "He will. But I work for Vice President Cortez. He will not want news of this in the papers with the election only a few days away. This man will go to jail, and he will do so quietly."

"The hell? He attacked you, Domina. I am *not* leaving you alone with him."

She rubs her swelling cheek. "Thank you for coming to my rescue, Leo. But you can go now."

In the distance, sirens start to blare, and the young couple from across the hall knock on Domina's open front door. "We called the cops. Is everything okay?" the man asks. He and his girlfriend are ex-pats. I met them a few weeks ago, and they're nosy as fuck.

"Everything is fine," Domina says with a wave of her hand. "Thank you. Do not worry."

The two stare at one another, then at the unconscious man on the floor. "Are you sure?" The boyfriend doesn't look convinced. Can't say I blame him.

As the young woman tugs on her partner's hand, clearly ready to bolt, he meets my gaze, and I give him a nod. "You can go back inside. Ms. Sanchez is okay, and the guy's restrained."

The couple rushes back across the hall, slams the door, and flips the locks.

Domina lets out a sigh, then rubs her shoulder. "The police will be here in minutes, Leo. I can handle this."

My instincts demand I stay. Stand over the asshole until he's in cuffs. But Domina limps to the couch and rummages in her briefcase. When she pulls out a can of pepper spray, I give up.

"Fine. If the police need a statement, you know where I'll be."

She brushes past me, a whiff of orange blossoms almost intoxicating. As she leans against the back of the couch, a small smile plays over her lips. "You can use the door this time. If you want."

"Probably smart." My nerves are on fire. A thousand daggers pierce my leg from ankle to hip. With each step, I have to stifle a grunt of pain. "Put some ice on that bruise and lock the door behind me."

I can't read the look she gives me, and I trudge back to my apartment, unsure how I ended up feeling like *more* of an intruder than the guy who attacked her.

CHAPTER TWO

Domina

MY DOOR CLICKS SHUT, and I'm alone with the man who—only moments ago—had his hand around my throat.

I can barely move. Pressing against the back of the couch, I stare down at him. My hand shakes, my fingers clutching the pepper spray so hard, they ache.

The sirens blare louder. Thank God the police are almost here. Every swallow hurts. The terror of being unable to breathe tightens my chest. But I will be fine. Everything is under control.

Still, I pray he doesn't wake up.

He was so angry when he saw me through the gap in the door. The security chain snapped like it was made of cheap plastic.

"You weren't supposed to be here."

The look in his eyes...it was the same one Papa would get when I refused to bring him another beer. Or when he would hit Mama.

With a shudder, I pull myself from the memory. "Focus, Domina. Distractions are dangerous."

I'd been distracted when I'd heard the doorknob rattling. All I'd wanted was a brief respite from my work. Five minutes out on the patio in the fresh air. The presidential election is only a week away, and Vice President Cortez has his final rally on Thursday. I need to finish writing his speech.

Shit. My notes. They are still scattered all over the couch.

Backing away from the intruder, I sweep my legal pad and wad of Post-its into my briefcase and fasten the buckle.

Once I tuck the leather bag next to the couch, I blow out a breath. Cortez would not be happy if he found out I let *anyone* see the speech ahead of time.

The man lying against the wall stirs, a weak grunt escaping his lips. The sound increases my panic by a thousand. I take aim with the pepper spray, but his eyelids only flutter for a moment.

Just as I get myself under control, the faint sounds of a football match trickle through the wall. From Leo's apartment.

"You know where I'll be..."

Maybe I shouldn't have kicked him out. He *did* leap onto my balcony like some sort of grizzled action hero. But my attacker is still mostly unconscious, tied up, and has a face full of cactus needles. I will be fine.

I let out a huff. Why did his voice have to be so deep that I cannot get it out of my head? The first time we passed in the halls, I noticed him. The silver in his chestnut hair. The neatly trimmed beard. The studs in his ears. And his limp. A recent injury? Or an old one?

"He is not thinking about you. Stop thinking about him," I mutter.

If only I could. He put himself in danger for me. And I thanked him by telling him to leave.

You did the right thing. You do not need a man to solve all your problems. You can handle this on your own.

But my cheek aches more and more with each breath, and I brush my fingers over the tender skin.

"Put some ice on that bruise."

Even after I was rude to him, he still tried to help me. And he was right. I need to stop the swelling or I won't be able to sleep tonight.

Do I dare turn my back on the man tied up on the floor long enough to get an ice pack from my freezer? I don't have much choice. But only two steps toward the kitchen, someone knocks. "Police! Open the door!"

Thank God. The officers will take this man away, and my life will go back to normal.

TWO HOURS LATER, the ice pack cradled to my cheek, I trudge out onto the balcony. The officers just left, and I am not ready to be inside—alone—just yet. It's peaceful out here, only a light hum of traffic from the causeway competing with the nightly birdsong.

The day started so well—a calm Sunday with nothing to do but work on Manuel's speech—and I want to forget everything that happened once the man broke down my door. If not for the bruises around my throat, my swollen cheek, and my aching shoulder, maybe I could.

"Shit!" the man growls.

My head aches where it hit the wall. Dark brown eyes bore into me. He's angry. Why?

"Let go of me!"

His free hand fists my hair, and I yelp. Fear wraps icy chains around me, and I can't breathe.

"Domina?"

I drop the ice pack and spin toward the voice. My memories recede into the background, the intruder banished by the shock of realizing I am not alone. With my fingers curled around one of the wrought iron whorls of the divider, I peer over at Leo, sitting in a chair only a few feet away. "¡Ayala vida! How long have you been out here?"

He pushes to his feet with a groan, then shuffles over to the wall separating us. "Since I left your apartment. You never shut your sliding glass door. I had to know if the police took care of everything."

"You listened in?" A part of me wants to tell him how rude that was, but there's something sweet about the gesture. Protective. Kind.

"Wait...I heard the football match. You did not watch?"

He shrugs his left shoulder and rubs his jaw. Is it swollen? In the semi-darkness, I cannot tell.

"Got a bowl of chips and can of soda on the coffee table. In case anyone came knocking. But no. I didn't watch."

I brace a hand on the railing, steadying myself as I retrieve the ice pack. "In case anyone came knocking?"

"I don't know why you said you'd 'keep my name out of this,' but I figured if the National Police wanted to talk to me, probably best they not find me eavesdropping on a member of the vice president's inner circle."

I snap my jaw shut. The police *would* have arrested him for that. "Mierda. I am sorry, Leo. I did not think..."

"It's okay. No one came. I couldn't hear much, but it didn't sound like they gave you any trouble. Did they?"

I shake my head, then regret the motion. The balcony spins around me. Grabbing the railing, I pray I don't pass out.

"Domina!" Leo's warm hand covers mine. "Slow, deep breaths."

I let him hold on—or maybe I will him to—until I feel

steady, then turn to meet his gaze. He's reaching around the partition at an awkward angle, and lines of pain tighten around his lips.

"I'm okay."

"The hell you are. You need a doctor. You lost consciousness. But I can see it in your eyes. You're not going. No matter what I say."

Despite his words, his voice is so gentle—and deep—that when he lets go, I feel the loss.

"Will you at least take my phone number?" he asks. "So you can text me if you feel sick in the middle of the night?"

"But if I lock my door, you will not be able to leap onto the patio and rescue me." My smile eases a small measure of my worry, but Leo's gaze is deadly serious.

"If you're in trouble, a locked door won't stop me."

The gravel to his voice—and his intense stare—tell me he is *very* confident in his ability to save me again if I need it. "Who *are* you? Rambo?"

His rough chuckle shouldn't be this sexy. And I *definitely* should not be leaning my back against the railing so I can get a better look at him. Or so he can get a better look at me.

"If you tell me you forgot my name already, I'm really going to be worried," he says. Then, one corner of his mouth lifts into a half smile. "Or insulted."

"Of course not! Your name is Mike. Or...Juan? No, wait. Brian." We both laugh, and I feel lighter than I have in days, despite my pounding head. "I have to know, *Leo*...where did you learn to fight? Or swing onto balconies?"

His shoulders hunch, and he turns to stare out over the courtyard. In the distance, lights from the seaside promenade twinkle like diamonds in the moonlight.

"Not easy to explain."

"Try?"

I touch the ice pack to my cheek and swallow a pained whimper. My eye is swollen half shut. My entire body aches. My neck, my shoulder, my back. All bruised so badly, I worry how terrible I will feel tomorrow. I need a hot bath, another handful of aspirin, and a full night's sleep. If only I could stop replaying the attack over and over again in my mind.

Leo pushes off the railing with a heavy sigh. "Domina, given where you work, anything I tell you puts me at risk."

"United States government, then." Shock plays over the left side of his face. The right doesn't move the same way, and I study his lopsided frown. "NSA? CIA?"

"Shit. No." Bracing his hand on the wrought iron between us, he meets my gaze through the intricate design. "I'm retired. Can we leave it at that?"

There's something in his tone, but I'm too tired and sore to figure out what it is. "You came to my rescue tonight, Leo. Even if Manuel—the Vice President—or the National Police asked me about you, I would keep your secret."

Resting my own palm against the divider, I thrill at the little zing as our fingers touch. The contact is...almost intimate. I should *not* be attracted to him. Relationships are dangerous. Just like distractions.

He nods. "Thanks." A spasm jerks his arm, and he takes a step back. "Been a long day." Swiping his phone from the table, he says, "Give me your number."

I rattle off the eight digits, and a moment later, my mobile vibrates in my pocket.

"And now you have mine. Don't be afraid to use it."

What am I supposed to say to him? Thank you? Have a good night? See you later? Or...nothing at all as he's already limping back into his apartment. When he shuts the door, I feel more alone than ever.

My phone's clock taunts me. I climbed into bed—after that handful of aspirin—but within ten minutes, I thought I heard someone rattling the doorknob, and I panicked.

Sitting in the living room is worse. Too many memories. I clean up the dirt and the remnants of the cactus pot, but a smear of my attacker's blood stains the tile, and I have no bleach.

A bath will help. But while the hot water soothes my aching muscles, my thoughts race. Even with the door locked, I jump at every sound.

By the time I slip back into bed, midnight approaches like an unwelcome guest, and I am no closer to sleep.

Picking up the phone, I intend to find a silly game to occupy my time until exhaustion claims me, but then I see the message.

Leo: Heard the vacuum. I'm an expert in sleepless nights. If you need anything, text me.

My cheek throbs, and I rub my swollen eye. "That was a mistake," I mutter to the darkened room, lit only by the glow from the screen. I should apologize for waking him. Or turn off my phone completely.

But instead of pressing the power button, I read Leo's message again. And again.

Domina: He broke the door chain.

My fingers tremble, and I hit *Send* by accident. The message disappears with a quiet *whoosh*. Shit. I sound like a helpless damsel in distress.

Do not stare at the phone. Turn it off. You vacuumed almost an hour ago. He must be asleep by now.

Yet somehow, I know he's not. Or if he is, he kept his mobile on. In under a minute, the device vibrates in my hand.

Leo: Wedge a chair under the knob. If you have anything that makes noise—bells or wind chimes—hang them from the chair. If they wake you, call me immediately.

Domina: Bells? Why would I have bells?

Leo: Because you love Christmas? Don't tell me you hate Christmas.

I laugh, then sink back against the pillows. He may be gruff, but then he says things like this, and I wonder if I have been wrong all these years. Keeping everyone at arm's length, only allowing a few people in my life to see the real me.

Perhaps getting to know Leo—as a friend—would not be so terrible.

Domina: I do not hate Christmas. I have a whole box of ornaments in my closet.

Leo: The last time I celebrated Christmas was ten years ago. You decorate? Get a tree?

Domina: An artificial tree, yes. But in Panama, we also paint our homes in early December. I will go to the store for the paint in a few weeks.

Leo: What color?

I had not given any thought to the color. Or to how this will be one more Christmas I spend with my friend Mina and her family. Watching them celebrate. Nursing a single glass of sparkling water all evening while her mom, aunt, *and* grandmother serve the tamales, fruitcake, and arroz con pollo. Being welcomed like I belong, though I know I do not.

Domina: Nothing special. White or beige. The landlord would not like it if I painted my walls orange.

Leo: Orange? Really?

With a huff, I shuffle out to the main room so I can wedge a chair under the front doorknob. Once I finish, I scroll through the photos on my phone until I find the right one. A picture I took of my apartment in San Miguelito more than ten years ago. The bedroom walls were a stunning shade of apricot, and they made me so happy every time I came home.

Domina: Do not mock my orange walls, Mr. Sleepless Nights. I loved them.

Leo: They're beautiful, and I'm sorry. How are you feeling?

He asked me that earlier, and I snapped at him. Told him I was fine when I knew I was not. What if the man who attacked me was searching for more than just an empty apartment to rob? What if he has friends?

Leo: Domina? Talk to me.

After another minute—maybe two—the phone rings.

Incoming video call.

My brain short-circuits. Growly, overly protective men do not call me in the middle of the night to find out if I'm okay.

The words flash across the screen three more times before I get the courage to answer.

"What are you—?" My words fall away when I get my first good look at him. Leo slumps against his headboard with a dark blue sheet pulled up to his chest. His right shoulder is mostly hidden, but the left? He holds the phone in such a way I can see the corded muscles all the way down to his elbow.

"Domina? I need an answer."

Shit. I did not even think about what *I* was wearing. A brief glance confirms my tank top covers everything it should, and I clear my throat. "You do not need to worry about me."

"The hell I don't. Your eye is swollen shut. Is it bleeding at all? Does it hurt? Any trouble breathing through your nose?"

The rapid-fire questions should annoy me—being *handled* is not something I allow. But at the moment, I am still too shocked I answered the call and let a man I have only just met see me in my bed at 1:00 a.m.

"I am not bleeding, and I can breathe. My cheek hurts, but I would be surprised if it did not." Settling back against the pillows, I focus on Leo's concerned expression. "I thought you were...*retired*. Not a doctor."

He blows out a breath and shifts his hold on the phone. Now, I can only see his face, and up close, his eyes are two subtly different colors. "We get basic medical training. How to check for a concussion, broken bones, signs of serious internal injuries. I should have insisted you call the paramedics."

I roll my eyes, though I probably look foolish since only one is open. "I am a grown woman, Leo. I do not need a man *insisting* I do anything."

"I noticed," he says, his voice even deeper than usual. Goosebumps race down my arms, and some of my irritation dissolves into longing. No one has thought to be protective of me for many years. I may not *need* his concern, but a small part of me cherishes it.

"I should go. Good night, Leo." I lower the phone to end the call but stop when he swears softly.

"Domina, I'm sorry if I overstepped. I'm not good with... people." He runs a hand through his hair and sinks lower in his bed. One corner of his mouth curves into a smile. "This isn't usually how I end up in a woman's bedroom."

I laugh, despite the storm of emotions churning in my belly. "No? What do you 'usually' do? Find a date on Love-Panama? Tinder?" I prop the phone against my bedside lamp and turn onto my side.

"Guys like me don't..." He shakes his head as his cheeks flush. "No one's going to swipe right on my profile."

"Why not?" Exhaustion barrels toward me, threatening to pull me under, but I have to know why this man who is so obviously handsome—and funny—thinks no one would want to date him. A single moment stretches between us, then snaps as all emotion drains from his eyes.

"Get some sleep, Domina. You put the chair under the doorknob?"

Drawing the blankets tighter around me, I nod. "I did. Good night, Leo—" He ends the call, and as I stare at the darkened screen, I suddenly feel utterly and completely alone.

CHAPTER THREE

Leo

THE BACKHANDED SLAP SENDS SHARP, stabbing pain through my ruined eye socket. "Wake up, cabrón."

"Like you shitheads would let me fall asleep," I manage. How long has it been? Four days? Five? Hell, for all I know, I've been here less than thirty-six hours, but it feels like a month. Bright lights, music—if you can call it that—blaring at ear-splitting volume, and the various stress positions haven't given me a moment's rest since they found me at Bar Rosario and shot me up with God-knows-what.

The metal chair I'm bound to jumps on the concrete floor as Asshole #1 kicks me in the chest.

With my right eye mostly gone and my left swollen half shut, I didn't see it coming. My diaphragm seizes. I strain against the wire binding my wrists to the arms of the chair.

Blood and fluid trickle down my cheek. Tears? Whatever the shit is—or was—inside my eye? Who the hell knows.

"Names! All those you work with in Venezuela, Colombia, and

Ecuador! Now!" A punch snaps my head back. The shock lets me draw in a wheezing breath.

"Fuck. You."

The sound of the switchblade makes me flinch. The last time Asshole #1 waved it in front of my face, he sliced through my eyeball. The sharp edge presses to my cheek. I grit my teeth—damn painful with what I think is a fractured jaw—and prepare for the worst.

Until Asshole #2 grabs Asshole #1's arm. "If he loses much more blood, he will be no good to us. Put the knife away. I have a better idea."

I jerk awake, the memory of a lead pipe shattering my temporal bone as fresh now as it was nine years ago.

Cursing as my right lid sticks to my prosthetic eye, I reach for the lubricating drops I keep next to the bed. After I smooth a bit over the acrylic, I can blink again.

The late night didn't do me any favors. Neither did the asshole who broke into Domina's apartment. My jaw aches, and when I push myself up to sitting, my right leg is nothing but pins and needles.

Great.

I ease myself onto the floor and reach for my therapy balls and trigger point rollers. It takes me half an hour of painful exercises and targeted pressure all along my back, my ass, and my legs for most of the sensation to return.

By the time I shuffle into the kitchen to start coffee, it's after nine, and I wanted to get to the El Chorrillo neighborhood well before noon in case the piece-of-shit I was hired to track down shows up at his mistress's apartment to take her to lunch.

After I pour myself a cup of wake-the-hell-up from the French Press, I scroll through the text messages I shared with Domina last night. I can't get a read on her. Vulnerable one moment, defiant the next.

The phone rings, and the number on screen sours my stomach. There's no name. No information at all from the cellular carrier. But I memorized it the day I arrived in Panama City and hoped to God I'd never have cause to see it again.

The CIA's Chief of Station.

AN HOUR LATER, I follow a low-level CIA officer through the halls of the United States Embassy in Panama City. "Right this way, *Mr.* Basher," the man says.

The subtle dig at my civilian status should annoy me, but I'm more concerned with the time I'm losing to work my case than petty shade thrown by a guy fresh off The Farm.

After two raps on an unmarked door, I'm ushered inside without a word.

Moses Ferrier—six-foot-two with more salt than pepper left in his closely cropped hair—braces his hands on his desk and stares me down. "You've been here for two months. Two goddamn months, and you never thought to check in? With anyone?"

"I'm retired."

"Retired is puttering around a house on the beach, fixing up an old boat or a classic car. Not bribing the Commerce Minister to get your P.I. license and gun permit fast tracked!"

With how the veins in his neck bulge, Ferrier has a serious blood pressure problem. Shoving my right hand into my pocket, I shift on my feet, trying to relieve some of the pressure on my rebuilt ankle.

With a shrug, I drop my gaze so he doesn't see my lopsided grin. "I didn't bribe anyone. I made a generous donation to the police union and asked nicely if there was anything that could be done to speed up the process. I track down cheating husbands, deadbeat dads, and the occasional embezzling accountant. Nothing you need to concern yourself with."

Ferrier's dark brown eyes narrow. "And what about the man you half-blinded *last night* in your own fucking apartment building?"

Shit.

"I will keep your name out of this."

So much for Domina's word. And for that asshole going to jail quietly. Why didn't I ask her what she did for the Vice President? For all I know, she's nothing but a secretary. Or his Chief of Staff.

"Are you listening to me, Basher?" Ferrier demands. "This is fucking serious."

"Yes, sir. But it's not. I defended one of my neighbors from an intruder. Nothing more."

Moses glares at me. "Your *neighbor* is the head speech writer for Vice President Cortez. You just put a target the size of the Pacific Ocean on your back."

Well, shit.

"One phone call, and you're on a plane to the States. Two, and I can get your fucking passport revoked. You step one toe out of line, and you're gone."

I narrow my gaze at him, straightening my shoulders so he has to look up at me. Ferrier's a good four inches shorter than my six-foot-six frame. "Which toe would that be, *sir*? Because three of mine never left Venezuela. Along with my right eye, a handful of bone fragments, and my spleen."

Ferrier sputters what might be an apology, but I've stopped listening.

"I did what any halfway decent spook—or person— would have done and I'd do it again. I'm not the CIA's lap dog, Ferrier. Not anymore. After twenty-two years, I'm finally free. Stay out of my way and I'll stay out of yours."

Slamming the door behind me, I lurch through the halls until I'm back out in the sunshine. My hands shake, and nerve pain snakes down my right leg.

"Tell us what we need to know, cabrón."

The memories swirl around me like a tornado. My captors' voices. The god-awful music they blasted nonstop. My own screams.

And what I did to each and every one of them just three months ago.

All I wanted was to spend the rest of my fucked-up life in a country where no one actively wanted to kill me. And Ferrier could put an end to that dream.

Time to put another call into Trevor and pray he can convince someone—*anyone*—to listen.

Domina

The morning briefing starts promptly at 9:00 a.m., and I slip into the room at the last minute. Despite my exhaustion, I only slept four hours. My alarm went off at six so I could transcribe my notes and *try* to finish the draft of Manuel's speech. I only finalized one page.

Even with all the makeup tricks my mother taught me, it still took me much too long to cover the bruises on my cheek and neck. My eyelid is still puffy, and the small bandage over the cut on my temple is only partially covered by my hair.

Manuel's campaign manager, Rafael Perez, leans against a podium at the front of the room. His eyes meet mine, then widen, disapproval furrowing his brow.

I was attacked. Not out partying until all hours. Jerk.

Rafael sweeps his gaze over the eight other men and women gathered with cups of coffee and pastries from the communal kitchen. "On Thursday, Cortez is giving the most important speech of this election. We are ahead in the polls, but Muñoz is stepping up his attack ads, and our win is not guaranteed. If we do not find a way to convince an additional five percent of the population that Manuel is the right choice for President, we may still lose, and all our hard work will be for nothing. Domina, do you have copies of the revised speech for everyone?"

Almost as one, the other members of Cortez's staff turn toward me. My assistant, Larissa, mouths, "*What happened?*"

The whispers set my cheeks aflame as I fumble for my tablet. "I do. But the last page still needs work." With a few taps to the screen, I send it to the rest of the team.

"You gave me your word the speech would be done first thing this morning," Rafael says with a frown.

Pushing to my feet, I do not bother to hide my wince. "Last night, a man broke into my apartment and attacked me. So please forgive me if I could not work after that. I will finish the last page by the end of the day."

With his shoulders hunched, Rafael mutters an apology and gestures to the podium. "Please read us what you have so far."

Most days, I would be happy to recite my words in front of my colleagues. But today, looking like someone's punching bag, I would rather chew broken glass.

Tucking my tablet under my arm, I make my way to the front of the room. After a moment to compose myself, I take a deep breath and begin.

"Panama stands at a precipice. The divide between the rich and the poor is growing every day. Our children learn from outdated books with missing pages and broken spines. Many have only a single meal each day or work for hours before and after school to help feed their families. We have failed them. We. Must. Do. Better."

The pain of last night's attack fades with every word. While I carefully crafted each sentence down to the dramatic pauses and emphasis Manuel will give them, it is *his* platform. His passion. His beliefs. When I move on to the lack of potable water outside the major cities, even Rafael looks impressed.

"And this is why there has never been a more important time for the people of Panama to come together and vote. Vote for hope. Vote for change. Vote for Manuel Cortez for President!"

The room is so quiet, I can hear my heartbeat in my ears. But a moment later, Larissa, Tomas, and Rafael applaud, Isobel whistles loudly, and even Omar Modelo, Cortez's chief of staff, inclines his head in approval.

"Do not change anything, Domina." Rafael claps his hand on my shoulder as I try to return to my seat. His palm hits one of my many bruises from last night, and I grit my teeth against the pain. "Excellent work. Send that to Cortez as soon as we finish the briefing."

"Thank you," I manage, ducking out from under his heavy hand. "But I must proofread the speech several more times. There was a spelling mistake on the second page, and at least two sentences on the final page need to be changed. They do not flow well."

"It sounded perfect to me," Omar says from the doorway. "You honor us with your talent, Domina. You're an asset to this campaign."

My cheeks flame, though my bronzed skin hides the worst of my embarrassment. "Thank you, Omar. But most of the credit belongs to Manuel. My words are only as good as his platform."

Larissa shoots me a look. If we were alone, she would tell me to take the compliment. That I earned it. Maybe I have.

I fought for this job when Cortez first ran for vice president five years ago. With each speech, I proved myself. I let Rafael nitpick every sentence. Demand tiny, insignificant changes so he could feel important. Or make me feel small.

But then, something changed. The newspapers started quoting Cortez's speeches—my speeches—in their articles. Cortez and José Garcia, Panama's current president, went from ten points behind to fifteen points ahead in under a month.

Now, everyone is counting on me to give them another miracle.

LARISSA FOLLOWS me back to my office, so close on my heels, if I stop short, she'll slam right into me.

"Tell me everything," she says when she shuts the door behind her. "Is that why you bailed on drinks with the rest of the staff?"

Sinking down into my chair, I rub my sore shoulder. "No. I wanted to come, but the speech still needed work. Around six, I took a break out on my balcony, and I heard something."

I tell her *most* of the story, minimizing Leo's part in saving me—and what I now know about him. But Larissa has worked with me for three years, and in all that time, I have *never* said more than two words about a man.

If she knew I answered his video call at 1:00 a.m.—from my bed—I would never hear the end of it.

"Did the police find out what he wanted?" she asks.

I shake my head, thankful the aspirin did its job. "He refused to say a word to them."

Larissa rests her elbows on my desk, her eyes wide. "Do they know who he is?"

"He had no identification. Unless his fingerprints are on record..." My stomach flips as I hear his words in my head.

"*You were not supposed to be here.*"

You. Not *no one. You.*

Did he know who I was?

"Domina? Are you all right?"

I jerk, and my travel mug rattles on my desk. "I'm tired. It was hard to sleep last night."

"You *stayed* at your apartment?" Shock plays over her heart-shaped face. "Honey, you should have gone to a hotel."

The police told me the same thing. But leaving my home? That felt wrong.

"Leo was next door. He gave me his number."

"His...*number?* You *like* him!" Larissa's voice rises half an octave. "I need to know everything. Right now."

I cannot tell her the truth. Leo would never forgive me. Larissa may be a friend, but she is not one to keep secrets. And Mina is traveling—three continents in four days—and I will not be able to talk to her until tomorrow.

"Leo checked on me after the police left. But there is nothing between us. We are neighbors. That's all."

If only I believed my own words.

CHAPTER FOUR

Leo

"WHAT PART of *'stay on Ferrier's good side'* was confusing?" Trevor asks. "Because I just got off the phone with your former SSO, and you're exactly one parking ticket away from being shipped back to the States, permanently."

"None of it. I'd *planned* to watch Panama beat Sweden on the pitch." My shoulders feel like two solid pieces of granite, and a tight band holds my head in a vise. "You think I should have let my neighbor get beaten up? Or worse? You would have done the same damn thing." Tearing the wrapper of a protein bar with my teeth, I sink down onto my couch. Traffic was a bitch getting back from the Embassy, and after barely sleeping, my body is one—or a thousand—raw nerves.

Trevor sighs. "Probably. Though I would have used the door. *And* found a way to keep my name out of the National Police's records."

"I didn't just hand over my driver's license, passport, and top secret work history. Give me a little credit, will you?

Domina said she'd take care of it. That no one would know my name. I believed her. Clearly, I was an idiot."

"Domina. Not 'my neighbor.' Just how well do you know this woman, anyway?"

"Met her last night." The protein bar tastes like shit, and I choke down the last bite before balling up the wrapper.

"Got a last name? I'll have Wren do a background check." Trev's all business now, but there's still an edge to his voice. One that tells me he thinks I fucked up. Big time.

"Not necessary. She's a neighbor. Nothing more."

Except she works for Vice President Cortez. And knows what I used to do for a living.

"Leo, if the Panamanian government finds out you worked for the CIA, you could be in deep shit. After the coup, things got a hell of a lot better between the United States and Panama, but we'll always be one fuck-up away from relations breaking down again."

Slumping back against the cushions, I close my eyes. Once, Trevor trusted me with his life. But then I spent the better part of a decade at the bottom of a bottle whenever I wasn't *actively* on assignment. I drowned that trust in rum, and I deserve to be treated like a first-year probie.

"Even at my sloppiest, Trev, I never broke cover. Leo Basher has a clean arrest record, an average-Joe work history with the Department of the Interior, and legal firearms and P.I. licenses for the country of Panama." After a beat, I add, "And is eleven months sober."

He doesn't say anything for a long moment. "Eleven months. That means you stopped drinking in..."

"January. Yeah. The night you and Dani showed up at my house? I'd poured my last bottle down the drain an hour before." I ball my left hand into a fist, so tight my fingernails dig into my palm. "Wasn't sure it was going to stick, but when you ended up in La Crypta, I promised God, the Universe, and whoever the fuck else would listen I'd never touch the stuff again if we could just get you out."

"Fuck me."

Warning bells go off in my head. That was too much information. Trevor doesn't open up. Hell, neither do I. Usually. We've both been through hell and didn't come back...whole. We have secrets the other will never know, despite once being almost as close as brothers.

"I didn't give it up for you, Trev. I did that for me. But when I get low, I remind myself of that promise. Someone up there looked out for you, so maybe they're looking out for me too."

AFTER THREE HOURS scrolling through security camera footage from a bodega at the edge of the El Chorrillo neighborhood, I reach for my eye drops. A series of pops all along my spine reminds me I was a fool for sitting in one position this long.

What was I thinking? Being a P.I. seemed like the logical career choice after the CIA. The best way to use my skills and not be in mortal danger on the regular. I wasn't counting on the endless hours at the computer or the constant surveillance that has me on my feet on my worst days.

Back in Venezuela, I spent most of my time going from coffee shop to bar to public market. Watching. Listening. Drinking when I could. As one of the few officers in country and the *only* one not stationed at the Embassy, I had it easy.

Now, though I don't have to work every day, when I do, it's hell on my aging body.

After I can blink easily again, I turn my gaze to the patio doors. The clouds rolled in a few hours ago, and sheets of rain fall at a steep angle, the wind howling all around the building.

A bright flash illuminates the room, followed by thunder so loud, it rattles the windows. Shit. I rush to unplug my laptop as the lights flicker.

That's my cue to give up for the night. Thank fuck I charged the battery pack for my tablet. If the storm is as bad as the news predicted, I won't have power much longer.

Lighting squat, long-burning candles in every room, I grab a can of club soda and yesterday's leftover pizza from the fridge. A blip in the constant hum of the air conditioning is almost immediately followed by another clap of thunder.

And someone knocking.

I shuffle over and check the peephole. All the anger and frustration from this morning come flooding back, despite how miserable Domina looks. If Ferrier had wanted, he could have sent me directly to the airport and back to the States. All because I tried to be a good guy.

I flip all three locks and open the door. "Something I can do for you? Make it quick. My former employer almost had me deported this morning. Figure whatever you need next should get me hauled off to jail within a couple of hours."

"What are you talking about?" Domina steps back, shock playing over her features. I take a second look at her. Her hair is drenched, and some of her makeup has washed away, revealing the dark purple bruise under her eye.

"You said you'd 'keep my name out of it.' Clearly, you didn't."

Domina straightens her shoulders, the fire returning to her eyes. "I did not lie to you, Leo. I told the police you knocked the man out, but that once you tied him up, I told you to leave. They did not ask for your name, and I did not offer it."

My anger fades slightly. I listened in as best I could the

previous night, and her story tracks. I step back and jerk my thumb into the room.

She blows out a breath and hikes her briefcase strap higher on her shoulder. "If you think I betrayed you, I am not coming in."

"Domina, get inside. This isn't a conversation we're having in the hallway." I soften my voice and slouch a little, trying to seem less threatening.

Before she makes up her mind, all the lights in the building go out.

Across the threshold, Domina flinches and darts a glance up and down the pitch-dark hallway. Apparently, this building doesn't have emergency lighting. Or it's not working. In the subtle glow from the candles in my living room, she's scared—terrified even.

"Domina? I'm sorry I was an ass just now. Come on in. You're soaking wet. Sit down. I'll get a towel for your hair, and we can talk. I promise you're not in any danger from me."

She holds my gaze for a long moment until someone in another apartment curses loudly in Spanish, then steps quickly over the threshold. "Only for a few minutes. So we can resolve this."

"Suit yourself." I flip the locks and turn to find Domina watching me.

"You do not have a chain," she says quietly.

I gesture to the couch and duck into the hall to grab a thick, dark blue bath towel from the linen closet. "Chains don't do shit. Even a hundred-pound kid can break a chain if he hits the door just right."

Domina's lips part, then she presses them together in a thin line. Shit. That was the wrong thing to say.

Handing her the towel, I move to the kitchen. The power might be out, but my USB mug warmer plugs into my tablet's battery pack. "Can I make you some tea? I don't have much. Chamomile or...shit. Chamomile."

"There is no power," she says simply, her brows furrowing as she squeezes sections of her hair in the towel.

I show her the little USB plug and the battery, then set a mug of water on top of it. "It'll take five minutes. If you want a better lock than the cheap-ass deadbolt the landlord installed, I'll get you one tomorrow and install it for you. Along with a motion alarm."

"I thought you did not trust me. Why would you do this?" Domina tugs her red blazer closed over her *very* wet white blouse.

I shrug, though my right shoulder doesn't rise as high as the left. "I didn't say that." Shoving my hands into my pockets, I stare at her from across the room. The candlelight casts flickering shadows over her face, and shit. She's so damn beautiful. Even with the bruises and obvious exhaustion. "The CIA's Chief of Station called me in this morning and reamed my ass for pulling a gun on a Panamanian citizen."

"How did he find out? I swear to you, Leo. I said nothing to the police." Domina rummages through her briefcase and pulls out a brown paper bag tied with a red ribbon. "If I had given them your name, would I have brought you Huevos de Leche from the bakery by my office?" She offers me a weak smile and shakes the bag gently.

The confections made from milk, sugar, and cinnamon are a local delicacy—one I rarely allow myself.

"You have Huevos de Leche?" I limp back to the couch and ease the bag from her outstretched hand. The ribbon falls to the floor, and inside, a dozen confections—each wrapped in a piece of colorful paper—bring a lopsided smile to my face.

"This bakery makes the best ones in Panama City. I thought...it was the least I could do." Domina swipes at her face with the towel, and more of her makeup disappears. "Whoever told your 'Chief of Station' you were involved did not hear it from me."

"I believe you." I shuffle back to the kitchen, pour the Huevos de Leche into a bowl, and add a chamomile tea bag to the heated mug. "Maybe that asshole was conscious when we were talking. Or he told the National Police how I jumped onto the balcony and they pulled my rental agreement."

With a shrug, I bring the bowl over to the couch and set it on the side table. "I'll call the Chief of Station again in the morning and see if I can get more information. Hopefully he won't tear me a new one or have me arrested."

"Oh, God. Could he really?" She pushes to her feet, reaches for my arm, and curls her fingers around my right wrist. Right over the scars from days spent bound with wire and ropes.

I jerk away before I can stop myself, and Domina gasps.

"Sorry. It's been a long time since anyone...touched me." After a beat, I add, "I've got cold pizza. A couple of protein bars. And all those Huevos de Leche. What can I get you besides tea?"

Domina stares down at my wrist peeking out from the pocket of my cargo pants. The scarring is mostly hidden, but she felt it. She knows it's there.

"I should not impose on you. Perhaps...if you have a flashlight, you could come next door and check that my apartment is...empty?" The hope tinging her tone does something to my heart I don't understand—or like. I want to take care of her— though I don't think she's a woman who lets anyone do that.

"I can't eat all six slices of pizza myself, and I'm sure as shit not going to open the fridge again until the power's back on. You can hang out here for a while, and if Premier Power doesn't have an update in two hours, I'll walk you next door and clear the apartment for you."

What the hell are you doing? Letting someone you don't know "hang out"? Someone who works for the Panamanian government? You're going to have to talk. Get to know one another. You're just asking to be deported.

Despite knowing this is a bad idea of epic proportions, there's something about Domina that calls to me. In rare moments, she's vulnerable in a way it's obvious she hates. Then, the next, she's all business. Totally capable, unable of letting *anyone* come to her aid.

I want—no, I *need*—to figure her out, and this might be my only chance to do it.

Handing her the mug of tea, I wait for her to take a tentative sip.

"All right. I will help you finish your pizza. As long as you share at least one of the Huevos de Leche with me." Her smile does what no candle ever could. Lights up the room like the sun. So much so, I'm surprised a clap of thunder doesn't immediately follow.

Shit.

This woman is trouble—according to my former employer—and I don't give a fuck. I want to get to know her anyway.

I hope to all that's holy, I'm not making the biggest mistake of my life.

CHAPTER FIVE

Domina

I SHOULD NOT BE HERE. But Leo has candles burning, and the apartment is lit by a warm, flickering glow as the storm rages outside.

If I leave, I will be alone, and while I do have candles—they are a must for October and November—I do not have a way to make hot tea. Or anyone to talk to.

He hands me a plate of pizza and a napkin, then nods at the couch. "I'll be right there. Unless you want to eat at the table."

"I do not even *have* a table. Only the breakfast bar," I admit with a small smile.

"You don't...entertain? Have guys—people—over?" He turns away to retrieve his own plate and mutters, "Shit. Way to be rude, Leo."

My cheeks flush hot, and I stare down at the cold slices of pepperoni and pineapple pizza. "I do not date."

He eases himself down on the other end of the couch with a wince. As far from me as possible. "At all?"

I take a quick bite of pizza to give myself a moment to decide how to answer him. It's surprisingly good. "I never thought I would enjoy pineapple on pizza," I say with a little chuckle.

"It's gotta be done right. Palermo's is the only place I trust. They use fresh pineapple, a jalapeño glaze, and thick-cut, spicy ham." After he settles back against the cushions, he casts a glance in my direction. "You didn't answer my question."

Even in the low light, the intensity in his eyes unnerves me. "I work more than ten hours a day. When the vice president calls—even if it is in the middle of the night—I answer. That does not make for a strong relationship. Or...any relationship. It's easier to be alone."

"Domina—"

I shake my head. "If you are about to tell me that is no way to live, keep your opinion to yourself."

"Whoa. I wasn't." Leo holds up his hand. Dressed in short sleeves and a pair of cargo pants, he doesn't bother to hide the scars along his arms. Or the very thick ones around his wrists. The candlelight makes them stand out even more than they did last night. On video. In his bedroom. "I was *going* to say that the right person understands when your job is important to you, and they don't ask you to change."

"Oh." I return my focus to the pizza. "Then clearly I have not met the right person." After a deep breath, I add, "Nor am I looking. It is easier to be alone."

The lie escapes before I think it through. Is it *easier* to sit in a stranger's apartment in the middle of a storm because I am too afraid to go home?

Yes. Because relationships are supposed to be equal. But they never are.

Leo and I eat in silence for several minutes, each of us

studying the other with furtive glances. "You're left-handed?" I ask. His right is balled into a fist, braced against the plate.

Little lines tighten around his eyes, and he shakes his head. "Not by choice."

"What does that mean?" Lightning illuminates the entire living room, so bright it's like a sunny day for a few seconds. The thunder follows quickly, and we both jump. Leo stares out the window into the darkness. With the power out, it's nothing but an abyss beyond these walls.

"Means I have almost no sensation in my right hand." He uncurls his fingers. Half a dozen red welts cover his palm.

"Oh, Leo. What happened?" Setting the plate aside, I take his hand in mine. The contact seems to surprise him. He tenses for a moment, closes his eyes, and blows out a breath before meeting my gaze.

"Your cactus is a dangerous weapon. Should probably license it with the National Police."

"Dios mio. Do they hurt?" Gently, I stroke my fingers over the wounds. His skin is a study in opposites. Calloused, yet still soft in places, and as I reach his wrist, I find smooth, almost shiny scar tissue obscuring the small veins there.

"Can't even feel them." He pulls his hand back, his entire body stiff. "I heal quick. They'll be gone in a few days."

"I should have asked last night." Shame has me staring at the polished marble floor, at my black pumps dotted with flecks of dirt from splashing through puddles to get to the bakery. "You risked your life for me, and I did not think you might have been hurt. I am sorry."

"Don't," he says sharply. "You had your own shit to deal with. I'm the one who grabbed the cactus. I knew what I was doing. And getting my bell rung? That's nothing."

With a frown, I peer over at him. "Getting your bell rung? What does that mean?"

His left eyebrow arches. "Taking a punch to the head. Jaw, in my case." He rubs his chin gently. "That asshole had some power behind his cross. At least my beard hides the bruising."

I touch my swollen cheek, then immediately drop my hand. "Why is it called that? 'Getting your bell rung'?"

Leo shifts on the couch so he's facing me, his back against the arm, and one of his legs bent at an angle. "Get hit hard enough, your ears ring. Like you're standing inside the bell tower of one of the churches in Old Town."

"You have been hit that hard before?"

He holds my gaze, and with the candles casting flickering shadows over his face, he looks so dark and dangerous. "More times than I can count."

I don't know why this surprises me. But my knowledge of what spies *really* do is limited to a few non-fiction books and action movies.

"Leo—"

Pushing to his feet, he takes a couple of uneven steps and grabs my plate from the end table. "You want another slice?"

"No. I..." He's already in the kitchen. I join him, mug in hand. The space is so small, we're almost shoulder to shoulder—or we would be if Leo were not at least eight inches taller than I am. "I did not mean to pry."

He spins around, but he's off balance and slams into the counter. "Shit."

I grab his hips to steady him, and his obliques tense under my fingers. Every inch of him is hard, strong, and...safe.

He slides an arm around my waist, pulling me even closer. "Domina..." His voice is deeper than usual, and despite the heat building between us, I shiver. "My right knee and ankle had to be completely rebuilt."

"Mierda. Why?" As soon as I ask, I know he does not want to tell me.

With a tiny shake of his head, he meets my gaze. Or, tries to. But only his left eye focuses on me. The right…is off somehow. "You see it now?" he asks.

The vulnerability in his voice shocks me. This is not the confident, protective man who saved me last night. This man is hurting.

"Your pupils are different sizes. That happens with head injuries. From last night? Do you need a doctor?"

He smiles—lopsided as usual—then taps on his right eyeball. "It's fake." I gasp and jerk against Leo's hold. His grin fades immediately, and he steps back with a muttered swear. "Shit. Sorry. I'm being an idiot. You didn't need to see that. Get your things. I'll walk you home."

Oh, God. He thinks I'm disgusted by him.

Pulling a flashlight from one of his kitchen drawers, he gestures to the front door. "Don't forget your bag. And take the Huevos de Leche. I don't want them."

"Leo, stop." With one hand on my hip, I block the narrow opening between the kitchen and the living room. "Before you lost your eye, if someone had done what you just did, would it have taken you by surprise?"

His mouth opens, but he must rethink what he was about to say, because he closes it again and nods.

"What happened…is that why your smile is crooked too?" I take a step closer. Then another and another, until we're almost back to our original positions.

"Yup." After a breath, he adds, "Not a story you want to hear."

I cock my head. "And how do you know that?"

Leo stares down at me, a look of vague disbelief on his face. "Because you're a good person, Domina. And good people don't enjoy hearing stories like mine."

"What does that mean? We met yesterday. You have no idea what kind of person I am." Glaring up at him, I notice it's not only his mouth. The whole right side of his face from his cheekbone down is affected.

"I'm *trained* to know. You're..." he reaches up and skims a knuckle along my jaw, "sad, lonely, and you've seen too much in your life. But you *are* good. And you don't need to carry my burdens next to your own."

Letting out a huff, I take a step back. Whatever shred of hope he carried in his eyes fades, and I reach for his hand. He's still touching me, his fingers cupping my face in a way that makes me feel...cherished. "Come sit. Please," I say, my words scraping and spilling over the lump in my throat.

Despite the frown curving one side of his mouth, he lets me lead him back to the couch, only this time, when he tries to flee to the far end, I take a seat right next to him.

We face one another, positions mirrored, bent legs touching at the knees. "You were not wrong about me." I fiddle with a button on my blouse, needing something to distract me. "Five years ago, the first man I had dated in a very long time left my bed in the middle of the night with only a text message saying 'this was fun.' He refused to answer any of my calls after that."

"He was an ass," Leo says. "But that's not why you're sad, is it?"

I shake my head. "My life has not been...easy. I fought for everything I have. I put myself through college in the United States because my papa spent all our money on beer and rum." Rubbing my hands up and down my arms, I try to banish the memories somewhere they will not hurt me. "We lived in a two-bedroom shack with a leaky roof and walls so thin, winds like these would have knocked them down. Mama had three different jobs for as long as I can remember. She left at sunrise and did not get home until after ten every night. I took care of the cooking, cleaning, grocery shopping...everything a young girl should not need to do. And when I sat down to do my homework—usually after midnight—I had to listen to Papa beat Mama because she refused to buy him more beer."

"Domina, I'm—"

"If you say you are sorry, this conversation is over. I do not need sympathy. Or pity. It was hard. I wish Papa had gotten help. I wish Mama had been home at night. Or had been able to take me to school every day. I wish I could have had a *normal* childhood. Or any at all. But I did not. So yes. I am all those things you said. Sad. Lonely. And more. Now that you know why, maybe you will realize I can handle whatever it is you tell me."

The storm raging outside is nothing compared to the tempest swirling in his gaze. A muscle in his jaw tenses, and he swallows hard. "It's...classified. The details. But I was taken by a terrorist group and held for eight days." His voice cracks, roughens. "They wanted information about other people I worked with, and I wouldn't give it to them."

"They tortured you."

He nods. "One of my buddies got me out. If he'd waited another day...they would have killed me." Scrubbing a hand over his jaw, he whispers, "I wish they had."

My heart breaks for the man across from me. The pain etched on his face, in his voice, in every muscle...I have only seen its equal once before. In my Papa's eyes when I told him I was leaving the country for college. He begged and pleaded, promised to stop drinking, but even *he* knew it was a vow he could not keep.

Scooting closer, I drape my fingers over Leo's wrist. He tenses at the contact, then blows out a breath. "Sorry," he says. "Not used to anyone...wanting to touch me." I start to pull away, but he covers my hand with his own. "Don't."

"Don't what?"

It's not pain in his eyes now. It's need.

"Don't go."

CHAPTER SIX

Domina

THE STORM RAGES OUTSIDE, though thunder no longer shakes the walls. Leo's admission hangs in the air, his hand still tight on mine. Without power, it's warm in his apartment—or maybe the heat is coming from whatever is growing between us—and I remove my blazer and fold it over the arm of the couch.

"How long does it usually take Premier Power to get the lights back on?" Leo asks, reaching for my hand once more.

I tighten my fingers on his and lean against the cushions, angling my head closer to him. "You have not lived here long, have you? In Panama?"

"I left Venezuela eight months ago. Went to Colombia for a few weeks. Then Brazil. But they didn't feel right. I've been here since mid-September."

"We have very reliable electricity. But today has been strange. We lost power at my office a few minutes after four, and they sent everyone home. The winds were still weak, and the rain had just started. But the bakery two blocks away was unaffected." I elbow him gently. "Lucky for you since they sell the Huevos de Leche."

He releases my hand and reaches for the bowl of sweets. The loss of his touch affects me more than I want to admit. How long has it been since anyone touched me like this? Four? Five years?

"Lucky for both of us," Leo says with a lopsided smile. "The rental agent left me six of these—along with a bottle of sparkling wine—when I moved in. Took me a full week to find out where she got the damn things."

I focus on peeling the blue and green wrapper from one of the round balls. "I have heard they pair wonderfully with champagne. Is it true?" I remove the last of the paper and stare at the confection. The entire night has been simple. Cold pizza, conversation, and now, one perfect bite of deliciousness. But I would not change a thing. "I do not drink. Not after seeing what it did to Papa."

Leo stares at me, his expression going blank in the space of a heartbeat. And then he takes a ragged breath and lurches to his feet, dropping his still-wrapped candy back into the bowl. All color drains from his ruddy cheeks, and he stumbles over to the patio doors to rest his head on the glass.

"Leo? Is something wrong?" Coming up behind him, I touch his shoulder, and he jerks. "Talk to me."

"I have to tell you something," he says, his voice gruffer than usual. "But...I'm afraid you're going to hate me once I do."

"Hate you? Why would I—?"

"I'm an alcoholic. In recovery. Eleven months sober."

I take a step back, my hand falling away. "You used to be—"

He whirls around and meets my gaze, but it costs him, weariness evident in every muscle, every movement. "A drunk,

Domina. To a point. You get too close to the bottom of the bottle in my former line of work, you die. Or you get your friends killed." After a hard swallow, he hangs his head. "I never blacked out. Never lost control. But that's no excuse. I still drank to quiet my demons, and it almost cost me everything."

Leo *is* sober. I know what drunk looks like. Even when someone—like my papa—is very good at hiding it, there are signs. But how many times did Papa say all the right things? Promise to quit? Even give up his beer for all of a day? Or two?

Whatever this is between us—friendship...or something more—can I really start *anything* with a man who carries this burden? Even if he has made it eleven months, would I ever truly be able to trust him?

"I am sorry, Leo," I say quietly. "I should go."

"Wait. Let me explain. Please." The desperate edge to his voice should not affect me so. Or stop me from leaving. But I don't move, and he balls his hands into fists at his sides. "One of the only men I trust in this world—the guy who pulled my dying ass out of that hell hole in Venezuela—had some trouble last year. Before that, I was getting pretty damn low. Twenty-two years in the field, alone, dealing with the worst of humanity..."

"You said 'before.' What about after?" I ask.

"He and his girl had to get out of the country quick. When they called, I was at home, staring at my last bottle of rum, trying to decide if I should drink it or dump it. I poured it out the minute I hung up the phone. Haven't had a drink since."

Tears threaten, and I blink them back. He says all the right things, and his eyes hold a lifetime of pain. But also truth. And an unwavering belief in his own words.

"What did you do with the wine?" I ask.

"The wine?" His brows furrow, and he shakes his head. "What wine?"

"From your real estate agent."

Leo relaxes slightly. "I left it down by the mailboxes with a 'gratis' sign on it." He shoves his hands into his pockets, holding my gaze. "Most days, I don't miss drinking. I *thought* it made my fucked-up memories easier to deal with. But all it did was make me hate myself even more."

I can see the truth in his one good eye. The burden he carries with him. I wish I could tell him I understand. That I could accept this part of him and not constantly wonder if—when—he'll slip. Or how far he'll fall.

"I have to go," I manage. "I cannot stay...here. Not..."

"Domina, please." He doesn't move. Doesn't take a step toward me or reach for my hand. But the desperation etched on his face stops me from fleeing back to the uncertainty of my lonely apartment.

"What do you expect me to say?" The first tear trails down my cheek, and I swipe at it, angry he put me in this position, angry I didn't have a *normal* childhood, angry I had to hide from my friends, my teachers, from everyone. But most of all, angry I have to walk away from him.

"I don't know." He staggers back until he hits the wall, then half slides, half falls to the floor and stares up at me. "I can't promise you I'll never have another drink. Anyone does that, they're a fool. But for the first time in eleven months, I'm not sober because it's the right thing to do. I'm sober because I don't want anything in my life that's not one hundred percent *real*."

"Is that what this is? Something real? There can be nothing *real* with a man I cannot trust!" The truth breaks me. Shatters my heart into a million tiny pieces. It shouldn't hurt this much. We only met yesterday. We are barely friends, but already I had started to want more.

"I have a code," Leo says quietly. "From the job. Just because I'm *retired* doesn't mean all that training goes out the window. Twenty-two years, and the only lies I told were because of the mission." His shoulders slump. "Or to myself. When I thought a glass of rum—or two or three—would quiet the nightmares. But I know the truth now. Nothing does."

The way he looks at me...I want to stay. But if I do, he could break my heart, and that is a chance I cannot take. I grab my briefcase and slip into the hall, leaving Leo still sitting on the floor, staring after me.

Leo

The door clicks shut with a finality that makes me regret everything. My entire life. My career. My decision—and declaration—that I didn't want anything that wasn't *real*.

Reality is overrated.

We only just met. Hell, it's barely been twenty-four hours. But I feel something when I'm with Domina. Felt, anyway, as I'm sure she's never coming back.

Spies make shitty romantic partners. Always have, always will. When you can't tell the truth about what you do—or who you are—it's damn near impossible to get close to anyone.

And after Trevor pulled me out of that warehouse on the edge of Caracas, I didn't even bother to try. Who'd want me? With my scars, my face, my eye? They drive most people away. Great when you're a covert CIA officer who needs people to largely ignore him. One hard look, usually followed by a horrified or disgusted expression, and anyone around me turns away.

But Domina *saw* me. Didn't even bolt when I jabbed myself in my prosthetic eye. And I went and fucked it all up.

Better now than later.

That single thought is my only solace. If I'd kissed her—and I wanted to—if we'd continued down this path from neighbors to...something more, and she'd found out in a month? I'm not sure either one of us would have come out the other side.

It takes me forever to get to my feet. My knee locks up, my ankle sends stabbing pains through my toes—even the three that aren't there anymore—and I spend a solid minute wondering why I should even bother.

Until the lights come back on.

The air conditioning hums, its cool breeze wafting over me, and I stare at the couch where we passed one of the best hours of my life. No fancy dinner, no perfect words. Just two people sharing stories in candlelit ease.

Shit. Domina's blazer is folded on the arm of the sofa. In her rush to get the hell away from me, she forgot to grab it. My limp is worse than it's been in years as I cross the room, each step something close to agony—though maybe the pain is more than just physical.

Lifting the jacket, I catch a whiff of sweet orchid and citrus. With the material pressed to my nose, I inhale deeply. We crashed and burned before we could even begin, but I take the time to memorize everything about her I can remember. Her light, sweet scent. Her laugh. Her smile. The way her hand felt on mine. The softness of her skin. The warmth in her eyes.

"Enough. This has to be enough."

It isn't. Not by a thousand miles. But it's all I'll ever have. Carefully, I refold the jacket and slide it into a paper bag. Grabbing a notepad and a pen, I tear off a piece of paper.

Domina, you left this. I'm sorry. For everything. If you ever need me, I'm here. No strings. No expectations. Just a friend who can wield a cactus with the best of them. -Leo

The hall is quiet, and I set the bag in front of her door.

Running my fingers over the apartment number, I whisper, "Be safe, baby." It's all I can do. Except turn on the television and hope I'll find some old movie to distract me from the pain.

CHAPTER SEVEN

Domina

SOMETHING CRUNCHES under my foot as I leave my apartment. A brown paper bag. Neatly folded. With something soft inside.

My blazer. And a note.

Tears burn my eyes.

"Just a friend who can wield a cactus with the best of them."

A friend. Could we truly be friends? Something more than neighbors? I spent most of last night tossing and turning, panicking at every sound—despite attaching a string of bells to the chair I shoved under my door.

My phone buzzes, and I check the screen.

Rafael: Cortez called a meeting. Be here by 8:00 a.m.

Of course. The one day I sleep past six, the vice president arrives at the office early. I hope the car service is waiting downstairs. Most of the staff don't drive themselves to and from the office. Not with the hours we work. Manuel pays for a car and driver for each of us. One more reason we are all devoted to him.

I pass by Leo's door. Is he awake? Is he all right? The way I left him was wrong. Until his admission, I thought there was a chance we might one day be...close. I had even wondered what it would be like to kiss him. Now...I know that can never happen.

But perhaps...friendship is not impossible. Not totally out of the question. Another alert dings on my phone, and I rush to the elevator. My driver is waiting, and with morning traffic, I will be lucky to make it to the office by 8:00 a.m.

WHEN I ARRIVE—ONLY three minutes late—Omar is rushing to the main conference room. Coffee splashes over the rim of his mug, and he swears under his breath before he sees me. "Domina, hurry. Manuel is about to begin."

I cast one last, lingering look at the coffee machine before following Omar. The energy in the office is *wrong* somehow. This close to the election, it should be tense, but still full of anticipation. Of promise. Not the uncertainty I feel in the air today.

Manuel sits at the head of the table, back straight, completely in control. Except for his eyes. The brown depths hold an exhaustion I have rarely seen in him.

I drop my briefcase and take a seat next to Larissa. Before I can apologize for being late, he clears his throat.

"Yesterday afternoon, the Institutional Protection Service alerted me to a security breach at El Palacio de las Garzas. President Garcia and I were both elsewhere at the time. Someone attempted to pilot an amphibious drone under the Cinta Costera causeway and onto the property. The device was destroyed, but the Presidential Palace was on lockdown for three hours."

"Who was behind the breach?" Rafael asks.

Cortez shakes his head. "We do not know. I tell you only so you are aware. We may need to address this in the next few days. Domina, there will be a full briefing sent to your email within the hour so you can craft our message."

"I will prepare several statements for you, Manuel. Is President Garcia holding a news conference today?" I pull out my notebook and pen.

"No. Until the election, we have more important priorities. But as much as we might wish to keep events like this quiet, the press often does not allow it." Manuel runs a hand through his white hair with a sigh. "I will be at El Palacio de las Garzas for the rest of the day. Tomorrow, we will finish preparing for the rally." He pushes to his feet and forces a smile. "Thank you for being here so early this morning and for all your hard work this past year. A few more days, and we can celebrate."

One by one, the rest of the staff follow him from the room, and I sink back in my chair. Several public statements —in addition to polishing his speech for Thursday's rally— all on less than five hours of sleep. If I expect to accomplish anything today, I need a very strong cup of coffee.

———

A FEW MINUTES AFTER ONE, I shut my office door. The National Police officers who arrested the man at my apartment the other night left me a voicemail, and I have not had a moment to call them back until now.

"How can I help you?" Detective Ortiz says when he answers the phone.

"This is Domina Sanchez. You left me a message this morning?"

"Ms. Sanchez, of course." The detective's voice wavers, almost hesitant, and anxiety forms a tight knot in the center of my chest. "The man who broke into your apartment Sunday night is no longer in custody."

I lose my breath for almost a minute until the detective asks if I'm all right.

"Why was he released?" I ask, my voice only slightly above a whisper.

A heavy sigh carries over the line. "Ms. Sanchez, I cannot answer that."

"Why not?" I shove back from my desk, needing to pace. "He assaulted me!"

"You misunderstand," Detective Ortiz says quickly. "I do not know why he was released. When I came in this morning, he was gone."

"Did he escape?" I am so confused—and scared that the man will come after me again. Or Leo. Shit. I need to let him know what happened.

"No. I questioned him several times yesterday and was able to learn his name—Daniel Pinzon—but he refused to tell me why he chose your apartment. We provided medical care for his eyes, though his injuries were not serious. The doctor believed he would suffer no long-term damage to his sight."

I don't care about the man's eyes. I was safe and now I am not. "What are you doing to find him?" I am not proud of the panic in my voice, with Manuel's news this morning put me on edge, and I cannot handle anything more.

"I sent his name and photo to all our officers. We will find him, Ms. Sanchez. And when I figure out who released him, they will be dismissed from the force. I am sorry I do not have more information for you, but I will keep in touch."

He hangs up before I can say another word, and I sink back into my chair.

Why did Leo have to tell me about his drinking? Before

he said a word, I thought perhaps we could have something real. Right now, I need real. I need to not be alone.

"If you're in trouble, a locked door won't stop me."

After what I did to him last night, would he still come to my aid? My heart says yes, but my head is not so certain.

A LITTLE AFTER 3:00 p.m., I take a can of Coke from the refrigerator and trudge out to the courtyard. Protected by high walls, it is one of the few places I can go in the middle of the day and feel completely at peace.

Sinking onto one of the benches under a giant palm tree, I close my eyes. Several times today, I thought about sending Leo a message. He needs to know Daniel Pinzon is no longer in custody. But is that really news one delivers by text?

I should leave early. Tell him in person.

"Foolish, Domina. You do not even know if he is home."

I never asked what he does with his days. Does he have a job? Or is he simply...*retired* from everything?

The soda tickles the back of my throat, and a gentle breeze wafts over me. I love this place. This small oasis in the middle of chaos.

A voice comes from the far corner of the courtyard. Almost too faint to hear. Until the conversation takes an angry turn.

"He is an idiot!" Tomas says. He stalks out from behind one of the bushes. "If he cannot do the job, we will find someone else."

I leave my can of Coke on the bench and duck around the palm tree, hoping I can make it back inside without him seeing me. Whatever Tomas is mad about, he thinks he is alone, and I should give him privacy.

"I don't have that information." A loud bang startles me,

and I peer around the tree trunk. One of the small trash bins lies on its side, and Tomas reaches down to brush off his shoe, pain twisting his expression. "I tried to—" After a brief pause, his shoulders slump. "I'm sorry. I will find another way."

He jabs the phone screen and shoves the device back into his pocket. I hold my breath as he turns on his heel and heads back into the building.

I wish we knew each other well enough for me to ask him if he's all right, but Tomas has only worked for the campaign for three months, and he keeps to himself. He likes coffee, though. Tomorrow, I will stop at the local roasters for a large bag of Gesha beans. We could all use something special this close to the election.

Leo

I drop the bag from the hardware store on the small kitchen table. The best deadbolt they had, a swing latch to replace Domina's broken chain, and the components I need to build her a motion alarm. It won't be as state-of-the-art as mine, but it *will* be loud enough I'll hear it should anyone try to break in.

"Stupid," I mutter as I pull a can of soda water from the fridge. "What makes you think she'll even answer the door? She made it pretty damn clear last night she wanted nothing to do with you."

I haven't been able to get her out of my head all day. The way she looked when she left. The hurt in her eyes. Dammit. Why do I even care? I'm better off alone. Always have been, always will be.

I doubt Domina will be home for another hour or two, so

I set up my tablet and check out the surveillance cameras I set up outside Marisol Ruiz's apartment this morning. They're hidden well enough I don't expect them to be stolen until at least tomorrow—not even in one of the worst neighborhoods in Panama City.

The wireless transmitters weren't cheap, and I hope to hell I can get them back. But if they help me find my client's ex, I'll earn enough to pay my rent for a good six months.

Maybe I should go to Taboga Island when this case is done. Or Bocas del Toro. Hell, even Casco Viejo. Anywhere Domina isn't. Clear my head. Find a woman who doesn't care what I look like to take the edge off.

As soon as the thought enters my head, I know I'll never go through with it. Any of it. Casual sex was never for me. Even when I was young and relatively good looking. Though you spend enough time on assignment, and you scratch the itch at least a time or two.

My vision blurs, and I rub my good eye. The surveillance footage plays at double speed, but I find only half a dozen drug deals, two muggings, and some light vandalism.

I save a few clips and feed them to a low-level officer with the National Police. I didn't lie to Ferrier. I didn't bribe anyone to fast-track my P.I. and gun licenses. But I *do* send an extra fifty bucks to the guy every couple of weeks to look the other way when I need to do something *less* than legal. Like install a wiretap on Marisol's phone line.

I should really call Trevor and see if he can hook me up with his firm's facial recognition software. Second Sight is the premiere security and protection firm in the United States, and their hacker extraordinaire can do things with a computer that shouldn't be possible.

My stomach growls, and I push to my feet with a groan. I've been sitting for too long. There's a tamale place on the corner, and I need to do something besides stare at a screen and these four white walls.

A whiff of Domina's sweet scent hits me as I limp past the couch. Damnit. Was it really only last night we were so close, we almost kissed?

Cursing under my breath, I grab my keys and head for an order of tamales to fill the hole inside me.

WITH A BOX of fried yucca tucked under my arm, I call out, "Hold the elevator."

A delicate hand stops the doors from closing, and suddenly, I'm face to face with Domina.

"Leo," she says softly.

Stopping two steps from the elevator, I hold her gaze. "I can wait. If you want me to."

Shock plays over her features, her lips forming a small *o* before she shakes her head. "Of course not."

I shouldn't notice how her cream-colored blouse drapes over her breasts. Or stand close enough to her, I can smell her perfume—something light and floral. "Thanks. I bought some better locks. If you want me to install them, I can. Or I can give them to the landlord."

The elevator dings as it reaches the fifth floor, and I brace my hand against the door until she exits.

"You did not have to do that." We walk side by side down the hall, and I'm surprised she doesn't try to put as much distance between us as she can.

"The standard ones don't do shit. I'll need a few days to assemble the motion sensor, but the deadbolt and security latch I can put in any time."

At our respective doors, Domina stops, her key in her

hand. "You could come over now. There is...something we should discuss."

"Are you okay?" She sounds so unsure of herself, so very unlike the woman who walked out on me last night—or the one who kicked me out the night before.

"Fine." Straightening her shoulders—which only serves to highlight her curves—she slides her key into the lock. "But I spoke to the police today, and..." With a quick glance down the hall, she shakes her head. "Come over whenever you are ready."

"Give me five minutes."

I can't open my door—or dig out my toolbox—fast enough. The way we left things, I was sure she never wanted to see me again. And while I know we'll never be more than friends, I'll take whatever I can get.

She answers less than a minute after I ring the bell, still wearing her black skirt and silk blouse. She kicked off her heels next to the couch, and her briefcase dangles from one of the tall chairs at the breakfast bar.

"Can I get you something?" she asks. "I have lemonade, tamarind soda, and tea."

"I'm good. But can I use one of those chairs? I can't kneel for long periods." As soon as the words leave my mouth, I curse under my breath. I feel like half a man needing to sit down to install a couple of locks.

"I have a desk chair. Would that be better?" she asks.

I nod, and she disappears into the bedroom. A moment late—are those...bells?—Domina drags a chair down the hall, a string of bells attached to the back.

"You got them." I grin as I take the chair from her. Domina's cheeks turn dark red, making her even more beautiful. "Did they make you feel safer?"

"A little. Thank you, Leo." She's so formal with me now.

Like we're strangers. But those few words still make up for needing the damn chair in the first place.

Sinking down with a sigh, I start unscrewing the flimsy deadbolt. "So, what did you want to talk to me about?"

Domina sits at the counter, turning her cell phone over and over in her hands. "I spoke to Detective Ortiz this afternoon. The man who broke in..." Her voice trembles, but she swallows hard. "His name is Daniel Pinzon. He refused to talk to them—or answer any questions."

The old deadbolt tumbles into my hand, and I drop it into the bag at my feet. "Not surprising. He was a grade-A asshole."

Popping the clamshell package for the best deadbolt on the market, I fumble for the screws. One of them slips through my fingers and skitters across the floor.

"There is more." Domina slides off the chair and retrieves the errant screw. When she drops it into my hand, her fingers brush my palm. A little zing of electricity passes between us.

Shit. How can I be "just friends" with her? Her words finally sink in, and I peer up at her. "Domina? What else did the police say?"

"Daniel Pinzon is no longer in custody," she says, and I drop the strike plate back into the bag.

"What?"

By the time she fills me in on the incompetence of the National Police, I'm seething. And more determined than ever to give her the best security money can buy.

Get a hold of yourself, asshole. She doesn't need you to scare the shit out of her because you can't control your anger.

The last screw goes in, and I test the new locks, giving myself a minute to calm down before I turn back to her and force a smile.

"I'll make some calls. See if I can find out anything more about the guy. But he'd be fucking stupid to come back here."

"Do you think so? Or are you telling me what you think I need to hear?" she asks.

From her tone, the question has more than one meaning, and I take a step closer, holding her gaze for a long moment. "I will never lie to you, Domina. I know what it feels like to have someone betray you. I can be an ass on my best day, but on my worst, I still wouldn't lie to anyone I...considered a friend."

"And you think we are friends?"

My training—knowing how to read people—has failed me exactly twice in my life. The first time, it cost me my eye. The second, it almost cost Trevor everything. If I'm wrong now, I could lose the first good thing to come into my life in years.

I blow out a breath, heft my toolbox, and pass her the new keys. "You're all set, Domina. Keep the latch in place whenever you're home, and until I get the motion sensor put together, keep using the chair under the knob."

"Thank you, Leo. For doing this after..." The sadness in her tone is like a knife to my heart.

"I meant what I said." Stepping over the threshold, I lift my gaze to hers. "You need a friend who can hit one out of the park with a cactus, you know where I'll be."

For a brief moment, I hold onto the hope that she'll say something—anything. But then the door closes softly, and I'm alone in the hall, wondering if Domina will ever speak to me again.

CHAPTER EIGHT

Leo

THERE ISN'T enough coffee in the world this morning. After I left Domina's, I stretched out on the couch with *Casino Royale* playing on my small flatscreen. But with her scent all around me—and those damn Huevos de Leche candies still in the bowl on the end table, my thoughts kept wandering. Back to *her*.

We were doomed from the start. I can't change my past any more than I can change hers. She'll never fully trust me, and I sure as shit won't ask her to. Not when she's so clearly been hurt before.

It's barely 8:00 a.m., and I sling my backpack over my shoulder and step into the hall. Is she already at work? Did she feel safer last night with the new locks?

Stop. You don't have the right to wonder anything about her.

Who am I kidding? Something about Domina has settled deep in my soul, and I'm afraid I'll never get her out of my head—or my heart.

My body aches, several nights in a row of shitty sleep not

doing me any favors. But a jolt of caffeine will help. I amble down the street to a little family-owned pastry shop and order a cup of coffee along with a half-dozen orejita—little pastries that are supposed to look like ears. But turn them on their sides, and they resemble hearts. Not sure why I never noticed that until today.

This was a terrible idea.

Señora Marquez brings the coffee over to my table and smiles down at me. "You look tired, Leo."

Tired is an understatement. "I didn't sleep well." I offer her a shrug. "But I'll be fine once the caffeine hits. How are you?"

With a cluck of her tongue, the woman pats my shoulder. "I am well. You are not." She nods at the steaming mug and plate of orejita. "No charge."

I protest, but she's having none of it. She and her husband open at dawn and close sometime in the afternoon—whenever they feel like it. She's never failed to remember my name or how I like my coffee. As strong as it comes with a single packet of sugar.

"Necesitas una novia," she murmurs as she heads back to the counter for her next customer.

There are days I think Señora Marquez is the most obser-vant person I've ever met. But she's wrong. I don't *need* a girl-friend. Certainly never wanted one. Not with my damage. But for an hour while the storm raged the other night, I thought Domina and I might be heading there.

My coffee is almost gone when another regular stops by on his way to some office job. The man—Sylvio, I think—and Señora Marquez chat about the weather, his kids, her grand-children...a little bit of everything. I should stop listening, but after twenty-two years on the job, eavesdropping is second nature.

"Did you hear?" Sylvio asks in hushed, rapid-fire Spanish.

"About the men who broke into Vice President Cortez's campaign offices this morning?"

My entire body tenses, and I reach for my phone. Domina said she worked ten hours a day. What if she was there? What if she's hurt?

Leo: Please tell me you weren't at the office when the break-in happened.

Señora Marquez makes the sign of the cross. "God was watching. The news said the building was still empty."

My right hand shakes, and I drop my gaze. My scars stand out dramatically against my white knuckles, and when I release my tight fist, small dots of crimson stain my fingers. Shit. I couldn't feel the puncture wounds tear open.

Domina's apartment. Then her office. Three days apart? Even at my worst, I wouldn't let that coincidence slide.

"Cortez is speaking in an hour," Sylvio says. "I wonder if the police know who's responsible? Do you think it was Muñoz?"

I give up all pretense of minding my own business and bring my empty mug up to the counter. "Has Cortez had problems like this before?" I ask.

Sylvio narrows his gaze at me. "Who are you?"

Señora Marquez starts to introduce us, but I hold up my hand. "I'm sorry, but this is important. Has anyone vandalized his offices before?"

They start talking over one another, the words blending together until my head starts to spin. Cortez's politics, Muñoz's dirty campaign ads, the rumored corruption in the last two presidential elections, and some outrageous claims about Muñoz having an illegitimate son who used to work for the Ministry of Public Affairs—Panama's equivalent of the CIA.

"I have to go. Thank you for the coffee, Señora Marquez." Digging a five-dollar bill and one of my cards out of my wallet, I slide them across the counter, then lean in and lower my voice. "If you see anything suspicious, especially around my apartment building, you call me. Okay?"

She stares at me like I'm a total stranger but takes the card and tucks it into the pocket of her apron. "You do not pay tomorrow, Leo! I insist."

———

SECURITY AT DOMINA'S office is a fucking joke. I'm through the outer doors without anyone giving me a second look. Not even the police.

As soon as I get a good look at the place, I shake my head. There should be cops all over the place, but I've only seen three of them. Half the chairs are knocked over, laptops and computer monitors lie broken on the floor, and there are papers everywhere.

The vice president must not be here or the Institutional Protection Service—the organization directly responsible for guarding the President, the VP, and the legislature—would be all over me already.

I brace my hands on the chest-high reception desk and scan the open areas. Only a handful of National Police officers around, and a few members of the Presidential Guard Battalion—glorified building security—but no one pays much attention to the angry, desperate American calling Domina's name.

She hasn't texted me back, and though it only took me ten minutes to get here, it feels like it's been hours.

When one of the police officers *does* finally notice me leaning over the desk, he barks out an order. "Arrest him!"

Oh, shit. "No, no." With two fingers, I snag the lapel of my jacket and hold it open. "I'm unarmed. I'm a private investigator, and my ID is in my pocket. I'm here to see Domina Sanchez."

Two officers converge on me, grabbing my wrists and pinning them behind my back as they shove me against the reception desk. My license slides halfway across the polished wood.

"Domina! Call Domina. She'll vouch for me," I grit out as they tighten the cuffs around my wrists.

"Leo?" Domina rushes around a corner, shock in her warm brown eyes. "What are you doing here?"

"A little help?" I manage. The metal is tight enough to eventually cut off my circulation, and the officers wrench my arms closer together, promising to make my life hell once they get me to headquarters.

She keys in a code, and the thick, plexiglass doors between me and the rest of the office whisper open. Marching over to the cops, she glares at them. "Let him go. Leo is not a threat. He is a...friend."

Is she saying that because they're about to haul me off to jail? Or because she actually means it? And if she does, is a "friend" more than I deserve or a hell of a lot less than I want?

"You know this man?" one of the officers asks.

"Yes. He is not responsible for what happened here, and he will not harm anyone. I demand you release him." When the officers don't make a move to uncuff me, she turns and calls, "Manuel? I need you for a moment, please."

Cortez? He *is* here?

The man striding around the corner is every bit as imposing in person as he is on television. Sixty-two years old, a full head of snow-white hair, and a dour expression. He's solid—at least two-hundred pounds—with a tailored suit that probably cost more than my rent for six months.

His detail tries to herd him back to safety when they see

the commotion, but Domina assures them that I'm no threat, then meets the vice president by the plexiglass doors, which I'm guessing are bulletproof. Otherwise, the IPS officers wouldn't let him anywhere near them.

"This is Leo," she explains in quiet Spanish. "My neighbor. He came to my rescue when the man broke into my apartment three nights ago. He is not here to harm you—or anyone else. He is here to see me." She pulls out her phone and shows him the screen.

The rest of the office staff whispers to one another, their gazes pinging between the vice president, Domina, and me. My right hand starts to spasm, the tremors racing all the way up to my shoulder. The motion angers the National Police goons, and they shove me harder against the reception desk. One of them grabs the back of my neck, forcing me to bend over so my cheek is pressed to the wood.

"Not helping," I grunt as I try to relieve some of the pressure on my brachial nerve.

"Shut up," the bigger officer snarls.

Cortez says something to Domina I can't hear, and at her nod, he gives a sharp wave of his hand to his detail. "Release Mr. Basher. He is a *guest* here." The vice president approaches the desk where my billfold—with my PI license—lies open and examines it closely. "You know, of course, that all official private investigators in Panama must be vetted by your own organization, yes?"

"Yes, sir," the officers grumble in unison. One of them unlocks the cuffs, and I rub my right wrist, willing the spasms to subside. Shoving my hands into my pockets would only get me shot.

Domina hasn't moved, and the uncertainty in her eyes drives an axe deep into my heart. She still doesn't want anything to do with me.

The plexiglass doors open, and Cortez waves me through.

"Come, Mr. Basher. I would like to meet the man who helped Domina the other night."

"Sir," one of the IPS agents says, "we have not vetted him."

"And you will be no more than two meters from me for the next *five years*," Cortez snaps. "Check him for weapons, then you will wait outside my office until we are done."

Stunned, I step through the doors, widen my stance, and hold out my arms so a dark-haired man wearing a gray suit and tie can pat me down. He takes his time, and if I didn't think it would earn me a one-way trip to jail, I'd make a joke about buying me dinner first.

The groper finds my cell phone and Bluetooth earbud, then rifles through my backpack. "We will return these to you when you leave."

"No problem, man."

The agent passes the bag to his pal, who locks it in a cabinet against the wall. "He has no weapons, sir. We will be right outside the door."

"Domina, I would like a moment alone with your neighbor. I will send him to your office when we are done." Cortez doesn't wait for her answer, but I shoot her a quick glance before I follow him down the hall.

Her lips are parted, her cheeks devoid of their usual color. I ache for even a moment to see if she's all right, but angering the man who will—in under a week—be the president of the whole goddamn country isn't a good idea. Not when he saved me from a very uncomfortable prison stay not more than two minutes ago.

"Sit," Cortez says with a tight smile as he rounds his desk. The office is simple. Understated. The Panamanian flag stands proudly in the corner, family photos line one shelf of a bookcase, and he shuts his laptop before folding his hands on the dark, antique wood. Windows behind him overlook a courtyard with tall fences, a single palm tree in the center, and ferns surrounding half a dozen benches.

"Thank you, sir," I say. "For stepping in."

He studies me, his stare so intense, I think most men would look away. "Domina has been with me for almost six years now. She is a brilliant speechwriter, but more than that, she is honest and kind, with a good heart. She told me about the attack this morning. I did not know her rescuer was American, though. Who are you, Mr. Basher? Besides a private investigator living in one of the nicer middle-class neighborhoods in Panama City."

Do I tell him the truth? Or the sanitized version of my life that keeps me out of the Chief of Station's crosshairs? Shit. With his contacts, Cortez could probably learn everything about me in under an hour. Hiding who I am won't end well.

"I left the CIA eight months ago and came here to live out my retirement in peace. To disappear."

His brows lift slightly. "Such honesty is surprising, Mr. Basher."

"Call me Leo. You'll verify who I am and where I used to work as soon as I leave this room. Lying would be pointless. It would only serve to put Domina's loyalty to you in question, and I won't do that to her."

"And your relationship with her is...?"

The urge to squirm in my seat is hard to ignore. I've never had to ask a father for permission to date his daughter, but I suspect it would feel a lot like this.

"We're neighbors. Friends. Nothing more."

Yet.

Leaning back in his chair, he steeples his fingers under his chin. "I have only one other question. Why did you come here? I heard you calling for Domina before the police stopped you. That was not the tone of a man who dropped by for coffee with a friend."

"You're a very observant man, Mr. Vice President. I heard about the trouble here this morning. Coming only two days after a man breaks in to Domina's apartment? Ignoring coincidences in my former line of work can get you killed. Or worse. I need to know the details—if you're willing to share them with me—but more importantly, I need to make sure Domina is all right."

Cortez's gaze softens for a moment before the mask of his position snaps back into place. "You will find her office three doors down to the right. But do not leave, Mr. Basher. I need to make those calls you mentioned. After I find out what I need to know, I may want to speak with you again."

He picks up the phone, a clear dismissal, and as I shut the door behind me, I sense her.

Turning, I expect to find anger. Pain. Betrayal. All the emotions I saw in her eyes the other night. Instead, Domina wraps her arms around me.

"You came," she whispers against my neck. She's trembling, and I pull her closer.

There's so much I want to say to her, but I can only force out three words. "I'll always come."

CHAPTER NINE

Domina

Leo's gentle touch at the small of my back reassures me as I lead him to my office. Throwing my arms around him was impulsive—even reckless—but this morning has been one stressful moment after another.

When I stepped through the doors at half-past six, I found chaos. Papers scattered over every surface, laptops in pieces, picture frames broken with glass littering the floor. I screamed, fled back outside, and called the police. Rafael was the next to arrive—only five minutes later—but I couldn't stop shaking until the National Police and the IPS started questioning everyone.

Then, I was numb.

They only returned my phone and laptop moments before Leo showed up. When I saw his message, I wanted to cry.

The worst part of the morning? Telling Manuel and his detail about the attack at my apartment. I should have reported it to the IPS the night it happened. Instead, I had to listen to the agents berate me until Manuel told them he would not stand for their rudeness.

After that, every time someone called my name, I almost jumped out of my skin.

And then I heard his voice.

Shutting my office door, I gesture to the visitor's chair, but Leo backs me up against the dark wood. "Lock it."

"Wh-what?" This close, with him pressed against me and his hands rubbing up and down my arms, my body comes alive in a way I've never felt before.

"You heard me. Lock it."

I fumble behind my back, and as soon as the lock *thunks*, Leo cups my neck and leans down to press his lips to mine. Gentle at first, then desperate. Small nips of his teeth, a single, bold stroke of his tongue, and I'm on fire. The world falls away, and there's only the two of us, fused together like our lives depend on it.

His fingers slide higher, into my hair, and he angles my head so he can deepen the kiss. Oh, my God. I've never felt so wanted, so...*needed*.

He draws back too soon. We're both out of breath, and I cannot bring myself to let go.

Warm, calloused fingers trail along my jaw. "I'm sorry. You don't want anything to do with me. But I had to know what it was like—just once—to kiss you." Stepping back, he shoves his hands into his pockets. "It won't happen again."

"What if I want it to?" Shock lifts his brow, and he snaps his mouth shut. "What I did...the night of the storm..." My cheeks—already on fire from that kiss—burn even hotter. "It was wrong. I asked you to trust me. But *I* did not trust *you*. I should not have walked out on you. Not the way I did."

"You had every right..."

"I did not. And I should have said all of this yesterday when you changed my locks. But we will talk about that later.

Now, I am more interested in why you are here. You were so certain I wanted 'nothing to do with you,' yet you came anyway?"

I grab his wrist, the scars smooth under my touch. The past two nights, I have tossed and turned, playing everything I know about this man on a loop in my head. The look on his face when I walked out? There was no deception in his gaze. Only pain. When he promised he would never lie to me, I knew he was telling the truth. He's a good man, even if he does not see it.

"I sent you a message when I heard about the break-in. You didn't reply, and...I had to know if you were all right." The rough edge to his voice raises goosebumps along the back of my neck. "Some asshole forces his way into your apartment three nights ago, and now this? They're related, Domina. I just don't know who the real target is. Cortez...or you."

———

HEARING Leo say the words is like a punch to the face—my second of the week—and I back up until I hit the edge of my desk. Panic lends a shimmer to the world, then darkness creeps in along the edges of my vision.

"Domina. Take a breath." Leo molds his hands to my hips, steadying me. But I cannot do what he asks. All morning, I managed to ignore the warning bells going off in my head. There was so much to do. All the interviews, working with the IT department to give them access to our computers and phones, cleaning up the fingerprint dust that covered *everything...*

But now, all I can think about is the danger I could be in. How can I ever go home? Or walk down the street unafraid?

"Look at me, baby. No one is getting to you when I'm around."

He sounds so certain. But he has no weapon. No agency behind him. I meet his gaze and find the strength to clear my throat. "Cortez—Manuel—he will provide security if there is a threat. I hope."

Leo sinks down into my guest chair and tugs me until I'm sitting in his lap, my legs draped across his. With his arms around me, I feel safe. Protected in a way I did not know possible.

"The Institutional Protection Service is highly trained," he says, "but their job is to guard the president and vice president. How many people work in this office?"

"Manuel has twenty-seven people on his staff at the Presidential Palace and sixteen of us working here, including me. Marissa is in Santiago—her sister just had a baby—and Artesio suffered a heart attack last week. He's still in the hospital."

"Does anyone here—besides Cortez—have an IPS detail?" Leo asks.

"Rafael. He is the campaign manager. He worked for President Garcia until last year. And Omar. He is Manuel's Chief of Staff."

Leo rubs circles on my lower back, and the motion calms me. Or maybe talking—answering questions—gives me a purpose amid all the chaos.

"Are either one of them here? Now?" His eyes cut to the door. Footsteps pass back and forth, the bustle of a campaign in the final days. Until today, I loved every minute I spent at my job. Even the stressful ones. Now, I wonder if I will ever find joy in it again.

"Domina? Are you still with me?"

Am I with him? I'm sitting in his lap. But...I know so little about him.

With a shake of my head, I shove my errant thoughts aside. "I am so tired, Leo."

"I know, baby." He threads his fingers through my hair, and I sink against him, wishing we were alone—truly alone—so I could kiss him again. "Cortez told me not to leave until he vetted me, but as soon as he's done, I'm taking you home so you can rest."

I want that. So much. But can I really sleep knowing someone might be after me? Ever since the attack, I've jumped at every person walking down the hall, every gust of wind, every little creak the building made.

A dozen times, I picked up the phone to text Leo, but I did not know what to say.

His words finally permeate the haze of my exhaustion.

"Wait...vetting you?" I rub my eyes and blink hard. "Shit. But then he'll know—"

Before I can ask Leo how bad this is going to be for him, someone raps on the door. "The Vice President wants to see the American in his office! Now!"

I scramble up, rushing to flip the locks. In the hall, two of Manuel's IPS detail stand with their hands clasped behind them. Black wires trail from the small communications units in their left ears down their necks. "Mr. Basher? Come with us."

"Not without Domina," Leo says, stepping in front of me, drawing up to his full height and filling the doorway.

The taller agent taps his ear and speaks into a microphone at his wrist. "Basher wants to bring Ms. Sanchez."

After a beat, the agent nods. "Fine. Both of you."

Leo

With Domina's hand in mine, the second trip to Cortez's office is much calmer than the first. She's definitely *not* okay, but at least she's safe. And she didn't protest when I linked our fingers.

Cortez stands when we enter, his gaze pinging between the two of us and the IPS agent behind us. "Chavez, we are going out to the courtyard. Wait here."

"Sir—"

"Wait here," he snaps. The man's orders carry weight. Not only that of his position, but of his very presence. No wonder he's the front runner. He exudes charisma, power, and command.

We follow Cortez down the hall, around a corner, and through a heavy, wooden door with another agent stationed just inside.

A gentle breeze carries the memory of rain. Cortez gestures to one of the benches, and I sit with Domina at my side. Hands clasped behind his back, the vice president stares us down.

"Leo Francis Basher. Twenty-two years of dedicated service to the United States Central Intelligence Agency. Awarded the Distinguished Intelligence Medal, twice. Missing and presumed dead for over a week until one of your colleagues went rogue on an extraction mission and found you in an abandoned warehouse at the edge of Caracas. Despite serious and debilitating injuries, you refused to return to the United States and take a desk job, choosing to remain in Venezuela, where you had a hand in the ousting of President Farías."

Domina gapes at me, and I offer her a weary smile. "Most of that is classified. I would have told you, eventually. If we'd—"

Cortez clears his throat. "Mr. Basher, I am a busy man. Tomorrow, I have a campaign rally at Pacifica Stadium. More than ten thousand people are expected to attend, and it will be broadcast across the country. Today was supposed to be a day of preparation—for me and my staff. But with this morning's events, I am sending everyone home after the press conference. May I continue? You and Domina can discuss your *business* later."

Domina drops her gaze to her hands folded in her lap, and I stare up at the man who would be king—or close to it.

"You're well connected. All that classified information in less than ten minutes? Did you find out my shoe size too? My high school GPA?"

His lips twitch once, but he gives nothing away.

"What exactly do you want from me, Mr. Vice President? You have the power of the Presidential seal and an entire security detail at your beck and call. If you contact the CIA's Chief of Station in Panama, he'll be more than happy to send me back to the United States on the next flight—in the cargo hold, if he can get away with it."

Next to me, Domina fiddles with the hem of her jacket. Her fingers tremble, and I reach over to still them.

"Mr. Basher, the IPS and the Presidential Guard Battalion are responsible for the security of this building. We have cameras over every entrance. They have a dedicated power source and battery backup. Yet they recorded nothing after 2:00 a.m. this morning. My safe was breached, and only *I* know the combination."

"Manuel?" Domina asks. "You said nothing earlier—"

I push to my feet. "You think this was an inside job."

His dark brown eyes shift to the building—and the shadows that move back and forth on the other side of the frosted glass. "I do not know. But a man in my position cannot simply 'hire a private investigator.' All my financial records are public. We are having this conversation outside because while my office is checked for cameras and listening devices every day, I do not know how else anyone could have gotten the combination."

"Mr. Vice President, I'm a has-been with one eye, very little use of my right hand, and a permanent limp. And you want me to...what? Put out some feelers? Why would you trust me?"

With a hearty laugh, Cortez leans his shoulder against the trunk of the palm tree. "Your reputation—once I found someone who would admit you existed—is of a wholly incorruptible intelligence officer whose powers of observation are unmatched. Even with only one eye." He arches a brow. "The person I spoke with also told me your sense of self-preservation was non-existent."

Whoever talked is going to regret the day they were born.

Trying to keep my anger in check, I dig the fingers of my right hand into my palm. "If this *someone* doesn't keep their mouth shut about me, I'll never be safe anywhere. Who did you call?"

"I am certain you can figure that out on your own. But I will give you a name if you agree to come to the rally tomorrow. Watch. Listen. Tell me if you see anything out of the ordinary. Through Domina, of course. Because you and I will never be alone together again."

I take a step back so I can rest my hand on Domina's shoulder. "I'll be her shadow for as long as she'll let me. Just to be damn sure no one hurts her again. Which means I'll come to the rally. But how the hell are you planning to explain *this* conversation to the IPS?" I ask. "Because unless they're shit at their jobs, they'll have a nice fat file on me by tomorrow, and they'll want me as far from that rally—and you—as possible."

Whatever Cortez *thinks* is going to happen? It's a pipe

dream. Even if I were willing to put my life on the line for him, I won't risk Domina.

"I cannot tell my staff whom they are allowed to date," Cortez says with a cocky grin. "I brought you out here to explain the delicate nature of having a relationship with a member of my campaign. You will look suitably warned when you go back inside. I will inform my detail that you are Domina's paramour, and that I have vetted you. They will still run a background check, but unless you have been careless in your retirement, they should only find what you wish them to find."

Damn. If he's half as quick in his debates, no one stands a chance against him.

Inclining my head, I sink down next to Domina and squeeze her hand. She's barely reacted to anything he's said, and I want to get her out of here. Back to my place where I know she'll be protected. "Are you okay with this, baby?" This time, the term of endearment is intentional. I need to know if she can pretend we're dating.

She turns to me, and some of the strain in her eyes fades. "Y-yes." Shifting, she links her arm with mine. "Manuel, are you certain you do not need me after the press conference? Tomorrow's speech—"

"Is perfect. As always. If I need any last-minute adjustments, someone will call you. I am certain you can make updates from home."

"She's not going home," I say. "She's staying with me."

Domina straightens her shoulders, the first hint of defiance shining in her eyes. "Is there some reason *you* cannot stay with *me*?"

There's the woman I met that very first night. The one who knows what she wants and isn't afraid to demand it. "Your place it is, then."

"Ask Rafael for a VIP badge before you leave," Cortez

says. "It will allow Mr. Basher to accompany you to the private areas of the venue tomorrow." Turning to me, he gives me a pointed look. "You will still be frisked by the IPS and sent through the metal detectors. Domina will be spared all of that by virtue of her position."

Got it. Any weapons go with her until we're inside.

"Understood." I get to my feet, stifling my wince as my hip protests. I jogged halfway here, and I'll pay for it the rest of the day. "Mr. Vice President, it was an honor."

He offers me his hand, and despite the nerve damage, I can tell his grip is almost crushing. "You may still regret this, Mr. Basher. I do not know who is after me or why, but this close to the election, I fear any answers you find will not be good."

Domina fits herself to my side, and her closeness settles me. "I'll do what I can, sir. You're married. Two kids?" He nods. "Then you'll understand what I have to say next. Domina comes first. Always."

Cortez looks between the two of us, then reaches down to twist his wedding ring on his finger. "I understand, Mr. Basher. I would expect no less."

CHAPTER TEN

Domina

NOTHING ABOUT TODAY SEEMS REAL. Finding the office in chaos, writing a spur-of-the-moment speech for Cortez to give to the media, Leo kissing me... What's next? A jaguar playing the flute?

In the large conference room, I scrub my palms over my thighs. A dozen reporters gather in the first two rows of seats, waiting for the Vice President's statement. They talk amongst themselves, gossiping, trading rumors about the break-in.

I stand with the rest of the staff against the wall. Though Manuel told us all to go home, not a single person has left. At a time like this, unity is important.

Leo comes up behind me, his hands molding to my waist. "Stay right here until I come back for you, okay?"

"Do you really think there's danger...here?" I hiss. "Now?"

He leans closer so his lips brush my cheek. "Not taking any chances, remember?"

The heat of him makes my core clench, despite how my heart wants to beat out of my chest. "Where are you going?"

"To find out if these reporters know anything *useful*." Leo's entire demeanor changes as he makes his way through the rows of chairs to find a seat directly behind the press.

He's calm in a way I have not seen before. Slinging his left arm over the back of the chair, he stretches his legs out and crosses them at the ankles. But as still and relaxed as his body is, Leo's gaze pings from one journalist to the next.

"What is he doing?" Rafael asks. "He's not press."

I turn, glaring at him. "Leo has a bad ankle. He cannot stand for long periods of time. There are plenty of empty seats."

"He shouldn't even be here."

Before I can tell Rafael to mind his own business, Manuel strides into the room. The chatter stops the moment he takes the podium.

"Good morning," he says, only a hint of strain to his voice. "Sometime after 2:00 a.m. this morning, one or more individuals vandalized my campaign headquarters. The building was empty, and the crime was not discovered until a few minutes after six. A dozen laptops were destroyed, and some of our confidential files were accessed. Given the timing of this attack, I will be speaking with my opponent, Eduardo Muñoz, and asking for his assurances that he and his campaign had no part in it. The Institutional Protection Service—along with the National Police—are investigating, and we will share updates as we get them. I will now take questions."

For ten minutes, he gives the practiced, official answers we crafted earlier.

Nothing was taken.

The files were all related to campaign finances.

No national security secrets were exposed.

"That is all the time I have today," Manuel announces,

holding up his hands. "I hope I will see you all at the rally tomorrow."

The journalists continue to call out questions until Manuel is nothing but a memory in the room. Leo doesn't move, waiting for each and every one of them to file out before he limps over to me.

"At least two of them are loyal to Muñoz. The woman from the *Panama City Business Journal* thinks elections are boring."

For the first time today, I chuckle. "Boring? Today has been anything but boring."

Leo reaches up and drags a knuckle along my jaw. "You're exhausted."

"I work for the man who will be president. I am always exhausted," I say softly. "We need to get your VIP pass for the rally tomorrow. Then we can go."

Taking Leo's hand, I escort him back through the security doors. All around us, people are packing up what little they have left. Thank God I brought my laptop home last night. My office was one of the few largely untouched, and I wonder why. Because my computer was gone? Or because whoever did this knew they would not find anything?

Rafael looks up when I knock on his door. "Yes?"

"I need a VIP pass for tomorrow's rally. Manuel authorized it."

"He would not..."

At my side, Leo tenses, but I quickly intervene before the two men come to blows. "Check your email."

Grumbling, Rafael picks up his phone. After a minute of scrolling, he shakes his head. "He's not thinking clearly. After this morning..."

"Leo could not have been involved with the break-in," I say. "He was with me." The lie should not come so easily, but we *are* supposed to be dating. "He has been vetted. If you have a problem with that...?"

"It's okay, baby," Leo says, releasing my hand and wrapping an arm around my waist. "If I were the vice president's campaign manager, I'd be suspicious of me too." He turns to Rafael and gives him a lopsided smile. "See you tomorrow?"

"Just stay out of the way," Rafael mutters as he slides the pass across his desk. "Get some rest, Domina. You look like you need it."

I'm too shocked—and too tired—to reply, but I hope my stare causes him at least a moment of regret.

Leo tightens his arm around me and guides me through the security gates. Once he retrieves his backpack and mobile phone, he leans in to whisper in my ear. "That guy's a dick. You're beautiful."

My cheeks warm. "I am a mess. I think I only slept three hours last night. Are you certain you don't need glasses?"

Outside, dappled sunlight filters through the clouds. I expect Leo to let me go now that no one is watching us, but he keeps me close until we turn the corner. "My eyesight is just fine," he says. "At least in the one eye I have left." His tone takes on a hard edge, and he positions me with my back against the wall of the building.

I'm about to ask what he's doing when he turns in a slow circle, scanning the small groups of people all around us.

"Can I take you to lunch? Preferably somewhere with outdoor seating?" he asks when he returns his focus to me.

"There is a sandwich shop only a block from our apartment building. They have an excellent takeaway menu."

He leans in, his lips brushing my ear. "Domina, I can't see much on my right side. It's a hell of a lot easier for me to make sure no one's following us if we can sit outside for a while. I know you're tired, but this is how I keep you safe." A light kiss to my neck, and he adds, "It's also an excuse to spend time with you."

Only his lips on my skin keep me calm. He really does think I'm in danger. And...he's kissing me. Out here, where no one on the campaign staff is watching. "I...I know a place. It's a ten-minute walk. Or I can call a car."

Drawing back, he cups my cheek. "Perfect. We can walk. And when we're in public together, stay on my left side, always."

"Your left?" I'm confused, but when he offers me his hand, I take it.

"I need to be able to see anyone coming for you," he says quietly. "And with how messed up my right leg is, it's easier for me to pivot on my left if I had to."

Glancing up at him, I try to read his expression, but he won't meet my gaze. He's looking everywhere *except* at me. The bodega on the corner with half a dozen customers. The small park across the street. At a man walking a fuzzy white poodle directly in front of us.

With Leo so focused on our surroundings, I let my mind wander, concerned only with directing us to Cucina de Mare, one of the nicer seafood restaurants in this area of Panama City.

A car horn blares, and I tighten my grip on Leo's hand. "You okay?" he asks.

"Not in the least."

He stops us from crossing the street, turning to me and holding my gaze. After a moment, he blows out a slow breath. "I wasn't thinking. I'll take you home. If we go the long way—double back once or twice—it'll be enough."

Despite the strain of the morning, my exhaustion, and my worry someone will come after me again, the idea of a *date* with Leo—even a fake one—had sent a little thrill through me. I do not want to give up what might be my only chance to spend a few, easy hours with him.

"We need to eat. Cucina de Mare is supposed to be excellent."

"You've never been?" He checks both sides of the street, and though up close, it is obvious how he has to swivel his head to see to his right, I don't think anyone else would notice.

"No." As soon as the light changes, we rush across the busy intersection. "Everyone has been working nights and weekends for months preparing for the election. Rafael set us up with expense accounts for Comida Móvil so we could have dinners delivered to the office or to our homes."

"Shit. When was the last time you had any fun?"

Embarrassment has me pulling my hand from his. "Mina's birthday dinner back in April? She's one of my oldest friends. But we haven't done more than talk on the phone in months."

Saying the words, I realize how little I have *lived* this past year.

"Once Manuel announced his candidacy, I gave up... everything. Muñoz is vicious. He believes Panama was a better country under Noriega." The idea of him taking the presidency sickens me, and I reach for my mobile, suddenly worried I might have missed a call or text. But there's nothing, and I do not know how I feel about that.

"We're here," Leo says. He offers me his arm—like a gentleman—and I tuck my hand in the crook of his elbow. In flawless Spanish, he asks for a table in the shade, but with a full view of the street, then holds my chair until I'm seated.

Once we have menus and glasses of sparkling water in front of us, he leans forward, his stare so intense, I want to look away. "Whatever is going on? We'll figure it out. And until we do, I'll keep you safe."

I shake my head, my eyes burning. "You cannot promise that, Leo. No one can."

Leo

I'm shit at the soothing and supportive parts of relationships. I went to the campaign office to protect Domina, and instead, I confirmed her worst fears. That there *is* someone after her or her boss—or both of them—and she's in danger.

And instead of telling her you wanted to take her out on a date, you made it about recon instead of her. Asshole.

We order plates of grilled corvina—a local whitefish—along with a cured chorizo appetizer and fried plantains, but when the server leaves, Domina fiddles with a delicate gold bracelet around her right wrist and stares over my shoulder at the water in the distance.

I don't know how to get her back—not that I ever had her —and as the awkward silence grows between us, my mind races, scrambling for *anything* that might let me catch a glimpse of the woman who shared cold pizza and tea with me the other night.

A group of teens pass by on skateboards, and I use them as an excuse to check up and down the sidewalk. Across the street, a guy wearing black jeans and a dark green t-shirt sits on a bench with a book balanced on his knee. The hair on the back of my neck prickles. I've seen him before.

Scooting my chair closer to Domina, I pull out my phone and tap the camera. "Smile. We're on a date, remember?"

"Wh-what?" She stares at me, confusion clouding her eyes. I drape my arm around her shoulders and hold the camera up.

"Trust me. Please?"

Domina's lips curve, and it transforms her face from beautiful to stunningly gorgeous. With a quick tap to the screen, I focus on the guy reading behind us. He hasn't moved or glanced in our direction, but I'm not taking any chances. After a couple of shots, I recenter the frame to capture one of just the two of us. It might be my only chance.

Being this close to her makes me want things I can't have. Pulling away leaves a strange, burning hole inside me, and I drag my chair back to the other side of the table.

"Probably nothing," I say. "But there's a guy across the street who looks familiar."

Her eyes widen. When she reaches for her water, her fingers tremble. The glass teeters, and she scrambles to catch it, a string of Spanish curses tumbling from her lips.

Shit.

"Domina, I'm sorry. I didn't mean to scare you."

She takes a tentative sip, then carefully sets the glass back down. The fire returns to her eyes. "You startled me, that's all. I am not so delicate you need to hide the truth from me. You have a job to do."

"Is that what you think this is? My job?" I ask. "Because if that were true, we'd be in the bowels of Rio Abajo or El Chorrillo. My *job* at the moment is finding a low-life piece of shit who left his pregnant wife three weeks before their kid was born so he could go fuck the nineteen-year-old who used to sell him coffee every morning."

Domina swallows her retort as the server delivers our appetizers. As soon as the man returns to the kitchen, she leans forward. "I can find my own way home, Leo. Go do your job and do not worry about me."

"I'll always worry about you." The admission shocks both of us. Domina's shoulders jerk, and I stab a piece of chorizo with my fork. "I know I don't have the right. But it doesn't stop how I feel."

She doesn't say anything for several minutes. I'm suddenly not hungry, but I force down another couple bites of chorizo. If I don't eat, I won't be any good to her.

"How do you feel?"

The question leaves me hollow. If I tell her the truth, she'll run—and she'd be right to. But I can't lie to her.

"I want to know you, Domina. Maybe even...*be* with you. And despite what you said in your office about that kiss, you clearly don't want to see where this goes. So let's have a nice lunch—as friends—and get home. After that, we can stop pretending we're something we're not. At least until tomorrow."

By the time the waiter brings us two cups of coffee and an order of flan, I don't know which way is up—at least where Domina is concerned. We passed an hour with light conversation. Favorite foods, movies we've seen, books we love.

"*Good Omens* is the one I go back to at least once a year," I say, grabbing a single sugar packet and dumping it into the dark brew. "Terry Pratchett was a genius. Thank God for the invention of eBooks. You move around as much as I do—or did—you can't keep a paperback collection safe."

Domina stares at me like I just committed a mortal sin.

"Shit. Don't tell me you hate Pratchett." Thumping my hand over my heart, I hope for at least a smile—if not a complete denial.

With a small shake of her head, she gestures to the delicate cup in front of me. "You did not strike me as a man who likes his coffee sweet."

"This is hardly sweet." I give the drink a quick stir, then slide it across the table. "Try it."

"You put a whole packet of sugar in there!" She makes a face, her nose wrinkling.

"Trust me, Domina. One sip."

She huffs, then gestures to her own cup. "Okay. But you have to try mine."

I reach across the table, and our fingers brush. It's only a moment. A blink. But I'll take whatever I can get until she sees how broken I truly am. Because when that happens, she'll run. So far and so fast, I'll never be able to catch her.

CHAPTER ELEVEN

Domina

For a short time while we enjoyed our coffee, Leo looked... lighter. Almost relaxed. But now that we're on our way to my apartment, he's back to the always-on-edge grump.

"What happens now?" I ask. He has not touched me since the restaurant, and every two blocks, he pauses to "window shop" or pretend to check his phone screen while taking a photo of someone he *thinks* he might have seen before.

The closer we get, the more my nerves tighten in my chest. At work, I know what to expect. Or did until this morning. But here? How am I supposed to spend the rest of the day with this man?

One minute, he kisses me with such passion, it curls my toes. The next, he treats me like he cannot wait to get away from me.

Leo takes one last look around, then reaches for our building's front door. "Need to stop at my place first." He sounds so tense—almost angry—and once we're in the elevator, I put as much space between us as I can.

"You do not have to stay with me. You are right next door. If anything were to happen, you—"

Whirling on me, he takes me by the arms. His grip is desperate, bordering on tight, but not painful. "Nothing's going to happen. Because I'm sleeping on your couch until we know for damn sure no one's after you."

"I am a grown woman, Leo. I can take care of myself."

Like you took care of yourself when Pinzon broke in? Or the last two nights when you could not sleep for hours?

With everything I am, I wish I could tell him the truth. That I bounce between scared and numb. That I want him to hold me until I fall asleep because the only place I feel safe is in his arms.

His gaze bores into me, pain tightening lines around his eyes. "Don't push me, Domina. This is who I am. *All* I am."

All he is?

"Leo..." The doors lumber open, and he pokes his head into the hall.

"It's clear. Come on."

We move so quickly, I don't say another word until he unlocks his apartment door and ushers me inside. "Leo, talk to me."

He is already halfway to his bedroom, so I follow. A king-size bed with a dark blue duvet, simple wooden nightstand, and matching dresser. No personal touches beyond two hardcover books—both Terry Pratchett—and some strange-looking exercise equipment on a yoga mat in the far corner of the room.

"Were you confused when I said 'I want to know you'?" he asks, yanking a duffel bag from under the bed.

"No. But I am now." I catch his arm, his muscles tense under the light canvas of his jacket. "You are angry with me."

With a jerk of his arm, he heads for the closet. "Can you

blame me? You expected me to leave you unprotected. How could you think I'd *ever* be okay with that?"

My own anger flares, made worse by my lack of sleep. "You made it sound like staying with me was the most terrible burden in the world."

"Fuck." Leo slams his right hand against a small safe at the bottom of the closet. With a heavy sigh, he presses his index finger to a small black square on the door and it pops open. A gun in a holster and two boxes of ammunition go into the duffel bag, and he rises with a groan. "Domina, you could never be a burden."

"Then what is it?"

His gaze softens, and for a moment, I think he's about to touch me, but then he drops his hand. "I wish our first date hadn't been a surveillance mission."

"Date?" My voice cracks. Swallowing hard, I shake my head. "No, we had lunch…"

Leo recoils like I slapped him. "Lunch? If that's what you want to call it, fine. This is going to take me a few minutes. Go wait in the living room."

Stalking into the bathroom, he slams the door. The vague sounds of cabinets opening and closing carry, along with the occasional curse.

Stunned, I don't move, though a part of me wants to leave and lock myself in my own apartment—and not let Leo in. But then I remember what he told me that first night.

"If you're in trouble, a locked door won't stop me."

So, I sink down onto his bed and wait.

When he emerges, the look on his face? He's angry in a way that should scare me—would scare me if he were any other man.

"I told you to wait in the living room."

Straightening my shoulders, I meet his gaze. "I wanted to wait here."

His limp is worse as he skirts the bed, then picks up three small, padded cylinders from the yoga mat.

"What are those?" I ask.

"Trigger point therapy rollers. Painful as fuck, but I need them to get moving in the morning."

Shit. I peer into the duffel bag to see a handful of prescription bottles, a tube of arnica, and a knee brace along with the rollers. "We should stay here."

"I'm not making you leave your home. We're going," he growls. "But I need another bag. I still have to pack my laptop, tablet, and a change of clothes."

"Idiota obstinado," I snap. "Why will you not listen to me?"

"Because all we did was *have lunch*."

I flinch, and tears burn my eyes. "That is no answer." Fishing my keys out of my briefcase, I stand. "Stay here, Leo. Put all of your things back where they belong. I do not want you in my apartment. You can either let me stay here with you, or I will go home alone."

"Don't push me on this." The words are hoarse, almost guttural, and his right hand, balled into a tight fist, shakes at his side.

"You are not my keeper. I will see you in the morning. We leave for the rally at nine."

I flee—that's the only word for how quickly I move—and though he calls after me more than once, Leo does not chase me.

MY APARTMENT FEELS EMPTY. Lonely. I don't understand why. Three years I have lived here, and I welcomed my solitude. My own space. Not luxurious, but comfortable. Not grand, but far from the run-down tenement I grew up in.

Tears drip down my chin. When did I start crying? I swipe at my cheeks, sniffle, and blink hard. This is not me. The last time I lost control like this was when my papa died.

My phone beeps.

Leo: If you insist on staying alone, I'm going to text you every hour. Text me back if you don't want me picking your locks.

Domina: I go to bed at ten. If you text me after that, I will block your number.

Dropping the phone on the kitchen counter, I make it all of two steps into the living room before the first sob rips from my throat. By the time I reach the couch, the pain in my heart is only matched by the fear that I will always be alone.

Leo

The sun sets, and though Domina has answered every one of my texts, it's clear she wants nothing more to do with me.

Are you surprised? You were an ass.

Half a dozen times, I've gotten all the way to my front door, determined to check on her. To apologize. Grovel. But if I piss her off more, she might leave for the rally without me tomorrow, and the VIP pass is still in her briefcase.

My back aches. When I get up for another cup of coffee—my fourth since lunch—my ankle pops and cracks with each step. Too much walking—and running—today.

I've spent hours analyzing the photos I took, and I found three different men in several of the shots.

Since I'm *retired*, I don't have a whole team at Langley to run facial recognition. Even if I still did have contacts at the agency, I have no authority to question anyone. No protection. No backup.

With half an hour before I need to text Domina again, I

bring my coffee cup to the couch and get mostly horizontal to give my back, hip, and leg a break.

He's going to hate me, but I don't have a choice. I need help, and Trev's the only person I trust.

"Three times in one week? This is a record," he says when the call connects. "Do I need to pick you up at the airport?"

"Ferrier hasn't kicked me out of the country. Yet. But I do need a favor. A big one." Taking a sip of coffee, I wait for him to tell me I used them all up yesterday when he managed to keep the Chief of Station from throwing me in the smallest, dirtiest jail cell in Panama.

"Name it."

The coffee burns a path down my windpipe. Sitting up, I cough and wheeze until Trevor asks if I'm all right.

"Fine, man," I choke out. "Hot coffee isn't supposed to end up in your lungs."

"Coffee this late at night? Now I know it's serious." A woman's voice floats over the line. "It's Leo," Trev says quietly.

"Leo?" Dani asks. "Put him on video."

I should protest. What I need from Trevor is so illegal, either one of us could go to jail for it. But Dani's wicked smart, and after working the political desk for the *Washington Post* and the *Boston Globe*, she has enough experience with foreign elections to give me a read on Cortez and Muñoz.

"Dani. How are you?" Despite working together to get Trevor out of La Crypta, we've only had half a dozen conversations, and most of those were strained at best.

"Better than you, from the sound of it. What's going on?" She sinks down on a beige couch next to Trevor, practically snuggling into his side.

I tell them everything. From the attack at Domina's apartment to the break-in at Cortez's campaign offices, to the three guys I think *might* have been following us today.

"What do you need?" Trevor asks. "I might be able to get

Vasquez to fly down there for a few days. Assuming Dax hasn't assigned him to any other cases by the time we get off the phone."

"I don't need Vasquez. Not yet, anyway." Running a hand through my hair, I wince at the headache that's starting behind my eyes. "But I do need help with facial recognition on half a dozen photos I took today. I don't suppose Wren—?"

"Nope. She's in the middle of another case, and Ry's a goddamn mess. He doesn't want her working more than five hours a day, and keeps threatening to lock up her computer." Trevor chuckles, and even Dani's smiling. "You can imagine how well that goes over."

"Is there a lock Wren can't open?" I ask.

"Nope. But she's exhausted." Trevor snorts. "She still regularly checks in at 3:00 a.m., but she is *trying* to cut back."

"Shit. I don't suppose you can access her tech?" I should be more concerned with Wren's health—she's Trev's family, even if I barely know her—but how the hell am I supposed to protect Domina if I can't figure out who's after her?

"He doesn't have to," Dani says.

"What?" Trevor and I both ask at once.

Dani's tone bleeds exasperation, and I'm pretty sure she rolls her eyes. "TJ, what exactly do you think my brother does with his time these days?"

"Fuck me." Trevor slaps his hand to his forehead. "Of course. Zephyr."

I sit up, wondering if I'm suddenly delirious. "Exactly what is a zephyr?"

"Not what. Who," Trev replies. "You remember Ronan?"

"Irish bastard with a serious attitude problem? Yeah. I was stuck in the van with him for almost three hours in Caracas while the rest of your team breached the prison. What's he got to do with anything?"

Dani grins. "He went and fell in love with the only

woman—only *person*—on earth whose skills might be a match for Wren's."

"Holy shit. And...she's available?" I cast a quick glance at my laptop. I'm not bad with tech. Better than most field officers—courtesy of being the *only* one stationed in Venezuela for the past ten years—but I can't hack traffic cameras, and the only facial recognition I have access to is no better than a child's toy.

"No guarantees, but she just wrapped up a couple big cases with Second Sight, and Ronan took her to Maine for a long weekend. They got back last night." Trevor nods at Dani, and she pulls out her phone, her fingers flying over the screen.

"How long until she gets back to you?" I ask.

Dani waves the phone at me. "About as long as it took you to ask the question. I'll send her your phone number. Be prepared though. She's intense."

"I can handle intense." It takes all the energy I have left not to stare at the wall separating my apartment from Domina's. "It's the unknown that scares the shit out of me."

Dani leans closer. "The unknown? Or Domina? Because I know that look. You have feelings for her."

Shit.

She presses a kiss to Trevor's cheek. "Talk some sense into him, okay?" As she moves out of view, she calls, "It was good to see you again, Leo. I'll send Zephyr your number now."

"Let me guess," I say. "That 'sense' has something to do with me going to apologize to Domina?"

"Maybe." Trevor settles back on the couch. "Or at least trusting her."

Trust. The last time I trusted someone—besides Trevor—I ended up losing an eye.

"Look," he says, exhaustion in his tone, "you don't think I get it? Gil was my best fucking friend. And he betrayed all of us. Gave you up to the Loma Collectivo, tortured Austin, and would have killed me too given half the chance." With a slow shake of his head, he adds, "You know, after you and Ry's team pulled me out of La Crypta, Dax reamed my ass for not telling him I'd grown up with Austin, Dani, and Gil."

"He did?" I reach for my mug, needing the rich scent of the coffee to keep me here in the present. The mission to save Trevor brought back a shit-ton of memories—none of them good.

"'When you get back,'" Trevor drawls, in what I assume is a spot-on impression of his boss, Dax Holloway, "'we're goin' to have a little talk about why you never told us you grew up best friends with the head of JSOC.'" His eyes unfocus, and he's not in Boston anymore. He's in that safehouse an hour outside of Caracas. Or worse. Back in that tiny cell in La Crypta. "The man didn't care about financing the rescue mission. Or anyone risking their lives to get me out of there. He only cared that I didn't trust him."

"Trust has never been my strong suit. You know that. Trust almost got me killed."

Trevor's laugh shakes the phone. "No shit."

"Eight days, Trev. Sleep deprivation. Only enough food and water to keep me alive. I can still *feel* the blade that took my eye. I trusted Gil with my life, and he did his damnedest to take it from me." My hand spasms, and I'm suddenly so tired, it's hard to focus. "Domina thought she was just 'a job.' If I want to make it through this, that's exactly what she has to be."

CHAPTER TWELVE

Leo

ZEPHYR IS as good as Dani's word. I have her encrypted mobile number before I end my call with Trevor. He tried to convince me to go talk to Domina, but I'm not ready. Not now —maybe not ever.

So I set up my tablet on the small dining table and pop in an earbud.

The video call connects, and a woman with bright teal hair, a sparkling eyebrow piercing, and a steaming mug twice the size of mine stares at me. "So, you and Trevor go way back?" she asks.

"We used to have the same boss." He and Dani trust this woman, but twenty-two years of hiding who I am can't be erased overnight. Even if she could probably find out all my secrets in under an hour. "And I know...uh...Ronan."

She arches her brows. "How?"

"Last year we spent some time in a van together down in Venezuela. It wasn't fun. I had to listen to him complain the whole damn time about being 'backup.'"

A wry grin curves her lips. "That sounds like him." Zephyr tucks a lock of hair behind her ear and takes a sip from her mug. "Dani said you needed help identifying some idiots who were dumb enough to be caught on camera?"

"Can't be sure they were following us, but I have at least three shots of each of them. Want me to email them to you?"

She shakes her head, leaning closer to the screen. The click of typing carries through the earbud, and then a link pops up in the chat window. "Install that app. Then use it to drop the photos into my secure cloud storage."

"ZEO?" I ask when the program launches.

"Zephyr's Eyes Only." She beams, pride clear in her expression. "Had to name it *something*, and 'Secure File Transfer and Chat' wasn't anywhere near as fun."

"S-F-T-C? Sounds like a bank. You coded this?"

"Yep. The first 'non-family' gig I took on for Austin, the client kept sending me unencrypted emails. *Huge* security risk. So now, all communication goes through this app. Next time you call me, you'll use ZEO. When I need to talk to you, same deal."

The interface is simple, but before it lets me in, I have to give it my fingerprint *and* a facial scan, then enter a ten-digit passcode. "I would have loved something like this when I was in the field."

"Well, you have it now. Drop me the photos, and I'll get to work. Expect to hear from me in an hour or two at most." She lifts the mug to her lips, takes a swig of whatever she's drinking, and offers me a mock toast. "And when I call back, you can tell me why these guys are following you and what you're going to do about it."

The screen goes dark before I can reply. I don't want to trust her. Hell, I don't *want* to trust anyone. But if she's working for Austin Pritchard—former head of the Joint

Special Operations Command and Dani's adoptive brother—
she's been vetted to hell and back. And without the CIA
behind me, I need all the help I can get.

THE MINUTES TICK BY, and though I have no right to be
impatient—it's almost midnight in Boston—I can't sit still. So
I pace, despite the pain shooting from my ankle all the way
up my thigh.

A soft knock stops me in my tracks for all of three
seconds, then I race for the door. I curse my lack of fine motor
control as my fingers slip off the deadbolt.

Domina. Standing right in front of me. Gone are the black
slacks, the red blouse that exposed the gentle swell of her
breasts, and her makeup. She's barefoot, a pair of yoga pants
clinging to her hips, and a peach tank sloping off one shoulder. She won't look at me, her gaze pinned to the floor, but
exhaustion shadows her eyes.

"Have you been crying?" I start to reach for her, but when
she flinches, I drop my hand. Until she lifts her gaze to mine,
and I have my answer.

"Come here, baby." Pulling her into my arms, I kick the
door shut.

Don't fuck this up. Whatever it is.

She doesn't break. Doesn't melt against me like I wish she
would. But she lets me hold her for a full minute before
pulling away. "Can we talk?" she asks softly.

Even if she only came over to tell me off, I'll let her. I'll
take anything she throws at me. As long as it gets me a few
more minutes with her.

Motioning toward the sofa, I pause only long enough to
set the locks before joining her, sitting close enough, I can

feel the heat of her next to me. She clutches one of my throw pillows like a shield but doesn't try to scoot away.

A dozen questions race through my mind. Did something happen? Why is she here? Did she lock her door? Does she have her phone? But before I can ask any of them, she clears her throat.

"I was wrong to walk out on you like that. Again." The sorrow in her voice crushes me. I pushed her away—on purpose—to hide how much I want to be more than her temporary protector, and she's blaming herself?

"No." I reach for her hand, twining our fingers. "I was the asshole. Getting mad at you for thinking it was just lunch? That was a dick move. I didn't ask you out. I practically dragged you there so I could make sure we weren't being followed."

Domina stares at me, utterly silent, her lower lip wobbling slightly.

Trev's words haunt me. *"If you want her to trust you, Leo...be honest with her."*

I force a deep breath, praying what I'm about to say won't make her run away for a third time. "I wanted it to be a date, Domina. Hell, I want *a lot* of dates with you. But only if you want that too."

Scooting closer, I bring our joined hands to my heart. "If we could start over, I'd introduce myself at the mailbox. Or when we passed in the hall. Flirt a little. Then after a week or so, I'd ask you out for coffee. Then lunch. Then dinner. I'd take it slow. Really get to know you before I kissed you for the first time."

A flush darkens her cheeks. "I would have said no."

"What?" My head throbs, and I drop her hand. Did I force myself on her at her office? Shame has me scooting halfway across the couch. "Shit. I—"

"To coffee," she says quickly. "The dates. Even the flirting."

She's about to say she doesn't want anything to do with me. This night can't get much worse. I push to my feet, bracing my hand on the wall for a split second when my ankle threatens to buckle. Limping into the kitchen, I reach for the coffee pot—again. But Domina follows.

"Why did you come over?" I ask. My hands aren't steady, and my mug rattles when I set it down. I don't offer her a cup. Not if she's just going to flee again.

"To explain." Domina leans against the counter across from me, hugging herself tightly. "I've been on my own since I was eighteen. My grades were good enough to earn a small scholarship to the University of California in Berkeley, but I worked two jobs the whole time."

After a sigh, she continues. "I told you about my last relationship. But not the one before that. Or the one I had in college."

"What happened?" The coffee forgotten, I face her, my hands shoved deep in my pockets. All I want to do is hold her, but the vibes she's giving off are clearly "stay back."

"I broke up with both of them after a few months. I told myself it was because they only wanted me to take care of them." She straightens, lifting her chin. "But it was not all their fault. Brian—I met him in college—was sweet. He used to bring me chocolate-covered espresso beans when I was studying. Even takeaway during finals week. But I never told him anything about my childhood. My dreams. My fears. Nothing."

Shit. She has no idea how to open up to anyone. Everything about her—the way she kicked me out of her apartment after the attack, her reaction when I told her I was in recovery, even shutting the door in my face last night—it all makes sense now.

"Domina..."

She sniffles once, then swipes at her cheek like she's angry at the single tear she let slip. "My entire life, I have been alone. I thought it was better that way. Until tonight."

"What happened tonight, baby?" If I thought she'd let me, I'd hold her, but she's not ready yet.

"I tried everything. A hot bath. Yoga. Meditation." She sniffles but straightens her shoulders. "I didn't *want* to be scared. But I'm always alone, Leo. Maybe...I don't want to be anymore."

Her eyes give everything away. Raw agony, made worse by years thinking she had to do everything for herself. "Has anyone ever taken care of you, Domina? *Really* taken care of you?"

"No. Not until you." Domina stares down at her bare feet. Her cheeks are even redder now. "I don't know how to let you. But I think...I know I want to."

All the pieces fall into place. "And demanding we stay here...that was your way of trying to take care of me, wasn't it?"

"I thought if I wanted us to have a relationship, that was what I needed to do. But...now I want to stay here because you're here, and you make me feel safe." A hint of a smile curves her full lips, and a small part of me settles. "I...I trust you, Leo."

Relief courses through me until she raises her head. "But I understand if you cannot forgive me. I made your actions, the sacrifices you were willing to make, all about me."

"It *is* all about you, baby." I cringe when the term of endearment slips—again—though the damage to my face hides at least some of the motion. "What you went through as a kid...I can't imagine. But trust issues? I've got those in spades. You don't have to explain yours to me—unless you want to."

"I do," she says, another tear spilling over. "But...not tonight. Tonight, will you just hold me?"

Domina

Leo wraps his arm around me and leads me into his bedroom. "It's close to midnight, and we have to be up early. Where's your phone? Your briefcase?"

"On my kitchen counter." I'm so tired. Crying for three hours was not how I expected to spend my evening. Until Leo's final text of the night, I still thought I would fall asleep in my own bed, alone and full of regrets.

"I'll go get them. Anything else you want?" He sinks down on the bed to lace up his boots. "Favorite pillow? Slippers? Eye mask?"

"I don't have any of those things. My phone and briefcase will be fine." Digging in my pocket, I pull out my apartment keys. "You will need these."

He gives me that adorable lopsided grin. "I don't, but the keys *do* make it easier. Be back in five minutes. Don't go anywhere."

The warning stings, but I don't blame him for not trusting me. I haven't given him much reason to.

Leo's front door clicks shut, and I stretch out on his bed. It smells like him. Like a rainforest after a storm. And something spicy, warm, and reassuring.

If only I understood my feelings for him. We have known one another for less than a week, and when I'm not with him, he's all I can think about.

A few minutes later, he's back with my briefcase and phone in his hand. "I expect Zephyr to call me back soon.

She's running facial recognition on the pictures I took today. You should get some rest."

Leo leans down and presses his lips to my forehead. It's so sweet, so utterly protective. Like he's promising to stand between me and whatever—whoever—comes for me.

"Don't go." I snag his wrist, pulling him closer. "I don't know who Zephyr is, but I don't want to be alone tonight. Stay with me, Leo."

I can see how conflicted he is. But I need this more than anything. Someone to hold me. To keep the darkness away. All night.

"Be right back." He waits for me to release him, then limps out into the living room. Two minutes later, he returns with his tablet tucked under his arm. "Zephyr is...shit. I don't know a damn thing about her—except she's trying to ID a few guys I took pictures of today and the only man *I* trust trusts her."

My heartbeat quickens, and I sit up. "You really do think there were people following us?"

Leo curses under his breath, sets the tablet on the nightstand, and sinks down next to me. "I won't lie to you, Domina. The chance that all three of them just happened to be going the same direction we were is about as good as me winning an Olympic medal for the hundred-yard dash. But for all we know, they could be working for Muñoz, keeping tabs on every member of Cortez's staff. They might not have anything to do with the break-in at your office *or* the man who attacked you."

"Are you sure we're safe here? Maybe we should go to a hotel..."

"We're safe." Opening the nightstand drawer, he pulls out a gun tucked in a black holster. "I have motion alarms over both the front and patio doors—loud enough they'll wake everyone at least two floors away. No one's getting in here without us knowing, and I'm a damn good shot."

Before I can respond, his tablet beeps. "That's Zephyr," he says. "I'll take this in the other room. You can get some sleep."

"No." I swing my legs over the side of the bed. "I want to hear what she has to say. Please…"

Leo offers me his hand and helps me to my feet. "Okay. We'll talk to her together."

CHAPTER THIRTEEN

Leo

"What did you find?" I ask the moment Zephyr's face appears on screen.

"Hello to you too." She shifts her gaze to Domina and smiles. "Leo didn't say who he was with today, but I recognize you from a couple of the pictures."

"I'm Domina," she says. "I work for Vice President Cortez."

"Shit. Really? And you're coming to *me* rather than working with...whatever Panama's version of the Secret Service is?" Zephyr asks.

"We don't know if we can trust them. Hell, Cortez isn't even sure." At my side, Domina stiffens. Dammit. I'm doing a bang-up job of reassuring her. "We'll fill you in on everything, but were you able to get IDs for the guys in the photos?"

To Zephyr's credit, she doesn't blink at the notion the Vice President's own detail might be corrupt pieces of shit. "Yep. Meet Larry, Mo, and Curly. Also known as Juan Alvarez, Umberto Vale, and Erick Romero."

Three Panamanian driver's license photos fill the screen. "Yep. Juan was sitting across the street from the restaurant when we had lunch. The other two took turns tailing us back to the apartment. I don't suppose you found anything linking these jackoffs?"

The pictures slide away, and Zephyr shoots us an "are you kidding me" look. "It's been less than an hour, Leo. Hacking into Sertracen for those licenses took some time. The U.S. DMV is a hell of a lot easier."

"But you'll keep digging?"

"If you tell me what I'm looking for..." She leans back in her chair, rolling her head around until her neck cracks. "The more I know, the faster you'll get results."

We tell her everything. The attack at Domina's apartment, the break-in at the campaign office, and my conversation with Cortez.

"And the Vice President didn't tell you what was in his safe?" Zephyr asks.

Shit. I've been out of the field too long. I'm losing my edge. "Cortez got an entire dossier on me in less than ten minutes. I was more concerned with ending up on the next flight back to the States—or in handcuffs."

"I can ask him tomorrow," Domina says quietly. "After the rally."

Zephyr nods. "Good. Anything you find out will help. I'll feed Daniel Pinzon's info and these guys' IDs into my algorithm and see what it spits out. But if this is politically motivated..."

I pinch the bridge of my nose, the headache that's been brewing half the day pounding like a bass drum. "The chances of you finding anything are somewhere between zero and negative two million."

With a delicate snort, Zephyr runs a hand through her teal locks. "Not that low. I'm *really* good at my job."

It's almost 1:00 a.m. by the time I double-check the locks and motion sensors, slip my holster into a special pocket on the side of the mattress, and pull back the blankets.

Exhaustion weighs me down, but Domina hasn't said a word since we finished talking to Zephyr. I don't want to leave her for even a minute, but I'm still wearing my khakis and t-shirt. I sleep in my boxers, but the idea of exposing Domina to what those bastards did to me...she doesn't need that. Not tonight.

Rummaging in my dresser, I find an old pair of pajama pants. Domina watches me as I disappear into the bathroom and shut the door. The look in her eyes? She's numb. It kills me that the fiery, proud woman who kicked me out of her apartment that first night is hidden underneath a shit-ton of pain and fear.

I shuck my pants and toss them into the small hamper. Scars crisscross my legs. Electrical burns, cigarettes, dozens of small—and large—cuts from all manner of knives, and five surgeries on my knee and ankle. What's under my t-shirt is even worse.

How the hell did I expect to have a relationship with her? She'll take one look at me and run.

When I emerge from the bathroom, she's sitting with her back against the headboard and her knees drawn up to her chest. "Come here, baby," I say and stretch out next to her. "Let me hold you."

She fits herself to my side, her arm around my waist. "If something happens tomorrow..."

"Shhh." I press a kiss to the top of her head. "Nothing's going to happen."

"You cannot promise that." The sorrow in her tone cuts deep. Domina sighs, her fingers curling around the hem of my t-shirt. "There will be thousands of people at the rally. If someone is after Manuel..."

I nudge her chin up and brush my lips to hers. "We'll stop it. I'll keep you safe, Domina. On my life, I'll keep you safe."

For a moment, I think she's about to argue with me, but then she blinks, and her entire demeanor changes.

"Kiss me." Her voice is pure sex and desire, making my dick twitch in my boxers.

"Are you sure?"

"Leo..." Her nipples pebble against my chest, the thin fabric of her tank doing nothing to hide her arousal. I'm already at half-mast, and any second now, she's going to feel it. "I want this."

Sliding one hand to her ass and the other around the back of her neck, I ease her onto her side. Domina's lips part, inviting me in, and I don't hesitate.

She tastes of mint, and I take the kiss deeper. Her fingers rake through my hair, a tiny moan deep in her throat sending blood rushing lower until my boxers can barely contain my hard-on.

She takes more than she gives, and I am *here* for this side of her. This bold, willing woman who wants me, despite knowing I'm damaged goods.

A lance of fear cools the fire burning through me. If we go any further, she'll see...everything.

"Domina..." I'm out of breath when I break off the kiss. Ready to strip her naked so my fantasies can become something real. But I can't do that if I'm not willing to let her *see* me. "We can't take this back."

"Do you think I want to?" Her eyes are bright with desire, her nipples so hard, they're begging for my touch. The sweet scent of her arousal fills the small bedroom. "I have not had many...relationships," she says, a hint of defiance to her tone. "But I am not so inexperienced as you fear."

"It's not that." Putting a few inches between us, I squeeze my eyes shut and swallow hard. Lights. If I turn off the lights, she won't have a chance to be repulsed by what she sees. Reaching over, I flick the switch on the bedside lamp. Darkness surrounds us, and I reach for the hem of her tank. "I want to taste you, baby."

Her body trembles as I lift her shirt. The material tangles at her shoulders, and she wriggles until it slides free. Exploring her body with the tips of my fingers, I find the smooth skin of her shoulder, then trail down her arm until I reach the heavy fullness of her breast. Domina shudders when I skate my thumb over her nipple. "Leo..."

"What is it, baby?" I ask, leaning in to kiss the hard nub. Only once. A tease. A promise of what's to come. She arches her back, and I chuckle. "More?"

"Yes." She reaches for my waistband, but I stop her, one hand capturing both of hers.

"Not yet. You come first." Carefully, I lift her wrists over her head. "No touching until I say."

Her sharp inhale stops me.

Shit.

"I like to be in control." Cupping her face, I relish the way she turns into my touch. "If that's not okay..."

"I am yours, Leo," she whispers. "I...trust you."

With a low growl, I kiss her until she's breathless. "Tell me to stop if anything is too much."

I feel, rather than see her nod, and trail my lips down the curve of her neck, along her collarbone, and over to her breast. When my teeth close over her pebbled nipple, she makes a sound something between a cry and a whimper. Her legs move restlessly under the sheets. A light dew breaks out over her skin, a hint of salt mixed with a delicious sweetness I might never get enough of.

I replace my mouth with my fingers, pinching lightly so I

can lavish attention on her other breast. She's panting, the occasional Spanish curse escaping her lips.

"These need to go," I say, tugging at her yoga pants. "Along with whatever you're wearing underneath."

Throwing the sheets back, I straddle her, my fingers curling around her waistband. Domina lifts her hips, allowing me to strip her naked with ease. I ache to be able to see her. All of her. The tight nipples, her pussy, but most of all, her face. Her eyes.

"Fuck," I groan as the scent of her arousal hits me, so strong, all rational thought flees. Surging up, I claim her mouth in a searing kiss. By the time I pull away, she's practically writhing under me. "I...I need to turn the light back on, baby."

Confusion furrows her brow. It's the first thing I see when the room is once again bathed in a gentle glow. Smoothing my thumb over the little wrinkle, I capture her lower lip between my teeth and tug gently.

"Gorgeous. Every inch of you," I say when I slide back down with my head between her thighs. Dark brown nipples, perfect, dewy skin marred only by the fading bruises on her shoulder and hip.

I should have been faster.

Black curls glisten over her mound, and she hasn't moved her arms from where they lie bent over her head, her fingers curled around the edge of the mattress.

But it's her eyes that hold me, that draw me deeper than I thought possible. Half-lidded, but still bright with desire. Watching her for any fear, any hesitation, I dip my tongue between her slick folds. She's so very wet for me, her hips shifting as she moans softly.

"More?" I ask, pressing a kiss to her curls.

"More...please, Leo."

God. The rough, throaty tone makes my dick even harder,

and I can feel the precum soaking into my boxers. Parting her lower lips, I trace patterns around her clit, teasing, taking her closer to the edge every time I lap at her tender nub. She's a summer storm, hot and wet and so sweet, I don't know how I'm ever supposed to let her go.

One finger slips into her channel, then two, and she's begging in quiet Spanish until her words dissolve into helpless mewls. Her hips shift and thrust until I have to lay my free arm over her stomach to hold her still.

She's so close, so ready, and I reach up to pinch her nipple with one hand as the other twists to find her g-spot. Trapping her clit between my lips, I give it one final bold stroke with my tongue, and she flies, her entire body imploding in wave after wave of pleasure.

My fingers are soaked with her release, and I suck them clean, needing all of her, before I ease myself onto my side and gather her into my arms. "I've got you," I murmur in her ear, then draw the blankets up over us. My dick begs to be freed, but when Domina's eyes flutter open, she's all that matters.

I'll give her anything she wants if she keeps looking at me like I'm her whole world, because I know for damn sure... she's fast becoming mine.

Domina

Held in Leo's arms, I feel protected in a way I never have before. He rubs my back, his fingers trailing up and down along my spine. I could fall asleep like this—except for the empty feeling inside me. I need more.

Stroking my hand over his chest to his abs, I find at least a six-pack, maybe more. "Take off your shirt," I whisper.

He stiffens, then stretches for the light. I wrap my fingers around his wrist, right over the thick scar.

"Leo? You have seen all of me." Being naked in front of him was not my plan when I knocked on his door. I wanted to be held. To fix what I had broken between us. To sleep without fear. But as soon as I was in bed next to him, I knew I needed more. "Leave the lights on."

He shakes his head, twisting his hand free. This time, I pull away, scooting to the far side of the bed and drawing the duvet up to my breasts. "What are you doing?" he asks. He's still hard, the sheet tented over his erection, and I wish I could let this go. Let him take me in the dark and not care that he feels he must hide from me.

"I trusted you. But if you cannot trust me, then this was a mistake." With each word, I feel Leo's pain even more. "I know you have scars." Trailing my hand down his right forearm, I trace one of the deeper, jagged troughs in the muscle. "Why do you think they matter to me?"

"Because they matter to *me*." He jerks back, fighting against the sheets. Stumbling to the far side of the bedroom, he presses his fist to the center of his chest. "Multiple surgeries on my ankle and knee. Skin grafts for the worst of the burns. I lost three of my toes. Spent six weeks in the hospital. *Months* in rehab before I could walk without a cane. And my eye...do you know what they do when you lose your eye?"

"No." I draw my knees up to my chest and hug myself tightly.

"You don't want to," he snaps.

"Yes, I do." Abandoning all modesty, I slip out from under the duvet and march over to him. "I want to know everything. Trust me, Leo." Taking a risk, I lift the hem of his t-shirt a few centimeters. This time, he doesn't stop me, but he does go completely still. Rigid.

His eyes closed, he tenses when I expose his abs. Burns

mar his torso. But they do not look like any burns I have seen before. They are deeper, somehow.

"Take it off," I say softly. "Please."

With a wince, he reaches over his head and grasps the collar. The shirt falls to the floor, but he still will not look at me.

His right shoulder bears most of the damage. I rise up on my toes and kiss a dark red surgical scar that stretches from his collarbone almost all the way to his nipple.

Following the trail, I explore his upper body. Up close, the ravages of torture and time are obvious, but they do nothing to make him any less handsome.

"Did you think I would run away?" I ask, palming his cock through his thin pants. He hardens so quickly, it takes my breath away. And makes my core clench. "I need you, Leo. All of you."

With a low groan, he opens his eyes. Our gazes collide, and he hauls me against him. Hands under my ass, Leo lifts me until I wrap my legs around his waist and carries me back to the bed.

Something's shifted in him. Gone is the angry, fearful, damaged man who half begged me to turn off the light. *This* Leo is confident, possessive, and completely in control.

"You're so damn beautiful," he says, his voice rough as he takes a step back and reaches for the tie on his pajama pants. They fall to the floor—along with a pair of black boxers, then his socks—and I gape.

His right leg is significantly thinner than the left, with more scars than I could have ever imagined. He's missing two toes on his right foot, one on his left. But the rest of him...is perfect. A thick, hard cock stands proudly amid wiry, light brown curls with a hint of gray.

My nipples harden, and a fresh wave of arousal washes over me. His gaze is almost predatory as he straddles me.

Dipping his head, he scores his teeth over my breast. God, I want him. All of him.

"I need to touch you," I whisper. I never thought I would want a man to take control in the bedroom, but with Leo, it makes everything so much...*more.*

He stares into my eyes, a hint of wonder in his own. "I'm yours, Domina. Touch, taste, anything you want. *For now.*"

The implication—that his dominant side will come out again soon—turns me on even more. I wriggle my hips, the underside of his cock rubbing between my folds.

His ass is like steel, hard under my fingers. With a nod, I arch a brow. "Lie down."

"What?"

"If I can do anything I want to you...*for now,* I want you to lie down." My earlier exhaustion is nothing but a memory, replaced with excitement at being *with* this amazing man.

I run my fingers through his hair. It's softer than I expected, long on top, shorter on the sides. The neatly trimmed beard and mustache scratch my lips as I kiss him. Leo reaches for me, and though I am tempted to stop him, I need his arms around me.

My teeth score the shell of his ear, and he groans. "Fuuuu-ucck, Domina..."

With my free hand, I reach for his cock. The smooth, hot length fills my palm, and he shudders when I close my fingers around him. Skimming my thumb over his crown, I capture a drop of precum, and bring it to my lips.

Leo watches me as I suck it into my mouth.

"I can't wait any longer." His voice deepens, and he rolls onto his back to yank at his nightstand drawer. Once he rolls the condom over his length, he turns back to me. "Hands around my neck, baby."

Gently, he positions himself at my entrance, balancing on

his elbows so he can hold my gaze. "Eyes on me the whole time."

I cannot look anywhere else. Not when I have him this close. So I do what he asks, and the connection it forges between us as he pushes into me is like nothing I have ever felt before.

"Gonna try to make this last, but..." he manages.

I wish I could tell him we have the rest of our lives. Or even tomorrow night. But there are no guarantees in life, and after the rally... I blink once, hard, and all my fears fall away. There's only me and Leo and his cock filling me so completely, we're one.

"God, you feel so good." Thrusting his hips, slowly at first, then faster, he claims me. Every rasp of his length against my clit—how does he manage to angle his body in just the right way?—brings me racing toward the edge.

"Leo...I am close..."

"Me too, baby. Don't let go." The raw emotion in his voice is all I need to send me into orbit, and when I cry out, Leo thrusts twice more, so hard we shake the bed, before he lets himself fly with me.

CHAPTER FOURTEEN

Leo

Domina's soft curves press against me, her dark hair tickling my chin. She saw me—all of me—and didn't run. I don't know what I did to deserve her coming into my life, but I'll do anything to keep her here.

A weak ray of light filters through a part in the drapes, but the sun hasn't fully risen. In three hours, we'll be on our way to the rally, and my gut is telling me by the end of the day, everything's going to change.

I don't want to wake her, but my back and right leg are locked up tight.

Easing her from my arms, I clench my jaw so hard, my teeth ache. But I manage to sit up without groaning. Not bad for an almost-fifty-year-old with enough titanium in his body to rival the Six Million Dollar Man.

But after three of my six daily exercises, I can't help myself. A painful trigger point takes me by surprise, and the sound I make is part grunt, part hiss, and part strangled cry.

"Leo?" Her voice is still husky with sleep, and it does

things to me that are damn inconvenient wearing only my boxers with a therapy ball under my ass. "Are you all right?"

"Fine," I manage and let myself topple onto my side. "This is my normal." I toss the knobby ball into the corner where I don't have to look at it again and shift to hide my mangled right foot.

She draws the covers to her chest, facing me as I reach for my least favorite torture device, The Stick.

"What is that?" Domina asks. "It looks like broken pieces of PVC pipe..."

Grimacing, I bend my right knee and start rolling the damn thing up and down my hamstring. "It helps with myofascial release." At her obvious confusion, I adjust the angle and add, "It loosens up the muscles and helps with blood flow. Or so my PT back in Venezuela claimed. Hurts like hell, but without it, my flexibility is shit."

"And the rest?" She gestures to the various therapy balls and foam-covered rollers lined up against the wall. "You need all of them?"

Admitting how fucked up I am shouldn't be so hard. She saw me completely naked last night and didn't blink twice. But *seeing* my scars is nothing compared to learning my body is FUBAR without half an hour of painful exercises each morning.

"Every day." The two words follow a deep groan as I move The Stick to the side of my leg and roll up and down along the ligament connecting my hip to my shin. I have to pause to catch my breath, the pain making my eyes burn. "I'll make coffee in a few minutes. I'm almost done."

Domina pats the duvet until she finds her discarded clothes. "I can take care of the coffee. But you need to add your own sugar." She feigns disgust and pulls on her tank top, giving me a brief glimpse of her breasts.

My body responds immediately, the earlier agony

forgotten in a heartbeat. "Or...we could go back to bed. We have a couple of hours."

She pauses, the sheet still covering her from the waist down. "Are you...*flexible* enough yet?"

Rising with only a little pain, I grin. "I'll manage, baby."

At promptly 9:00 a.m., a black sedan with tinted windows pulls up in front of our apartment building. Domina hasn't stopped fidgeting since I taped a thin switchblade to her back. I hope to all that's holy Cortez was right and they won't frisk her or send her through the metal detector.

My Glock 19 and chest harness are hidden inside the lining of her briefcase. The most dangerous weapon I have on me? My phone.

"That's your usual guy?" I ask, my hand tight around her wrist while the uniformed driver holds the back door open.

"Yes. Viejo picks me up every morning." She glances over at the man and smiles. "This is Leo. My boyfriend. He meant no offense."

With his dark sunglasses, Viejo's expression is damn near unreadable. "Sorry, man. This is my first political rally. Wasn't sure what to expect."

In the back seat next to me, Domina tugs at the labels of her tailored blue jacket. Every few moments, she shifts in her seat, clearly uncomfortable.

I cover her hand with mine and lean in to whisper in her ear. "No one's going to know unless you keep fidgeting."

She huffs, wriggling one last time before she settles. "This is all new to me, Leo. My life—despite my career—is boring. *Normal.* Two years ago, Manuel treated the entire staff to dinner at a five-star restaurant. Until this week, that was the most exciting thing to happen to me in as long as I can remember."

I try for a wink. "So the bar for amazing dates isn't very high? Lucky me."

With a weak smile, she shifts closer to me. "Maybe after the election, we could try boring for a while?"

We.

My entire world tilts on its axis. It doesn't matter that I felt something for her the first day we met. That yesterday—when I wasn't panicked about her safety or convinced I'd ruined everything between us—was one of the best days of my life because I spent it with her. Or that sex with her was so intense, it felt like my first time.

"Leo?" she asks. "Did you hear me?"

I give her hand a squeeze. "If you want boring, you get boring." With my lips pressed to her ear, I add, "Except in the bedroom."

A blush darkens her cheeks, and she looks away, focusing on something outside the tinted windows. But a sexy little smile curves her lips.

If we weren't so new, I'd tell Domina how she's changed me. Everything with her is *more*. Every experience. Every sensation. Every emotion. Hell, if we burn so hot, the flame dies in a week, I won't be shocked. But I don't know that I'd survive it either.

Traffic grinds to a halt as we approach the soccer stadium. "The rally doesn't start for another hour," I say, checking out the cars around us. "How early can the public get in?"

Domina checks her phone. "The gates opened twenty minutes ago. We hired a local band to play until 10:00 a.m., then the speeches will begin."

"Shit. We should have left an hour ago. Or more."

Next to me, Domina frowns, her shoulders hiking halfway up to her ears. "Why?"

"So I could have walked the perimeter. Checked for holes in the vice president's security. Anything to avoid diving into a three-ring circus, blind." Digging the fingers of my right hand into my palm hard enough my knuckles crack, I check behind us again.

Who am I kidding? Unless someone's following us in a fucking clown car with a flashing neon sign on top, I won't see them.

It's not until the sedan stops by the north-west entrance gate that I return my focus to the woman next to me. And curse myself for being a complete ass. She stares straight ahead, her jaw clenched tight. Even when I taped the blade to her back, her gaze held a faint glimmer of excitement. But now, there's only fear.

"Domina, look at me," I say, keeping my voice gentle. When she doesn't move, I nudge her chin toward me. "Stay by my side, and everything will be okay. In a few hours, we'll be back at the apartment—yours this time—and tonight, I'm taking you out on a proper date. Anywhere you want to go."

"I just want to be safe," she whispers.

Wrapping my arms around her, I press a kiss to her forehead. "You will be, baby. You will be."

Domina

Leo presses his hand to the small of my back and guides me through the outer gates.

Just inside, six National Police officers stand shoulder to shoulder. I withdraw my ID and pass it to them. "Domina Sanchez. I am a member of the vice president's staff."

They scrutinize my badge for a full minute before a tall,

bald National Police officer waves me through. "You may pass, but *he* must be searched."

Leo pulls his mobile out of his jacket pocket and holds it up. "This is all I've got on me."

Another officer takes a thick, black wand and runs it up and down Leo's body. It beeps at his ankle, and everyone tenses. The bald officer rests his hand on the butt of his gun.

"Relax," Leo says, carefully tugging up the leg of his black pants. "Titanium pins in my ankle. I wear a brace. Check it yourself. No weapons."

He has to pull off his shoe, sock, *and* brace, then endure a very thorough pat down before the officers are satisfied.

"I'm sorry," I say when we enter the tunnel to the locker rooms. "They did not need to be so rough with you."

Leo takes my arm and draws me into an alcove next to a water fountain. "If it keeps you—and everyone else—safe, they can do whatever the hell they want to me." His hands slide around my waist, tugging the hem of my blouse free from my skirt. Deft, calloused fingers skim my lower back until he finds the knife taped under my bra. "Ready?"

"Do it quickly." I clench my teeth, and he pulls the tape in one fluid motion. It stings less than I expected, but my eyes still water.

His lips brush mine, firm, insistent, and I forget all about the pain. Leo twists his hand in my hair, tipping my head back so he can deepen the kiss. A flood of arousal makes my knees weak and my panties damp.

"Domina!" Rafael snaps from the end of the tunnel. "What are you doing?"

Leo sidesteps me, sliding the knife into his pocket as he moves. "Sorry, man," he says with a shrug. "I thought we were alone."

"You were wrong. And the vice president is waiting." Rafael crosses his arms and stares at us, the harsh lights turning his expression from angry to livid. "Are you going to stand there all day?"

"We will be right there." I make a show of tucking in my blouse, and Rafael turns, heading into the locker room and muttering the whole time.

"Is he always such an ass?" Leo asks as he opens my briefcase and withdraws his gun and shoulder holster from inside the lining.

I help him on with the harness—a move we practiced this morning—and he shrugs back into his jacket. "Rafael is... difficult. But he is a master of political strategy. Without him, Manuel and President Garcia would never have been elected."

"Well, if he keeps talking down to you, he's going to get a black eye." I start to protest, but he quickly adds, "After the election."

"Do I look all right?" I ask, smoothing my hands down my blouse.

He cups the back of my neck, his eyes locked on mine. "You're perfect."

The first sliver of excitement stirs deep inside me. Rallies are overwhelming—even frightening. But there is no better feeling than hearing *my* words inspire people.

"Come. Manuel and the rest of the staff will be waiting."

"FINALLY," Rafael says under his breath as Leo and I enter the locker room. Manuel stands in front of a full-length mirror while his stylist—a point of contention between him and Rafael—brushes lint from his jacket.

"Mr. Vice President, are you certain you do not want the light blue shirt?" the man—I think his name is Michael —asks.

"Yes. Now leave me alone. If I do not have a few moments to myself before the speech, I will be no good to anyone."

The stylist throws up his hands. "I will be waiting at the end of the tunnel, sir. For any last-minute needs."

Cortez steps off a wooden box in front of the mirror and turns to the rest of the staff sitting on benches around the room. "We have come far, my friends. You have all worked miracles over the last six months. I would not be here without you, and I am grateful," he says with his hand over his heart, "so very grateful. On Sunday, we will celebrate our victory. For Panama!"

Everyone applauds, even Leo. He leans close to whisper in my ear. "How much of that was you?"

"None of it." Smiling as Manuel makes his way around the room to shake everyone's hand, I explain. "What you hear outside? That is me. But this? Manuel was born to lead. In almost six years, I have never seen him be anything but genuine."

"Domina. And...Leo, is it?" Cortez asks when he reaches us. He offers Leo his hand, and the two share a brief, intense look. "Thank you for coming."

"Wouldn't have missed it," Leo says. "And for what it's worth, Mr. Vice President, if I were a citizen, you would have my vote."

"You are too kind. I am afraid I must leave you now so I can take a few moments to prepare, but my staff is gathering at Estrella Brillante after the rally for a small celebration. I do hope you can join us there as well."

Rafael edges his way between Manuel and Leo. "The coach's office has been readied for you." He snaps his fingers, and one of the aids rushes in with a thermos—Manuel prepares for speeches with lemon ginger tea he brings from home. "Domina and her *guest* can make their way to the staff box."

His dismissal stings, and Leo tightens his grip on my hand. "After the election," he grumbles. "That prick is going to—"

"He will be the communications director for the President of Panama," I hiss.

"On election night, then. Before the winner is declared but after the polls close."

I stare at him, certain he must be joking, but his expression is deadly serious. "Leo, you cannot. Rafael is harmless. And very good at his job. Ignore him. Please?"

He sighs, slides his hands up my arms and presses a kiss to my forehead. "For you, I'll give him a pass. But he damn well better start treating you with more respect."

My heartbeat quickens. This is what a relationship should be. Leo cares for me. Since the moment we met, he has done nothing but try to protect me. From Daniel Pinzon, from whoever broke into the campaign offices, even from Rafael.

"You okay, baby?" Leo asks.

He's so concerned, and I smile up at him. "I did not expect...you."

"Me? I don't understand." He drapes his arm around my shoulders and guides me out of the locker room. The crowd cheers from the stands as one of the other speakers finishes.

The rest of the staff—all but Rafael—pour into the tunnel. Larissa grabs my arm. "Come *on*, Domina! We need to get to our seats."

Omar and Tomas flank us. I glance over at Leo and mouth, *"Sorry."*

"We're finishing this conversation later," he says with a chuckle.

Excitement stirs inside me. Along with panic. Leo is about to hear *my* words. Why does that terrify me?

It gets brighter with each step. Louder.

"Cortez! Cortez! Cortez!" the crowd chants.

At my side, Leo murmurs, "Holy shit."

Even Omar, Tomas, and Larissa are shocked at the number of people packed into the stands. The rest of the staff climbs the steps to the stage but the National Police officers block Leo and me from following.

"VIP guests are not allowed on stage." One of the officers points to several empty seats in the first row of the stands. "You can sit there."

"The hell I will," Leo grits out, but I rest my hand over his heart.

"You will only be a few meters away." Leaning in, I brush my lips to his. "Ten, fifteen steps. I will be fine."

He wraps his arms around me, pressing a kiss to the curve of my neck. "The *minute* he's done, get back down here, okay?"

Goosebumps race over my skin, and I hold on tight. "I promise."

CHAPTER FIFTEEN

Leo

"The people of Panama deserve better!" From the stage set up in the center of the pitch, Cortez pounds his fist on the podium. The crowd lets out a roar of applause. His wife and two adult children sit to his left, and to his right, Domina and her coworkers.

She's beaming. Cortez's Chief of Staff, Omar, leans over to whisper something in her ear. I'd give anything to be up there with her. To *feel* the joy radiating off of her.

Every word, every line, every pause for dramatic effect... they're all perfect. Cortez may be good at his job—and genuine—but it takes more than noble intentions to stir a crowd like this.

I've never been one for politics—the CIA doesn't care how you vote, only that you can follow orders—but even I'm moved.

Focus. You're not here to watch Domina. You're here to observe.

Sitting in the first row of the home team seats doesn't give me the greatest view of the rest of the stadium. Every few minutes, I twist around, feigning a sore back—not much of a stretch—so I can scan to my right.

Situation normal. So far.

Another burst of raucous applause, and something catches my eye. Across the pitch, a small group of people in the stands shove at one another. Security swarms the area.

From this far away, I can't tell who's winning the fight. Until the uniformed National Police officers start muscling people down the steps and out of the stadium.

I don't like this. By my count, at least fifteen arrests. No one on stage notices. A quick check of my phone tells me Cortez has been speaking for almost thirty minutes. He has to be almost done.

Pushing to my feet, the weight of the gun in my chest harness familiar and reassuring, I grab the railing while I take one last look around.

A flash of light from the top of the scoreboard sends ice flooding my veins. What I wouldn't give for binoculars. Was I imagining it? Most of the time, my limited depth perception and field of vision isn't a problem. But now?

Fuck!

There it is again. Only one thing flashes like that.

I vault over the railing. Landing hard, my knees buckle, and my palms scrape over the concrete.

Move! Get up and move!

Sharp, jagged pain surges through my right leg, but I force myself up and sprint for the stage.

"Sniper! Get down!" Waving my arms, I shout louder. "Get. Down. Now!"

Three IPS agents converge on me, weapons drawn.

"Sniper! On the scoreboard!" I have to get them to understand. Have to get to Domina. Up on the stage, no one notices me. They're all focused on the Vice President.

"Together, we will build a better Panama! For us! For our

children!" The cheers are deafening. The agents shout at me, but I can't hear what they're saying. Shit.

I could die for this, but I yank open my jacket so they see the gun under my right arm.

Someone slams into me from behind, sending me sprawling onto the pitch. My arms are pinned, wrenched behind my back. A zip tie binds my wrists. "No. Get to Cortez!" I manage. "Domina! Get down!"

Dammit. I can't *see*. The stage is to my right. I twist, kicking at the agent straddling me.

"Sniper, you dumbfuck! On the scoreboard!" This gets their attention. The weight pinning me down lifts, but before I can react, I'm flipped over.

A dark-haired man in a black suit snarls at me, "You are going to regret the day you were born, American." He wrenches the gun from the holster and slams it across my cheek.

Stars burst all around me. I blink, hard, and see agents racing to the stage, heading straight for the Vice President.

A hush falls over the crowd. Domina screams my name. The terror in her voice gives me the strength to push up on one elbow. Cortez stumbles back, blood staining his bicep, and the agents take him to the ground.

Someone kicks me in the ribs. "Search him," one of the agents shouts. When they find the knife in my pocket, fists rain down on me. Jaw. Stomach. The side of my head. Restrained, I can't defend myself. Can't even turn over with how they're on me. I taste blood.

"Leo! I have to get—" Domina cries. Where is she? Why can't I see her?

Two sets of hands haul me up by my arms. My legs won't hold me. They drag me, my shoes scuffing on grass, then concrete. We're moving away from the stage. Away from Domina.

Shaking my head, I try to focus. A group of agents hustles the Vice President off the stage and back down the tunnel. The National Police surround the rest of the staff. Where is she?

"Domina! Call...Zephyr! I need—" I manage before another punch to the gut makes me retch.

"Shut up, American," one of the agents barks at me. "You are under arrest."

We're moving faster now. They're not taking me down the tunnel. One of the tall, black gates looms in front of us. "No. I'm...with Domina Sanchez. Cortez. Is he all right? Please—"

"You ask for *nothing*, asshole." An SUV idles just outside the fence. If they get me into that thing, I'll disappear.

With the last of my strength, I plant my feet and twist as hard as I can. The man on my right stumbles, but the other agent tightens his grip on my arm.

Pain explodes across the back of my neck. It's like a black cloud blocks out the sun. Everything slows. The screams and shouts from the terrified crowd deepen, and the world turns soft.

Domina's safe. She has to be safe.

It doesn't matter what happens to me. I did my job. Cortez is alive. I hope. The wound...where was the wound? His arm. High up. He'll live.

I land half on the back seat of the SUV, half on the floor. My head spins. A door slams. The car speeds away from the stadium, and I hope to God I live long enough to see Domina again.

Domina

For half an hour, my life was perfect. Thousands of people cheering for Manuel, *my* words inspiring them. I could see Leo in the stands, and though he spent most of his time scanning the crowd, our gazes locked more than once. He smiled —that adorable, lopsided grin—and my heart skipped a beat every time.

"Manuel!" He's ten meters ahead of me. So many IPS agents surround him, all I can see is the top of his head. The white hair, now mussed. And every few steps, a light tinge of red high up on his arm.

Two National Police officers flank me. We're halfway down the tunnel when I realize the rest of the staff is ahead of us. Together. Omar has his arm around Larissa's shoulders. Rafael and Tomas are side by side.

Manuel and his detail rush off to the right, down another tunnel that I think leads to a back exit. The staff follow, but one of the police officers takes my arm. "You will come with us," he says sharply.

I stop—or try to—but he pulls me to the left. "No. Where is Leo Basher? He is my guest. My boyfriend. I need to find him."

"Your *guest* smuggled weapons into the rally. He is going to jail. The Institutional Protection Service wants you detained and questioned." We're still moving. The tunnel starts to slope up. After another corner, sunlight shines far ahead.

The officer on my other side reaches for my briefcase, but I clutch it to my chest. "No. I need my phone. I have to call Manuel. He can straighten this out."

The bag is yanked away. I stumble in my heels and fall.

I lunge for the officer, desperate to snatch my briefcase from his hands, but the other one jerks me back to my feet.

My shoulder burns, and tears spring to my eyes. "You are making a mistake."

"No mistakes, Ms. Sanchez. You're coming with us to the station. You will tell the IPS everything you know about Mr. Basher, and *they* will decide if you will go to prison along with him."

This cannot be happening. Minutes ago, I was watching Manuel give the penultimate speech of his campaign. And now...? The officers force me to walk faster. We are almost to the end of the tunnel, and a police car, lights flashing, waits.

The officers pat me down. My cheeks burn, but I fight for control. Until one of them pulls out a set of handcuffs.

"No. Please. You do not need those!"

Shouts come from somewhere to my left. "Look! They're arresting someone! Get video. Now!" a woman shouts.

The handcuffs snap around my wrists, cold and tight. A news crew runs toward us. The woman—with her perfectly pressed red suit and coiffed black hair—calls out, "What are you arresting her for? Who is she?"

The police officers ignore her. One puts his hand on the top of my head and guides me into the back seat of the vehicle. The door slams shut, the finality of the sound signaling the end of my career. Of whatever I might have been building with Leo. Of...everything.

EXHAUSTION MAKES my swollen eyes burn. Before this week, when was the last time I cried? I can't remember.

"How long have you and Mr. Basher been seeing each other?" Detective Franco, the gruffer of the two officers sitting across from me, asks for what feels like the hundredth time.

"He came to my rescue when Daniel Pinzon broke into my apartment on Sunday. You know this. Where is my mobile phone? I need to call my lawyer." My voice wobbles. If they do not let me go soon, I will break down completely.

They have been at this for hours. Question after question about Leo, how he got the gun and knife past security, whether I knew anything about the weapons. I panicked the first time they asked me, and said I had no idea he was armed.

Was that right? Or will my lie cause him even more trouble? They will not tell me where he is, how he is, or if I will ever be able to see him again.

"Weapons were not allowed inside the stadium. As one of the Vice President's staff, you should know this. We could arrest you right now," Franco says, leaning halfway across the table to sneer at me. "Tell us the truth!"

"I am! Leo is my neighbor and my boyfriend. That is *all* I know!" My tears spill over, and I swipe at my cheeks. "You will tell me nothing about him. Or Manuel. I do not even know what time it is!

Covering my face with my hands, I give up trying to be strong. I have to get out of here. Leo told me to call Zephyr, but how will I even get in touch with her? If he's been arrested, they will have searched his apartment. Probably taken his tablet, but even if it *is* still there, I would have to unlock it. And his door.

Someone knocks, and I jerk upright. Since they brought me here, I have only seen the two men across from me. No one else has come in, and I'm not facing the door. The few times they've left me alone, I have not been able to see anyone in the hall.

Please, let it be Rafael or one of Manuel's lawyers. Anyone who will listen to me.

Detective Franco opens the door a crack and speaks in hushed tones to someone I cannot see.

"What do you mean?" he says sharply. After a moment, he snorts. "Why? She knows something. I can feel it!"

More quiet words, but from the tone, whoever he's talking to is not happy with him.

"Fine. But it will be *your* name on the paperwork." He turns to me and jerks his head toward the door. "Get up. I have orders to let you go."

Relief makes my muscles tremble. When I stand, the room spins for a moment, and I hold on to the back of the chair for support. "Where is my briefcase?"

The door swings open, and a tall, older man pushes into the room. "Ms. Sanchez, I am Sergeant Montoya." He holds out my bag, and I snatch it from his hands. "You are free to go. But I must warn you not to leave town. We may have more questions for you tomorrow."

"Where is Leo Basher?" I ask. A small voice inside my head warns me not to anger Montoya, but I have to know.

"That is none of your concern. Go now before I change my mind." He points down the hall to the left, and I don't hesitate.

My shoes echo on the dingy linoleum, and from how quiet it is at the station, the darkness outside the windows, and the way my stomach turns over on itself with every step, it has to be well after eight.

Outside, the warm evening air holds the promise of rain. I dig in my bag for my phone so I can call a taxi, but before I can unlock it, the device vibrates in my hand.

Unknown: Install this app right now. Then get somewhere private. -Z

I do not understand how Zephyr found my phone number or why the message arrived the moment I was outside the police station, but I don't care. She is the only way I will find Leo.

The app is the same one Leo used to talk to her. I recognize the name. As it downloads, I hurry away from the station until I find a bench a few blocks away. It's well lit, and across the street, a bar is crowded enough I should be safe here for a few minutes. I reply to the text message, telling her I'm alone, and within seconds, the app dings.

"Zephyr?" I ask.

"What happened? Where's Leo? I remote-locked his phone and tablet less than an hour after the assassination attempt, but—"

"The...what?" My entire body starts to shake. I can barely hold onto the phone.

"Domina, focus," she says. "It's all over the news, even in the United States. I pulled the footage from the rally. Only limited angles, but from what I can tell, there was a sniper on one of the scoreboards. Leo saw him, but those IPS idiots beat the crap out of him and dragged him away rather than thanking him for saving Cortez's life. I'm sorry it took me so long to get you out of custody, but we had to get *someone* to admit they had you first."

I sink against the back of the bench, fresh tears burning my eyes. "*You* convinced the police to let me go?"

"No. But I activated the Bat Signal. You'll have backup in five or six hours, tops."

My head hurts, and her words mean nothing to me. "I do not understand. What 'Bat Signal'?"

A tight laugh carries over the connection. "Leo might not believe this from what Trevor told me, but he actually *does* have friends. Ones with enough clout and resources to make things happen. Get somewhere safe and stay there. They'll come to you."

"Is...is my apartment safe? I do not have anywhere else to go."

Zephyr sighs. "I don't know. But I'd feel a hell of a lot

better if you were somewhere no one can find you. Hang on a minute."

While she does whatever it is that requires her to type faster than anyone I have ever heard, I check my text messages.

Larissa: Where are you? Cortez got shot! He's okay, but the police questioned all of us. They think your guy had something to do with it.

Rafael: Don't bother coming back to work. Your boyfriend almost got Manuel killed. You're fired.

I choke back a sob. Everything I have worked for is gone.

"Domina? What's wrong?" Zephyr asks.

"Everyone thinks Leo is responsible for the...attack." I cannot bring myself to say the word. Assassination.

"Fuck. I was afraid of that. Is there any way you can change your appearance? Hide your hair? Get different clothes? I booked you a room at the Hotel de Palmas under a clean alias. You just have to get there. But your face has been all over the news tonight. Some reporter caught the police handcuffing you and putting you into the back of a squad car."

My heart hurts. Even sitting here is dangerous. "I have nothing with me. Just my wallet, my tablet, and my phone. Lipstick."

More keystrokes, and then she whispers "yes" under her breath. "There's a store at the end of the block to the south. See it?"

I turn, and she's right. The little bodega is lit with colorful lights, and a man sweeps the sidewalk out front. "Yes."

"Please tell me you at least have cash."

Digging in my briefcase, I check my wallet. "Twenty dollars, yes."

"Buy something to cover your hair. A t-shirt if they have one. Sunglasses. Then call a cab and get to the Hotel de

Palmas. Go to Room 422. I'm sending the hotel's keycard app to your phone. Use that to open the door. Then do *not* leave until reinforcements show up. When they do, they'll identify themselves as Clark and Jimmy. If *anyone* else knocks, you call me immediately. Got it?"

"I...no. Zephyr, you have to find Leo..."

"Focus," she says sharply. "I'm working on it, but if I don't get you secured first, Leo would never forgive me. Hair. T-shirt. Sunglasses. Hotel de Palmas. Room 422. Clark and Jimmy. I need to know you understand."

"Yes." My hand shakes as I dry my tears. "I understand. Please...just find him."

"I will." The call drops, and I take a deep breath. I can do this. Rising, I stare up at the wispy clouds. "Please, God. Keep Leo safe."

CHAPTER SIXTEEN

Leo

THE EMPTY CUP of water mocks me from the corner of the room. With my wrists shackled to the table, I can't stand up.

Who are you kidding? Even if they took the cuffs off, you'd still be fucked.

I passed out minutes after the IPS agents muscled me into the SUV. When I came to, they were dragging me down a long hallway to God knows where.

Strip searched, beaten until I couldn't stand on my own, and thrown in here. No shoes, no belt. They even took my fucking ear studs.

My legs are half numb. I can't make a fist with my right hand. My eyelids feel like they weigh a hundred pounds each. Every time I put my head down, someone slams the door so loud, I jump.

I don't know how long I've been here. No windows. No way to mark the passage of time other than my exhaustion. They won't let me sleep. No food. Only a few ounces of water and that was hours ago.

The door bangs open, and I jerk against the cuffs. Peña, the one who asks all the questions, holds a steaming cup of coffee, and fuck. It smells like heaven.

Reyes, his partner—whose only contribution to the party is his fists—leans against the wall to my right. Fucker must know I can't see shit on that side.

"Mr. Basher, you do not look well," Peña says and takes a long sip of coffee. "We can bring in a doctor if you tell us what we want to know."

"Listen, dumbfuck—"

Reyes kicks the chair out from under me. The metal cuffs dig into my wrists. My ass hits the cement floor and sharp pain lances through my shoulders.

It takes me three tries to get to my knees. The room spins, Peña's expression fading in and out of focus. "If you're going to kill me," I say, "just *do* it already."

"We do not wish to kill you, Mr. Basher." Peña smiles, takes another sip of coffee, and folds his hands on the table. Reyes rights the chair, grabs the waistband of my Dockers, and shoves me back into the seat. Before he returns to his favorite spot, he punches me in the side.

Wheezing, I grab the bar welded to the table to keep from sliding back down to the floor. "Without me," I manage, "Manuel Cortez would be dead."

Peña throws his paper cup against the wall, the last of the coffee dripping down to the floor. "Without you, I would be asleep in my bed right now. You brought a loaded gun through security to a presidential rally, Mr. Basher. For that alone, you will go to jail for many years. Threatening members of the International Protection Service? Attempting to assassinate the Vice President of Panama? You will never see daylight again."

"I saved his fucking life. Your people didn't see the sniper.

I did." My voice is fading, and the split lip Reyes gave me hours ago burns with every word.

Peña arches a brow. "If you will not talk to spare your own life, maybe you want to keep your lover out of prison."

I sit up straighter, ignoring the throbbing pain in my back. "What have you done to Domina?"

"We have done nothing to her, Mr. Basher. But the National Police are preparing to bring charges against her. Helping a terrorist smuggle weapons into a secure location is a very serious crime." He smiles, and if I weren't locked to this goddamn table, I'd snap his neck.

"She's innocent, you fucking bastard." Desperation has me yanking on the cuffs, and blood slicks my wrists. "If you hurt her..."

"You will do what? And how? You are handcuffed to a table, in a locked room, somewhere no one will ever find you. I *own* you, Mr. Basher." Peña nods to Reyes. The bigger man ambles over to the door and punches a long string of numbers into a keypad. The locks disengage, and he retrieves a bucket from the hall and hands it to his partner.

"By morning, perhaps you will be more...talkative." Peña drops the bucket next to me, then follows Reyes from the room. "I would tell you to get some rest, but we both know that will not happen."

The locks engage, and I scream obscenities until my voice fades away completely. The way I feel now, I'll be completely fucked by morning. The only chance I have? Zephyr. She'll know something's happened to me. Maybe she'll tell Trevor. Or Austin.

And what the hell are they going to do?

At least when Trev was taken, we knew where the fuck he was. This place is a black site. Minimal staff—I think I've only seen one other person besides my two interrogators—thick walls, probably several stories below ground. They'll never find me.

But they can help Domina. As long as she's safe, I don't care what happens to me.

I lay my head on the table. If everyone went home, maybe I can catch an hour or two of sleep. But not more than a minute later, an ear-splitting cacophony fills the room. I jerk up so quickly, I lose my balance. The chair tips over, and so do I.

Twisting so I can peer up at the ceiling behind me, I curse —silently. I didn't notice the speaker mounted high on the wall. No sleep. No food. No water. I'm fucked.

Domina, I'm sorry. I should have protected you.

Domina

I am so tired, but when I try to sleep, all I see is Leo fighting against three IPS agents. I do not care how dangerous it is. I want to go home. This is one of the nicer hotels in Panama City with luxurious sheets, a feather duvet, and a mini-bar— that is now empty of everything but the alcohol. The National Police did not see any reason to feed me, and as soon as I opened the small refrigerator, my stomach reminded me I had not eaten since breakfast.

I took a shower, but I still feel dirty. The new t-shirt is scratchy, my eyes are dry, and the emptiness inside me aches. I need Leo, and I'm afraid I will never see him again.

When I arrived, a little after 10:00 p.m., I sat on the bed and watched the local news coverage of the rally. I cannot bring myself to call it what it was, despite the reporters repeating the two words—*assassination attempt*—over and over again.

My name flashed across the screen every ten minutes. *"Domina Sanchez, the Vice President's speechwriter, was arrested only minutes after the shot was fired. She has yet to be charged with a crime, but the National Police say it is only a matter of time."*

Huddled under the duvet, I hug my knees to my chest and stare at the bedside clock. The numbers blur, and I jerk when someone knocks on the door.

"Who is it?" I ask as I check the peephole. The two men carry themselves with authority. Like Leo.

They exchange glances, either amused or annoyed, I cannot tell, and then the taller one clears his throat. "Clark and Jimmy."

I cannot unlock the door fast enough. "Have you found Leo?"

"Inside," the shorter one says. The look in his eyes...it's the same one Leo had when he told me about his scars. But I think...this man carries pain with him every day of his life.

"I'm Austin," the older, taller one says after locking the door. "That ray of sunshine is Trevor."

I nod, backing up until my legs hit the bed. "Where is he?"

"We don't know," Austin says. "Yet. Zephyr hacked into Panama City's traffic camera network, and she ID'd the SUV they put him in. But after ten minutes, it went through a dead zone. She won't stop until she finds him, and President Garcia is getting a very unpleasant wakeup call any minute now."

"The President? I don't understand." I'm so tired, nothing makes sense.

"Pritchard—Austin—used to run the United States Joint Special Operations Command," Trevor says. "Basically, he's a big fucking deal and knows people who know people who know your president."

"My God. And you...know Leo? How?" I ask.

Trevor's shoulders hunch, and he stares down at his boots. "Austin and Leo had to get me out of a jam in Venezuela a while ago."

"One of the only men I trust in this world had some trouble last year. He and his girl had to get out of the country quick."

Leo's words haunt me every time I close my eyes. But I understand now. Who Trevor is. "Leo's friend. From the CIA. That was you."

Trevor nods. "I retired seven years ago. I work for a security company in Boston now. That's how we got here so quickly. Without going through Customs."

"And armed," Austin says. "West, Inara, and Graham—they're based in Seattle—are on standby. If we need them, they can get here in a little over eight hours."

I stare at the two men, amazed they are even here, let alone with *more* help potentially on the way.

"Domina?" Austin asks, holding out his hand. "Do you want to go home?"

Tears sting my eyes. "More than anything. Or...can I go to Leo's?"

Austin chuckles. "Zephyr was right."

"There's something in the water," Trevor adds. "Everywhere."

"What are you talking about?" I ask, hands on my hips. "Leo has been missing for"—I check the bedside clock—"fifteen hours. Panama is *not* a place to be an American in prison. We have come a long way since the days of Noriega, but, if you do not find him..."

"Domina, we found you. Well, Zephyr did," Austin says with a small smile. "She had to check the camera feeds for every police station in Panama City, but once we knew where you were, it only took us an hour to get you released."

I gape at him. "You..."

"You didn't wonder why they suddenly let you go?" Trevor pulls out his phone and checks the screen. "A couple of phone calls and the captain was shitting his pants. We're going to find him. But right now, you probably want to change—or sleep a while—and we need to set up shop and contact Zephyr. We have a car parked by the side door. You ready?"

I grab my briefcase from the foot of the bed and clutch it to my chest. "Yes. Do I need the hat and sunglasses?"

"Not with us." Austin opens his jacket to reveal a pistol under his left arm. "Anyone even *tries* to get close to you, they're going to regret it."

THE TWENTY-MINUTE RIDE to my apartment passes in a blur. Trevor drives, and Austin texts with Zephyr the whole way. As they find a parking spot on the street next to the building's back door, Austin turns to me. "We know of ten separate black sites within an hour of the city. Leo's in one of them."

"You're certain?"

Austin opens my door, then helps me to my feet. "The IPS doesn't have their own interrogation facilities. They use the Ministry of Public Service sites, and those..."

The two men flank me, Austin to my left, Trevor to my right. "What?" I ask. "What are you not telling me?"

"The assholes who run them were trained by the same sadistic fucks who worked for Noriega." Trevor punches the elevator call button, his voice taking on a rough tone. "Leo knows how to survive. But the longer he's there, the worse shape he'll be in when we find him."

"I knew I should have brought Griff," Austin mutters. "You're a ray of fucking sunshine, Trev."

"I'm a realist. Who's been where Leo is right now. Remember?" he spits out. "And Griff is in San Diego. Two flights are a hell of a lot harder to hide than one."

The elevator doors open to the fifth floor, and Austin pulls his gun from the holster. "Domina, stay between us. It should be safe, but..."

I nod, and we move as one to the end of the hall.

"Shit," Austin says. "Leo's door is open. Trev, take Domina next door until we know his place is clear."

"Unlock it, then let me enter first." Trevor holds his own gun, the barrel pointed at the floor.

My hand shakes as I slide my key into the lock. This is not my life. Worrying about someone waiting to harm me. My boyfriend—friend, protector, whatever Leo is to me—somewhere so terrible, Trevor cannot bear to think about it.

"Clear," Trevor says when he's checked my bedroom, bathroom, closets, and even behind the shower curtain. "If you want to stay at Leo's, pack up whatever you think you'll need for at least twenty-four hours. The less we have to go back and forth, the better."

In under five minutes, I have a small suitcase with several changes of clothes, my toothbrush, makeup bag, and power cords for my phone, laptop, and tablet. "Ready."

Trevor taps his ear. "Jimmy, we clear?" After a beat, he nods. "Okay. Let's go. Stay behind me."

Two steps into Leo's apartment, I stop short and gape. All of his kitchen cabinets are open, mugs and plates broken on the floor. Deep rips mar his couch cushions, bits of stuffing strewn everywhere. The bedroom is even worse. The mattress is askew, pillows ripped open...even his yoga mat is torn.

"The safe," I manage. "In the closet."

"Gone." Austin holsters his weapon, frowning. "But Leo wouldn't keep much there. His gun, maybe his Visa paperwork. There's another hidey-hole somewhere in this place no one would ever find. Except maybe us. That's where he'll have his go bag, passport, fake IDs…"

He and Trevor muscle the mattress back into place. The sheets are piled in a corner, and I pick them up and toss them onto the bed. "He cannot come back to this."

"He won't. Austin, get our tech set up in the main room. I'll help Domina."

The older man nods. "Got to get the gear first. I'll let you know before I come back in."

"Roger that." Trevor grabs one corner of the fitted sheet and tucks it around the mattress. "In a few minutes, I can go back to your place and get your pillows. These are obviously FUBAR."

"FUBAR?"

"Fucked up beyond all recognition." He chuckles, but there's no joy in it. "Don't know what we'll do about the couch cushions. My sewing skills are limited to stitches."

I stare at him, trying to decide if he is serious or not. Until I remember what I wanted to ask him. "Why did you call Austin 'Jimmy' at my apartment?"

Trevor turns his head and points to his ear. "When we're in the field and using comms, we all have codenames. I'm 'Superman' or 'Clark.' Austin's 'Jimmy' or 'Stars and Bars.' You're 'Diana' and Leo is 'Steve.'"

"Clark and Jimmy I know. But who are Diana and Steve?" Tucking in the sheet, I reach for the duvet.

"From *Wonder Woman*. Lois was already taken," he says with a small smile. "And Perry White…well, I doubt Leo would have taken too well to that one."

Trev cocks his head, then taps his earbud. "Got it. I have to go to Diana's. Need pillows." Another tap, and he reaches for his weapon.

The front door opens and closes, followed by Austin's deep, "Back. All clear."

"You're safe here, Domina," Trevor says, his voice gentle. "Shower, sleep...whatever you need to do. We'll let you know if we find *anything*."

CHAPTER SEVENTEEN

Domina

DESPITE WHAT THE POLICE—OR the IPS—did to Leo's apartment, his bed still smells like him. Or us. But as tired as I am, I only manage three hours before I wake up with my heart pounding. Leo could be anywhere. Hurt. Afraid. Alone.

"Call Zephyr! I need—"

He was depending on me. It doesn't matter that Zephyr found me. Or that Austin and Trevor are in the next room. It's been more than eighteen hours.

In the main room, I find Austin sitting at the small dining table with two laptops, a mobile phone, and more weapons than I could have imagined strewn around him. Trevor sleeps on the sofa, still wearing his shoulder harness and gun.

"There's coffee," Austin says quietly with a quick jerk of his head toward the kitchen.

I pour myself a cup and join him at the table. "Is there any news?"

He sits back, stretching his arms over his head with a wince. "Zephyr eliminated three of the black sites we identified. No activity within five kilometers at any time in the past twenty-four hours."

"But that still leaves seven." The coffee smells wonderful yet twists my stomach into knots.

"Domina, we *will* find him. President Garcia's aide messaged me a few minutes ago and said he'd take my call." He offers me an earbud. "Want to listen in and hear the most powerful man in the country shit his pants?"

"President Garcia is a good man. He and Manuel have been friends for years. But if it will find Leo, I will listen to anything."

Austin dials, and after a moment, the President answers, his voice rough with sleep. "Mr. Pritchard, I understand you have very powerful friends. But what is so important you had to get me out of bed at 6:00 a.m.?"

"It's former *Major General* Pritchard, asshole. The first call you received from me was at 11:00 p.m. last night. Since then, I've tried to reach you every hour on the hour. *You* chose to ignore me until now."

"I am a busy man."

"And I'm an angry one," Austin snaps. "Your vice president would be dead right now if it weren't for Leo Basher. And your precious Ministry of Public Service is hiding him in one of your fucking black site prisons. If this is what you do to people who *save* your citizens' lives, what the hell happens to the guys who pose an actual threat?"

"I know nothing about this...Leo Basher," Garcia says. I clench my hands under the table. After being fired without any chance to explain or defend myself, I shouldn't care about being loyal to anyone in power. But I still believe Manuel had nothing to do with it.

"You're the goddamn president. Make some calls and find him. He left the Pacifica Stadium in the back of a black SUV with government plates at 12:15 p.m. Ask me how I know that."

President Garcia doesn't answer, and Austin is getting angrier by the minute.

"You want me to shut down the IPS? Or the Ministry? Or tell the people of Panama what they *really* do? Or maybe I call the newspapers and tell them how you sold your soul six years ago to get on the presidential ticket?" A muscle in Austin's jaw ticks, and after a beat, he continues. "*Paying* your rival five million dollars to disappear? Do you think you'll be able to retire quietly to the countryside after that? You'll lose everything. Including the accounts you maintain in the Cayman Islands."

From the couch, Trevor adds, "Don't forget the escorts. All those private videos he uploaded to the cloud could be 'not so private' with a few keystrokes."

I gape at the man, still prone, eyes heavy with sleep, while Austin relays the information. "So, what'll it be, Garcia? Release Leo Basher or lose everything?"

"I will call you back in twenty minutes," President Garcia says. The connection drops and I stare at Austin, convinced he's out of his mind.

"You threatened the President of Panama! We have to leave. Now. He will know where we are, and the IPS will come to take us all." Rising, I dart a gaze around the room. There is nothing of Leo here. Nothing of Leo *anywhere*. The only evidence he lives here is the clothes in his closet.

"Domina." Trevor comes up behind me, and I whirl around, hands on my hips. "No one's coming after us here. No one who wants to see another sunrise, anyway." He touches the butt of his gun, as if he needs to know it's still there.

"But they will try." I hate the tremble in my voice. The weakness. In only a week, I have gone from never needing anyone—or so I thought—to weak, terrified, and helpless.

"No. They won't." Austin stands, turning one of the laptops so I can see the screen. And half a dozen chat windows. I take a step closer so I can read the names.

"That's...the Chairman of the Joint Chiefs of Staff," I whisper. "And the Secretary of Defense?"

"Plus the Secretary of the Navy and the Chief of Staff to the Vice President of the United States," Austin adds. "Can't tell you where the others work. Or worked. Garcia's well aware how connected I am. Even though I 'retired' a year ago, I still have some damn powerful friends."

Austin's phone rings, and he taps his earbud. "Garcia, you better have answers for me."

"Go to 1801 Avenida de Cedro. The Ministry of Public Service does not report to me. I did what I could. You should not face any resistance, but I cannot guarantee it."

"Good to know you're not a complete idiot," Austin says. "Your next call better be to Manuel Cortez. Because as soon as we get Basher out of that hell hole, we need some goddamn answers, and he's the only one who can provide them."

Austin doesn't wait for Garcia to reply. Tucking his phone into the pocket of his tactical pants, he slams the laptops closed. "Trev, get Domina set up with protective gear. We leave in ten minutes."

Leo

"Wake up, American." The punch sends me crashing to the floor. My legs are numb. The pain racing down my arms is like a thousand volts of electricity all the way to my wrists.

"Didn't need...a fucking...alarm clock," I slur. I shouldn't be thankful to see—or hear, since I'm so dizzy, I can't see shit

—Reyes and Peña again, but anything's better than the godawful "music" they played all night to keep me awake.

"Tell us who you work for!" Peña shouts. Reyes grabs me by the throat and shoves me back into the chair. "Or we will take you to another cell that is much less comfortable than this one."

"Fuck off." Lifting my head is damn near impossible. I blink hard and meet Peña's gaze. He's desperate. Why? Something's changed.

God, I need to be able to think.

He slams his hands down on the table, leaning so close I can smell the coffee on his breath. "Where would she go?"

She?

Another punch—this one to my side. Then a boot presses down on my right foot. The pain pulls a groan from my parched throat.

Without my shoes, it's easy to jerk my leg and slide my toes out from under Reyes's sole. "Not saying a word...until you give me some water."

A hand fists my hair. Before I can blink, Reyes slams my head against the table.

Darkness closes in. Peña's face shrinks before my eyes until all I can see is his blurry pock-marked cheek.

I wish I could stop fighting to survive. Pass out and let them do whatever the fuck they want to me. But I didn't survive eight days of torture in Venezuela to die at the hands of these two incompetent assholes.

"Again," Peña snaps.

This time, I'm fast enough to jerk away. My head pounds. The room spins around me, but Reyes only grabs a couple strands of my hair. He swears, lunges for me again, but the door bangs open.

"Get the American up," another man says. I'm so shocked,

I don't pay attention when he lowers his voice and switches to Spanish.

Peña protests, something about them almost breaking me. "Give us another hour, Robles."

"Quickly," the new guy says. "Or he's coming in. Garcia warned me—"

"You have thirty seconds, shit stain. Or my friend here is going to start shooting. And he does *not* miss."

I snap my head up, forgetting all about the pain. I know that voice. The slight east coast accent.

"Wait," Robles manages before he's shoved back against the wall.

Austin Pritchard fills the narrow doorway, his gaze sweeping around the windowless room. "Get those goddamn cuffs off him right fucking now." For good measure, he repeats the order in Spanish with his hand resting on the pistol strapped to his hip. A shadow moves behind him. No. Two of them.

Reyes pulls a small key from his pocket. His hands shake as he unlocks the cuffs. I'm too weak, too sore to do more than let my hands fall to my sides.

"Leo, can you walk?" Austin asks.

I stare up at him, convinced he's a figment of my sleep-deprived brain.

Gentle hands frame my face, and the scent of wild orchids and orange blossoms replaces the stench of sweat and blood clinging to me. "Leo? Put your arm around me. Please. We need to go."

She's here. I didn't think I'd ever see Domina again, but she's touching me. Draping my left arm over her shoulders. Trying to stand with me held against her.

"Get your ass up, dude," Trevor shouts from the hall. "Got to go."

Austin takes my right arm, and together, he and Domina

get me vertical. But when I try a step, I collapse. My head barely misses the corner of the table. Domina cries out, and it's like a knife to my heart.

"Legs are numb," I grit out. "Sorry..."

"Take this and stick close to Trevor," Austin says. "I'll get Leo."

I'm too dizzy and tired to focus on what he passes to Domina. Only on the fear in her eyes before she rushes into the hall.

"Guess I'm in bad shape," I say when Austin slings my arm around his shoulders and hauls me up.

"You look like shit."

In the hall, Trevor leads the way, drawing down on anyone we meet. Domina follows, a pistol in her hand aimed at the floor. The whole place is nothing but gray cement walls, harsh lights, and echoes.

In the main room, four men stand shoulder to shoulder, blocking the elevator. "Move or you each lose a testicle," Trevor says. Domina raises her gun, and he adds, "Or worse. *I* might spare your lives, but she won't."

"Get out of the goddamn way," Austin snaps. He pulls his Glock from the holster. "President Garcia doesn't have operational authority over you assholes, but he can still make you *disappear*. Then again, so can we. You want to fuck around and find out?"

The men exchange glances—I think, as my vision isn't completely clear—and the one on the left nods. "Step aside," he orders. Domina presses the elevator call button, and the four of us put our backs to the doors, Trev, Austin, and Domina still ready to shoot at any moment, until they slide open.

But by now, I can feel some of the tension leaving Austin's shoulders. He knows they won't stop us. I don't understand how he can be so confident—or how he and

Trev are even here—but I don't care. Domina's safe, and that's all I need.

No one says a word as the elevator climbs. Three dings before we're back to ground level. In a small, plain room, a single man sits behind a desk reading a magazine. "Anyone dead down there?" he asks, his voice completely monotone.

"No," Austin and Trevor say in tandem.

Satisfied, the man returns to his reading.

The sun blinds me the second we step outside. Letting my head fall forward, I stop struggling against my heavy lids. I'm breathing free air. And I'm not alone.

"Leo? Please wake up." A gentle hand strokes my cheek, and I turn toward the touch. "You need to drink something."

A car engine rumbles all around me. The regular *thump, thump, thump* of tires hitting seams in the pavement. I'm lying on something soft. In the back of a car? My eyes are so dry, I'm not sure I can open them.

"Trevor?" Domina asks. "When do we worry?"

"Awake," I rasp. "Kind of."

"Thank fuck, man. It's been almost an hour." Trev's voice carries almost as much strain as Domina's, and I force my left eye open. He's sitting in the front seat of the SUV, Austin behind the wheel.

Domina smiles down at me, tears glistening on her cheeks. "Take small sips," she says as she holds a bottle of water to my cracked lips.

Water hasn't tasted this good since the last time I was held, interrogated, and almost died. She takes it away long before I'm ready, but I know she's right. Too much too soon is dangerous.

"Can you...even...shoot?" I ask.

From the front seat, Trevor and Austin chuckle. "Of course that's the first thing he'd ask," Austin says. "Not, 'how the hell did you find me,' 'why did it take you so long,' or 'what are you two dumb fucks doing here'."

If I could glare at the man, I would. But I'm too exhausted and I can't look anywhere but into Domina's eyes.

"I know how to use a gun. In college, I joined a paintball team." She brushes my hair away from my forehead. "I won many games."

"You shouldn't have brought her." My voice is still so weak and hoarse, I don't know if Trev and Austin can even hear me until Trevor turns in the passenger seat, his brown eyes blazing.

"You think we should have left her alone at your apartment? Where anyone could have gotten to her? Give us a little credit, man. And don't even *try* to suggest she'd have been better off in a safehouse. Not with your head in her lap. Doesn't matter that you're in bad shape. You'll still end up on the floor."

"It wasn't safe." Talking is a herculean effort. My eyes close, the lids too heavy for me to keep them open a second longer.

"Leo?" Her voice sounds like it's coming from a mile away. "Drink more, please."

After another couple of sips, I whisper, "Need to sleep, baby. I'll be okay. Just...don't leave me."

"Never again."

With those two words, I can let go, and I drift off, knowing she'll be here when I wake up.

CHAPTER EIGHTEEN

Leo

BY THE TIME we reach my apartment, my legs are no longer numb. But every step is torture, even with Austin and Domina supporting half my weight.

"He needs a doctor." Domina glares at Austin, then Trevor in turn.

"I'm okay," I grit out in the elevator. "Nothing's broken."

"You look..." Her voice cracks, and tears shine in her eyes.

"Trev's had some medical training," Austin says. "Enough to know if we need to find a doctor we can pay to keep quiet."

Domina huffs, but when the doors open on the fifth floor, she swallows whatever she was about to say. The two ex-pats from across the hall are waiting to get on the elevator, and Trev steps in front of me. "You didn't see us," he says, his tone deadly calm. With a single jerk of his head, he gets them to step back and give us a wide berth.

They whisper to one another as we head down the hall, but I'm too tired to care. They can spread rumors about me to every apartment in the building as long as I can shower, eat, and sleep.

Austin lowers me onto the couch. Despite the lumpy, ripped cushions, I could pass out right here. Especially with Domina sitting next to me, her fingers linked with mine.

Until Trevor kneels down and shines a bright light into my eye.

"Shit. I told you, I'm fine."

"The hell you are." Only the rough edge to his voice stops me from shoving him away. "Austin? Find Leo something to eat. Broth, crackers, toast..."

"It's been less than twenty-four hours," I mutter. "I can handle more than toast."

I don't fight when Trevor unbuttons my shirt and starts checking the various bruises along my ribs and stomach but draw the line at stripping down to my boxers for him.

"No doctor. Yet," Trevor says. "But if any of those bruises get worse..."

"Internal bleeding. I know." I try to get to my feet, but the room spins around me and I'm back down in two seconds flat. "Fuck. I need a shower. And sleep."

Trevor helps me up, but before I can tell him there's no way I'm letting *him* in the shower with me, he passes me off to Domina. "You got this?" he asks. "Austin and I need to call Zephyr, then it's his turn to catch a few hours."

"Yes. I can do this. You will wake us if you hear anything... important?" She braces one hand against my chest, and I cover her fingers with mine.

"Anything time sensitive. I promise."

I meet Trev's gaze, and the look that passes between us? He understands what I need most right now is the woman at my side. Though we're going to have a long talk later about why either one of them left the safety of the United States to come rescue me.

Each step toward the bedroom is easier than the last. Especially with Domina's arm around my waist. She leads me into the bathroom, lets me lean against the counter, and starts the shower. But when she undresses me without saying a single word, then peels off her black yoga pants, the worry I've carried since the moment I saw the sniper spills over.

"Baby, talk to me." I gather her in my arms, relishing the way her breasts pillow against my chest. Her tank top falls from her hand, but she's still wearing her bra and panties. "I'm okay. I promise."

"How can you say that?" Tears spill down her cheeks, and she shatters, sobs wracking her body. "We couldn't find you. Not even Zephyr...no one knew...President Garcia...he refused to talk to Austin...Cortez will not return my calls...no one—"

"Domina. Stop." I press my lips to hers. She tastes of salt, her tears stinging so many cuts from repeated punches to the face. But I don't care how much it hurts. She's kissing me back.

Until her tongue tangles with mine, and her teeth scrape against my split lip. I jerk away, hissing in pain.

"Leo?" Domina cups the back of my neck. Her eyes narrow, and it's like she's seeing me for the first time. "Dios mio. You need to rest."

"I need you." But when I try to unhook her bra, I lose my balance. Only her arm around my waist keeps me from falling over.

"We can do both." Domina slides the bra straps down her arms, giving me a delicious view of her breasts. Despite my exhaustion, I'm hard for her before she takes off her panties.

If I had the strength—or the energy—I'd have her right here on the counter. And in the shower. And on the counter again. Instead, I let her wash my hair.

I can't hold a thought in my head. Not with Domina touching me. It was less than twenty-four hours, but it feels like I haven't seen her in a year.

"Hold on to me," she says, stepping closer so she can run a washcloth down my back. "You are about to fall over."

"Haven't slept." My words feel thick, unwieldy, and I rest my cheek on her shoulder. "They wouldn't...let me." She tries to draw back, but I hold on. "It's okay, baby. I'm here. I'm alive."

Domina

Voices from the next room wake me. Austin and Trevor. They don't sound angry or upset, thank God. I'm not sure if I should be happy they let us rest or relieved.

Leo sleeps soundly at my back, an arm curled around my waist, and his soft breaths tickling my cheek.

Outside his bedroom window, the day gives way to night. I stare down at his hand splayed over my hip. A bright red welt mars his wrist, and I skim my finger above the swelling. Suddenly, all I can see is him, handcuffed to that small table, his face twisted in pain.

I start to shake. If we had been an hour later, if Austin had not been able to sway President Garcia...

"Domina?" Leo's deep voice rumbles in my ear. "Breathe, baby. Everything's okay."

If only a few deep breaths would fix all our problems. I do try, but the panic chaining my heart only intensifies. "Rafael fired me, Leo. Cortez won't take my calls. I cannot even talk to Larissa. The police...they put me in handcuffs outside the stadium and the entire country thinks I had something to do with the assassination attempt. *Nothing* is okay."

He pushes up on an elbow with a groan. "That pissant *fired you*?"

Rolling over, I stare up at him. His color is better, but his face is a mess of bruises and cuts. His lids are puffy, and his right eye only opens halfway. "It isn't important."

"The hell it's not. You were attacked. Probably by the same people who tried to kill Cortez. You did *nothing* wrong. But they punished you because you were with me." He skims a knuckle along my jaw. It's rough, which makes the contact even more intense and arousing, despite how scared I am. "When I see that asshole, I'm going to punch him into next week. The election be damned."

I take his hand, brushing a kiss to his knuckles. "You should not be punching anyone. Not until you heal. I will find another job. Somewhere."

His low growl makes me feel protected. Cared for. Cherished. All the things I never knew I wanted or needed. Gently, I kiss him, careful of his split lip.

"I want you, baby," he says, and we're both breathless when I pull away. "But..." He darts a quick glance at the wall separating us from the main room.

"You are in no condition for...sex." My cheeks catch fire—along with my core—but Leo has to be in terrible pain.

"Domina, I spent almost twenty-four hours thinking I was never going to see you again. Or touch you. Or kiss you." He cups the back of my head, his fingers carding through my thick curls. "This is my second chance, and I'm not going to waste a minute of it."

Crushing me against him, his lips graze mine. Only the

gentlest caress at first. Testing. Teasing. His tongue tangles with mine, and he plunders my mouth in ways I never knew I wanted. I'm his, completely, and all he's doing is kissing me.

My nipples tighten, hard and aching. We fell into bed completely naked after our shower, and the rasp of his chest hair against my breasts fans the flames inside me.

With his free hand, Leo grabs my ass, his fingers digging into the soft globes to pull me closer. He's hard for me, the firm length of him pressing to my mound.

For a brief moment, we come up for air. "Are you sure?" I ask him. "We have..."

...the rest of our lives...

I cannot say those words to him. Not yet. But I know now. I knew when I saw him locked to that table, bloodied and tortured and desperate. I am falling in love with him, and for the first time in as long as I can remember, I am not scared of needing someone. Of *wanting* someone.

"We have what?" Leo skims his teeth along the shell of my ear. Goosebumps race along my arms. Slowly, he kisses a path down the curve of my neck, all the way to my shoulder. "Domina?"

"We have each other." Cupping his jaw, I urge him to meet my gaze. "We were supposed to be pretending."

"We were." He takes one of my nipples between his thumb and forefinger, rolling it until I writhe against the pillows. "It was always real for me."

My eyes start to burn, tears threatening, until he sucks the other tight bud into his mouth. Then there's nothing but *need*. For him to fill the emptiness inside me, for release, but also for the truth. All of it.

"It...Leo, stop."

He lifts his head, worry in his gaze. "What's wrong?"

"I wasn't looking for anything...real. I thought I was happy alone. And then you came leaping onto my balcony.

That should have been the end of it." Taking his hands, I hold on tight. "I thought…in a few days, we will go back to being neighbors. Nothing more. But you kept showing up. Helping me. Even when I treated you badly, you were there."

I lean closer, touching my lips to his for a brief moment. The connection gives me the strength to go on. "I cannot tell you it was *always* real for me. I didn't know what *real* was. But it's real now. It has been real since you came to my office after the break-in. Since you first kissed me. I thought I lost you, and now that we're together again…"

Leo wraps his arms around me, easing me down so we're on our sides, face to face. "Domina, I've never felt this way about anyone before. I broke my promise at the rally. I was supposed to protect you. To keep you safe. I don't know why you'd trust me again, but—"

"I do. Completely." Fusing our lips together, I claim him, giving him everything I am so he knows without a doubt, I'm his and he's mine.

No more words pass between us as Leo takes control. He kisses each of my palms, then brings my arms over my head so I can curl my fingers around the edge of the mattress. Parting my thighs, he slides between them. He devours me, long strokes of his tongue against my clit, two fingers pumping in and out of my channel, finding my g-spot and bringing me right to the edge a dozen times, but never letting me fly.

I grab his pillow and press it to my face to muffle my helpless whimpers and desperate cries. I need to come, but I think he needs this—to bring me pleasure—even more.

"I want…to be inside you," he says between nips to my thigh. "Will you…?"

Pushing the pillow aside, I meet his gaze. "Yes. Please, Leo. I need you."

He gives my clit one last, hard stroke of his tongue. I

almost fly off the bed from the sudden, intense tightness in my core. On his knees, his cock hard and glistening, he yanks open the nightstand drawer.

"No." I grab his arm, digging my fingers into the corded muscle until he looks at me. "You are the only man I have been with in five years. And I'm on birth control."

A low growl rumbles in his chest. "I'm clean."

"I want all of you."

It's more than that. I want Leo to be the only one who has ever been inside me like this. Nothing between us. Completely for each other.

He braces himself on one elbow, using his other hand to guide his cock to my entrance.

I feel...*everything*. The thickness of his crown. His solid, pulsing length. How he hardens even more when his balls brush against my ass.

"Hold on to me, baby. I can't be gentle. Not today." The rough edge to his voice turns me on even more. Wrapping my arms around his neck, I angle my hips.

How can it feel like he's splitting me in two and completing me all at the same time? I dig my heels into his ass, needing to take him deeper.

He starts with one hard thrust. I cry out, but he swallows the sound by ravaging my mouth. I never knew I could feel *so much* and still survive. Unless this is heaven.

We battle for control of the kiss, back and forth with each thrust of his hips. I'm so close, so ready to surrender to the storm of sensations building inside me.

Sweat slicks our bodies. Leo moves faster, thrusts harder, until he tears his lips away. "Mine."

The single word is rough, gritty, and utterly possessive. It frees me, and I shatter. Wave after wave of pleasure washes over me. I'm drowning in them, and if I never come up for air again, I don't care.

Tears swim in my eyes. HIs face shimmers over me, and when he surrenders to the vortex swirling around us, I know nothing will ever be the same again.

CHAPTER NINETEEN

Leo

FOR ALMOST AN HOUR, I've been able to pretend my life isn't a clusterfuck of epic proportions. Domina is everything I'm not. Brilliant, poised, and beautiful...a good person. Now that we've danced too close to forever, I have to tell her everything. What happened to me in Venezuela *and* what I did after.

I can't do this naked. Even if she doesn't care about my scars, I need armor. Because when she finds out, I'm afraid it'll be the end of us.

"We should get dressed," I say, planting a soft kiss to her forehead. "No telling when Trev and Austin are going to come barging in here with an update."

"Mmm-hmm." Her eyes are still closed, and fuck. I don't want this to end. Our legs tangle under the sheet, and she strokes a hand absently up and down my side. When I'm with her, everything is better.

Even the bruises and cuts from the assholes who interrogated me for eighteen hours don't bother me with her in my arms.

But we're running out of time. Sooner or later, they'll expect us to join them, and I'll lose my nerve.

She doesn't have to know. You could take this to your grave.

My inner voice is dead set against what I'm about to do. It's probably right. But she deserves to know before things get any more serious.

I ease her from my arms and get to my feet. Every step brings more pain—evidence that I'm about to do something colossally stupid—and I limp over to the dresser.

It's almost 7:00 p.m., and my stomach rumbles. I should have eaten something before we showered, but I was so damn tired.

By the time I pull on a pair of khakis, Domina's dressed in a pair of black yoga pants that leave nothing to the imagination, a black tank, and a lacy, scoop-neck sweater in a pale cream that makes her look like an angel.

"Wow." I sink down next to her on the bed and tuck a lock of hair behind her ear. After this, I might never touch her again, so I lean close enough our lips meet.

Kissing her chases all my demons away. I can almost believe I'm a good man. Except for all the horrors I can never forget. They brand me. Spy. Victim. Killer.

"What we just did..." I shake my head, unsure how the hell to even begin. "I want a life with you, Domina. For however long you'll have me."

She sucks in a breath, and I hold up my hand.

"I don't expect you to tell me you feel the same. I know this is fast, and I won't rush you. If all you want is what we have right now, I'll give it to you. If you decide you want more someday, say the word and it's yours. But I can't ask you for any of it without telling you what happened to me in Venezuela."

"Why not?" She turns slightly so we're almost facing and takes my hands. "I know you were tortured, Leo. I can see what they did to you. If you need to tell me every detail, I will listen. But do not do it because you think it will change how I feel about you. It won't."

God, I wish that were true. But as caring and accepting as she's been since the day we met, some things are unforgivable. And unforgettable.

"It might."

In the living room, Austin laughs at something. Pulling my hands from hers, I wipe them on my thighs. "Whatever happens, Austin and Trevor will stay with you until we know any threat has been neutralized. You won't be unprotected. Ever. If you ask me to leave, I will, but you'll stay here with them."

"You are scaring me, Leo." The tremble in her voice destroys me, and I push to my feet. I need distance. Something more than just a few inches between us.

Leaning against the wall by the window, I shove my hands into my pockets and take a deep breath. "I was stationed in Venezuela for twelve years. The CIA was after this terrorist group—the Loma Collectivo. They ran drugs, guns, women... anything profitable. Anyone who got in their way disappeared. Sometimes a few body parts would be found a few weeks later, but that was rare—only when they needed to make some sort of *statement*."

Domina wraps her arms around her knees, watching me. I could stop. Tell her I was wrong. That she doesn't need to know any of this.

Too bad my brain won't listen.

"Being a CIA officer isn't like what you see in the movies. It's not all chasing bad guys and running covert sting operations. There's a lot less running, fighting, and shooting than most people expect. We listen. Observe. Analyze patterns." I angle a glance through a part in the curtains, checking out the street below. Light traffic. A couple of pedestrians. Nothing suspicious.

"No one ever knew the assholes running the Loma Collectivo, but we had dossiers on a few dozen of the lower-level guys. They were spread out all over Caracas, Barquisimeto, Valencia, and Maracay. The first week of April, we intercepted a call between two of their grunts. A member of the Venezuelan government was causing trouble, and they were planning on putting an end to him. My SSO sent Trevor and Gil—he was Austin's adopted brother—down to Venezuela so the three of us could stop the attack."

"Wait," Domina says. "I thought Dani was Austin's sister? And she's with Trevor."

I nod. "Gil was Dani's brother. Different fathers, same mother." Even saying his name brings back too many memories. I wish I could pace without pain. Or even open the damn window. I need to move. To feel fresh air on my cheeks. Anything to keep me in the here and now.

"Was." Sadness laces her tone. I'm not surprised. She doesn't know what Gil did. Yet.

"The op was a success. We killed two members of the Loma Collectivo, kept the Deputy Finance Minister safe, and Gil and Trevor went back to the U.S. We'd been careful. No one from the Loma Collectivo had any idea who we were or how we got our intel. My SSO and I agreed I should stay at my post. I had all the contacts, knew the language...hell, I was at the top of my game."

I'm parched and grab the half-full glass of water off the nightstand. My hand shakes as I set it back down again, empty.

"Two days later, I went to a bar. No current mission, so I figured I could tie one on without any consequences beyond a hangover." I can't look at Domina now. Not and admit what happened next. "I don't know how they got to me. Whether they spiked my drink or shot me up with something…I was at least three drinks in. But I woke up bound to a chair in a room not much bigger than this one."

"Leo…" It's concern in her voice now. Concern I don't deserve.

Shaking my head, I turn to the window. The drapes may be closed, but I can still see a sliver of the street. "I'd never seen the guys who worked me over. They weren't from Caracas. Made a special trip. Just for me. Six of them."

Their voices haunt me—along with my own screams.

"You will pay for what you have done, cabrón. But not until we break you."

The punch takes me by surprise. I can't see shit with a bright light pointed right at my head, and I'm groggy as fuck. Blood fills my mouth, and I spit it onto the floor.

"Break me?" I laugh. "You don't know who you're dealing with."

"Leo Francis Basher. CIA Senior Field Officer stationed in Caracas for the past three years. We know everything about you."

"They took turns. Two or three at a time." I let the curtain fall closed and turn back to Domina. Pinning my gaze to the corner of the bed, to her slim, bare feet, I list off my injuries. "Broken arm. Four cracked ribs. Metal pipe to my cheek— that's what caused the facial paralysis—crushed fingers and toes…"

Rubbing the back of my neck, I force another breath. "They cut out my eye, broke most of the bones in my knee and ankle, had lots of *fun* with a car battery… There's more, but…" I shrug. "The only time I wasn't in constant agony was when I passed out. They wouldn't let me sleep. Loud music, bright lights, stress positions. Every enhanced interrogation technique they could think of. After eight days, I knew I was dying. Still hadn't talked, and they were about to take my other eye."

"Do it," Asshole #2 says. "And after he can no longer see, take his dick too."

"Even without...my dick...I'll still be...twice the man you are," I manage. My right leg is completely numb, but the left is on fire. Blood drips onto the floor from both wrists. Asshole #1 swapped out the thin ropes for razor wire hours ago. I can't hold my head up, so Asshole #2 grabs my hair.

A quiet pop, and blood paints my face. Another one, and the switchblade clatters to the floor, followed by two bodies.

I find the strength to look around me. I'm alone. The other four left hours ago, saying they'd be back tonight.

"Redemption," a man whispers.

The lump in my throat makes it hard to speak, but I manage a single word. "Deliverance."

"Trevor had to carry me out of there. He came alone, against orders, because after eight days, everyone else at the agency believed I was dead."

"Dios mio. What about the other four men?" Domina asks. Twice now, she's made a move to get up, but I've stopped her. What I've told her so far? That was the easy part. What comes next? She'll never look at me the same way again.

"I didn't know their names—or anything about them. They disappeared. Fled back to whatever rathole they'd climbed out of. For almost nine years, they were in the wind."

"Were?"

My entire body runs cold, and I brace my hand against the dresser. "When we got Trevor out of La Crypta last year, we also rescued a member of the resistance. Dani's birth father. He and his brother had been fighting against the Loma Collectivo for more than twenty years. A few weeks after Trev and Dani went back to the states, I got an email. Four names. Four photos."

"The men who hurt you." She'll put it together now. All of

it. Even if I don't say another word. But it doesn't mean a damn thing unless I confess my crimes. Out loud.

"It took me less than seventy-two hours to find them. Another two weeks to learn their habits. And less than a day to kill them."

Domina doesn't say a word. One minute. Two. Three. I raise my head, convinced I'll find horror, disgust, or betrayal in her eyes.

Tears threaten to spill over her lower lids, and she rises, crosses to me, and wraps her arms around my waist.

"What are you doing?" I ask. "I just told you I killed four people in cold blood *nine years* after they left Caracas."

"Did you make them suffer?" She tips her head up, and tears slip down her cheeks.

"No. Double-tap to the head. Close range. I made sure they saw me—recognized me—but I made it quick." Cupping her cheeks, I brush the tears away with my thumbs. "You're not running."

"You killed the men who tortured you. How is that any different than what Trevor did to save you?" Rising up on the balls of her feet, she presses her lips to mine. "I understand why you told me. And why you did not want to. But this changes nothing for me. I care for you, Leo. More than I thought possible. I know you have a past. That you have killed, and that you are capable of killing again. But I also know you are a good man."

"I don't deserve you." Despite my words, I don't let her go. She's seen the darkest parts of me, and she's still here. Still staring up at me with what just might be love in her eyes.

After we came together for the first time—was that really only two nights ago?—I thought I might be falling for her. Now? She's my entire world, and there's nothing I won't do to keep her safe.

CHAPTER TWENTY

Domina

Leo has not stopped touching me since he admitted killing the men who tortured him. We sit on the bed, holding hands, close enough the heat of him seeps into my side.

I want to stay here forever. Safe and protected in this little bubble we have made together. But whoever shot Manuel is still out there. With the election in three days, they will surely try again. And soon.

"What do we do now?" I ask.

With a heavy sigh, Leo shifts to drape his arm around my shoulders and pull me closer. There is something desperate in the motion. Like he's afraid to let me go. "We go talk to Austin and Trevor. See what they've managed to find out in the past few hours. If we can't get in touch with Cortez through Austin's contacts, maybe he can talk to Garcia again. The man might be packing up his shit at the Presidential Palace, but he still has influence. At least for another few days."

Someone raps on the bedroom door, and we both flinch. "Leo? Zephyr's going to call in five minutes. You awake?" Austin asks.

"If I wasn't, I would be now," he says, a hint of annoyance in his tone. "Be right there."

I try to pull away—to stand so I can help him up—but he tightens his arm around me.

"Domina? Trev and Austin don't know."

For a moment, I don't understand. Until I see the shame in his gaze. He thinks they'll judge him for the men he killed. "I will not tell them. But, these men are your friends. They will understand."

"And what if they don't?" He stares down at the floor, his body suddenly weary. "I can't protect you on my own. I'm too broken. Too old. Too slow. I thought I could, but look what happened? I need them on our side until we neutralize any threat."

I want to tell him he's wrong. I saw how worried Austin and Trevor were when Leo was missing. The man they spoke of was more than an acquaintance. More than someone they used to work with. Leo is practically family to them. But he doesn't see it, and the two minutes we have left before Zephyr calls is not enough time to convince him.

"Come. We need to get out there." I wriggle out from under his arm and hold out my hand. "I will keep your secret, Leo. I promise."

TREVOR AND AUSTIN sit at the small kitchen table, enough laptops, tablets, and mobile phones around them to fill an entire electronics store.

Leo's limp is worse than ever, and lines of pain tighten

around his eyes and lips. He leans on me, his arm around my shoulders, until we reach the couch. The ruined cushions are lumpy, but Trevor spread a blanket over them.

"About time the two of you got up," Austin says. "We have pizza, donuts, and yucca cakes. Anything else you want, I can get once we talk to Zephyr."

"I want my goddamn couch fixed," Leo mutters. "As if I'd actually hide anything in the cushions. That's always the first place the police look."

"Sorry, man." Trevor stretches his legs out, crossing his ankles, and twists in his chair until his back cracks. "I did what I could. Had to get you out of that hell hole first."

Leo swallows hard, clutching my hand like it is the only thing keeping him grounded. "About that..."

Glaring at Leo, Trevor arches his brows. "Stop right there. You didn't hesitate when Dani and I showed up in the middle of the night with half the Venezuelan government after us. Or when Ry called you and asked you to find Franco Rojas. Did you really think I wouldn't have come?"

"Yes." Leo's stomach rumbles, and he swears under his breath. "Shit. I haven't eaten since yesterday morning."

"Sit. I will get us food." I squeeze his hand, then head into the kitchen to rummage in the refrigerator. "No pineapple?" I ask after pulling out slices of pepperoni pizza. Trevor and Austin stare at me like I've just asked them for ants on top. "What? It's delicious. If you order it from Palermo's."

Leo chuckles, the first truly happy sound I've heard from him since the rally. My eyes sting, and the lump in my throat threatens to choke me. "Converted you, huh?" he asks.

Trevor snorts from his seat at the table. "I went for the first pie shop I saw. You want something better, give me directions. Later."

"I'd eat glue and oatmeal right now," Leo says. "Or mud,

as long as it had some sort of flavor to it. But when this is all over, we're getting Palermo's."

Austin's laptop dings as I set two cups of strong coffee next to the plates on the coffee table. "That's Zephyr," he says and taps the screen.

"Let me see them." Her demand surprises me, as does the worry on her face when Austin turns the laptop. "Thank God." Zephyr almost collapses back into her chair. Her shoulders heave, and she calls out, "He's okay, Ronan."

After a brief silence, a man comes up behind her and leans down so his face is next to hers. "I told ya' he was too much of an arse to die."

"Fuck you too," Leo says. Despite his words, a hint of warmth infuses his tone. "Heard you're not confined to the van anymore. Congrats."

I don't understand what's going on between the two men, but they obviously know one another.

"Thanks. I'll leave ya' to it, but if ya' need backup, Trevor..."

"I know. West, Inara, and Graham are on call too. Right now, we don't want to raise any more eyebrows. But if that changes, I'll let you know."

Ronan gently nudges Zephyr's chin so she turns to him, then plants a hard, fast kiss on her lips. "Don't be stayin' up all night now, luv. Unless ya' want me to..." He lowers his voice to whisper something in her ear, and her cheeks turn bright pink.

"I'll get you for that one later," she says and points behind her. "Leave me be. Important shit going on." As soon as the door closes, she huffs and shakes her head. "Sorry. We haven't had much time together the past couple of weeks, and it's getting to him."

Austin clears his throat, and he and Trevor move their chairs around so Zephyr can see all four of us at once. "Want to tell us what you found? Now that Leo and Domina are awake, we need to get in touch with Cortez. Get her job back and find out what happened after the IPS dragged him off that stage."

"Right." Zephyr taps a few keys, and her face disappears, replaced with video footage from the rally. "I couldn't get a clear shot of the sniper." She zooms in on the top of the scoreboard. "Sunglasses, knit cap, face mask...facial recognition won't do shit. But he's light-skinned, black hair, and right-handed."

"That only describes a third of the men in Panama," Austin mutters. "You said you had intel we could *use*."

The video footage disappears, and Zephyr's face fills the screen. "Boss, don't take this the wrong way, but you're being an ass."

Leo smiles, and Trevor starts laughing so hard, he has to set his coffee mug down. "What, exactly, would be the right way for him to take it?" he asks.

Zephyr grins and bats her eyes at the camera. "With love. I've done almost a dozen jobs for Austin, but this is the first time we've worked *together*. I'm getting to the good parts. I promise."

Those last two words carry weight, and Austin sighs. "You're right. I'm tired and I'm not used to being away from Mik for so long."

Leo's lips brush my ear. "Mik is his fiancée."

"She's fine, Austin. Dax and Evianna's house is a fortress. Tank and Vasquez are doing drive-bys every few hours." Zephyr turns her focus to me. "Domina? Dax is Trevor's boss at Second Sight. Evianna's his wife. Tank and Vasquez work there too."

"Oh. Thank you. I wondered, but..." Shrugging, I settle closer to Leo. "I did not want to interrupt to ask."

"The night after Ronan introduced me to everyone, I was

so overwhelmed, I made him print out pictures and write their names on the back." She grins, and it's so obvious she cares for all these people. A pang of regret slams into me. Who do I care about? Mina. Larissa. Manuel. And Leo. Everyone else I work with? That is all they are to me. Coworkers.

The screen switches back to video from the soccer stadium. This time, it's footage of the crowds in the stands. "I didn't have anything for you until now because running more than ten thousand faces through facial recognition is a hell of a load on the system. Not to mention all the red flags I had to sort through. Drug convictions, assault charges, domestic violence complaints...every one had to be investigated. Had to pull in Ripper this morning. We're down to nine men and one woman."

Ten photos fly onto the screen like playing cards. Zephyr gives us a summary of each. Name, occupation, violent crimes, bank account balances... So much information, it makes my head spin. Leo's too from the way he sinks back against the cushions and pulls me to his side. Austin and Trevor, though, scribble notes on their tablets and ask questions every few minutes.

"And then there's this guy," Zephyr says. "Domina? Take a good look at him."

Sitting up, I narrow my eyes at the screen. "I have seen him before. But...I don't know where."

"He's a low-level staffer on Eduardo Muñoz's campaign. And for the last ten minutes of the rally, he was on his phone, right next to the west gate. When Cortez's detail went on full alert, Gustavo Bernal slipped out of the stadium and into a black SUV with *no plates*. I lost him when a bus blocked the traffic camera a mile from the stadium. Maybe he just wanted to see how the crowd reacted to Cortez's speech. But maybe..."

Leo straightens with a muffled groan. "Maybe he knew exactly what was going to happen. Or thought he did. And when the sniper didn't land a kill shot, he rabbited."

"Give the man a gold star," Zephyr says as her face fills the screen once more. "Rip agrees with me. This is the guy to start with." She taps her keyboard a few times, and Austin and Trevor's phones vibrate on the table. "Sent you all the info we could get on everyone. We'll keep digging—look for offshore bank accounts, spouses, parents, kids with accounts beyond their means, all of it. But this should be enough to get you started. Oh, and Leo?"

"Yeah?" He's still exhausted, and his right hand shakes until he balls it into a fist and his knuckles turn white.

"I wiped all the data from your phone and tablet. The Ministry of Public Service still has them, and they've been trying to break your encryption non-stop. If they do, the only thing they'll find is a truly unhealthy obsession with puppies dressed up in Halloween costumes."

Leo's shoulders slump, and he nods. "Shit. There wasn't much on there I can't recover, but...I didn't back up the last few pictures..."

"Oh, please," Zephyr says. "Like I'd let you lose data. Austin has new tech for you, and I've already restored everything. Even gave you a new lock screen." She winks, then stifles a yawn. "I'm going to catch a few hours before Ronan comes to drag me out of here. Call me if anything breaks."

The screen goes black, and Leo staggers to his feet. "Phone," he says to Austin. "Now."

The man chuckles and digs in a small duffel bag on the floor. "I *was* going to surprise you with it. Should have known Zephyr would put an end to that plan."

Leo taps the power button, and the screen lights up.

Oh, my God.

It's a picture of us. Smiling, having lunch at Cucina de Mare.

"I didn't back up the last few pictures..."

The ones of us. The last few photos were all of us.

CHAPTER TWENTY-ONE

Leo

I CAN'T STOP STARING at the phone. I was too out of it when Austin, Trevor, and Domina found me to even think about what the Ministry might be doing with my tech—or my apartment—but as soon as Zephyr said she'd wiped everything, I realized what I'd lost.

Having this picture—the only one of just the two of us—soothes me in a way I didn't know I needed.

"Leo?" Domina's right next to me, her hand on my arm, squeezing just above my elbow. "Did you hear Trevor?"

I blink hard, and dammit. I need my eye drops. The lack of sleep combined with repeated blows to the head didn't do my prosthetic—or my eyelid—any favors. "No. Sorry. What did you say?"

Trev shoots me a look of disbelief. "You need a solid eight hours, man. Not another cup of coffee."

"You want me coherent for the call to Cortez?" I fill my mug, then Domina's. "No amount of caffeine in the world will keep me up much longer, but I need to know we'll be safe here tonight."

"What do you call all of this?" he asks, gesturing to the firepower and tech strewn about my living room. Three M4 rifles, six handguns, enough ammunition for half a dozen firefights, comms units, GPS trackers, night-vision goggles, tactical gear... They thought of everything. "Give us some credit, Leo. We might be 'retired' from government work, but we still know our shit."

I slump against the counter, exhausted, in pain, and embarrassed at just how much of an ass I'm being to one of my only friends in this world. "Sorry. I'm wiped. Not thinking straight."

Trevor ambles into the kitchen, shoots Domina a quick glance, and angles his head toward the couch. "Give me a minute with him?"

"I have some extra blankets next door," she says. "If you and Austin are going to sleep here..."

Pritchard stands, tucks one of the comms units into his ear and holsters his Glock. "That'd be great. We'll be right back."

Fear prickles along the back of my neck. I don't want Domina out of my sight for even a minute. But Austin won't let anything happen to her. Hell, he's a better protector than I'll ever be. He's got two working eyes, and only minor shrapnel damage to his shoulder. In a fight, I'd bet on him every time.

"Five minutes," I manage before they unlock my door. "Be back in five minutes."

"We'll be back when we're back." Austin shoots Trev a look I don't understand before shutting the door.

"I set up cameras in the hall, the elevator, and at all exterior exits. No one's getting in," Trevor says, clapping me on the shoulder.

"Don't fucking touch me." I jerk away, stumble, and crash to my knees in front of the fridge. "Goddammit!"

Trev thrusts his hand out in front of my face. I don't have much of a choice. After the beating those Ministry assholes gave me, I'm more broken than ever. Clasping his forearm, I let him help me to my feet, but shake off his hold so I can limp to the table under my own power.

"Want to tell me about that giant stick up your ass?" Trev asks when he takes a seat across from me. "Because when I was in your shoes, I didn't understand *why* Dax and Ry would fly halfway around the world for me, but I sure as shit wasn't an ungrateful bastard about it."

He's right. But admitting it? I don't know how.

"I work alone." Staring down at my right hand, I flex the fingers that no longer feel a damn thing. "Twenty-two years, and all but maybe a dozen of my ops were solo."

Trevor's brown eyes darken, and he runs a hand through his hair. "So were mine, dumbass. Try again."

I stare at the door, willing Austin and Domina to return. Both because I can't stand having her out of my sight and to save me from this conversation.

"They're staying at Domina's until I tell Austin you're done being a colossal jerk."

I'm out of the chair so fast, the room starts to spin. Even dizzy, my reflexes aren't total shit, and I grab Trevor's arms, hauling him up and pinning him against the wall. "You had no fucking right!"

"I had every fucking right." The lethality in Trevor's tone warns me to step away, but I don't listen. He doesn't move, doesn't fight me, doesn't do a damn thing but hold my gaze. "I haven't gone on mission since Venezuela. Traveled with Dani a couple of times, but that's it. Dax and I agreed. Unless it's a member of *this family* in trouble, I stay in Boston."

"Then why are you here?" If my voice weren't so hoarse,

I'd be shouting, but instead, the words aren't much more than a harsh whisper.

"Don't you get it?" Trevor shakes his head. "You're family, asshole. For years, you were one of the only people I could talk to. When Dani and I needed help, you got us out of the country. No questions asked. And even though you were stuck in the van with Ronan—trust me, I know how unpleasant that is—without your help, I'd be dead. One more victim of La Crypta and that piece of shit Ochoa."

Shock steals my words and any fight left in me. I stagger back, unsteady on my feet until Trev takes my arm and guides me over to the couch. "Sit before you end up on your ass again."

"I can't protect her." Dropping my head into my hands, I pull at tufts of hair, needing the pain as some sort of penance. "I'm too old. Too slow. Too fucked up to keep Domina safe."

"The hell you are." The couch creaks as Trev drops down next to me. "When I found you in that warehouse nine years ago, I thought you were dead. It took me almost an hour of recon before I could get into position, and I heard...*everything*."

I can't look at Trevor. It doesn't matter that he's my friend. That he's seen me at my worst. That he—unlike anyone else in this world—understands how easy it is to break a man. And how hard it is to put yourself back together.

"You survived." This time when he touches my shoulder, I don't slap his hand away. "Hell, you did more than that. You had another *nine years* in the field. Took down more members of the Loma Collectivo than any of us."

"And I couldn't get through most days without a drink. Or three," I manage.

"So?" Trev asks. "You're sober now. I saw the video, Leo. The sun reflecting off the scope? Half the operators I know wouldn't have seen that with two good eyes. You did. You fought off Cortez's security detail long enough to convince them of the danger. No. You're not going to beat anyone in a fifty-yard dash. Except maybe a five-year-old."

I choke out a laugh. "You find any five-year-old criminal masterminds, I'm your guy."

"Nah. We save those for the probies at Second Sight and Hidden Agenda. Everyone needs an easy win their first op." Trev leans forward, elbows on his knees. "You never wondered why your SSO didn't confine you to desk duty?"

"Every damn day." I glance over at him, wondering why we've never talked like this before.

"You're too damn smart. Observant as fuck. And your instincts are better than anyone I've ever met. Balin knew you were still the most valuable asset he had—even with only one eye and more titanium than bone in your ankle."

"Balin's an asshole. After rehab, I asked to be assigned anywhere but Venezuela. He denied my request. I didn't stay in Caracas because I *liked* it there. I stayed because I didn't have a fucking choice."

For what feels like forever, neither of us say another word. Until Trevor sighs. "I didn't know."

"No one did. Balin left me alone. He didn't care that I ended most my days with too much rum or that my reports were always late. And I didn't care that all I could do was gather intel. It was a shitty life, but it was mine. Until..."

"These men are your friends. They would understand."

Domina was so certain Trev and Austin wouldn't judge me for what I did. But I can't take that risk. Not until she's safe.

"Until what?" Trevor asks.

I shrug. "Until I stopped drinking. But the memories were just too much. I thought I could start over here. Alone. Then I met Domina." I turn to him, desperate to fix whatever I broke between us. "She's everything I never knew I needed. I can't protect her without you, Trev."

He meets my gaze, and where I expect to find pity, there's only understanding. "You don't have to. You're not alone, Leo. You never were."

DOMINA ROLLS a small suitcase behind her when she and Austin return, then disappears into my bedroom. I shoot Austin a questioning look, but he grins and shakes his head. "I'll tell you what I told Griff when I sent him to protect a model in Zurich last year. Three days into the assignment, he knew Sloane was it for him. They've been together ever since, and I've never seen him happier."

Three days?

I'm shocked, until I realize I've only known Domina for six.

"What we do, the stress we're under, the danger we're in every day when we're on mission? It cuts through all the bullshit you'd find in a *normal* relationship. Helps you see what really matters."

"She matters. She's all that matters." Before Austin can give me shit for falling so fast and hard, it makes my head spin, I stagger into the kitchen for a can of club soda and a protein bar. We still need to call Cortez—or try to—and I'm fading fast. Five hours of sleep after what those assholes did to me isn't nearly enough.

At the table, Austin plugs his phone into his laptop. "We'll try Cortez first. If he won't take my call, it's back to President Garcia."

"Back? What the fuck happened while I was...gone?"

Domina trails her hand down my arm, and I stifle my flinch.

She's on my right side, and I didn't see—or hear—her come into the room. "Austin threatened to tell the press that Garcia bribed his opponent in the last presidential race. Five million dollars."

Sadness laces her tone, and I turn so I can see her eyes. "You liked Garcia."

With a sigh, she nods. "He has been good for Panama. Under his administration, we rose from 75th in the world for education to 53rd. He championed prison reform, better healthcare, lower cost prescription drugs... So much has changed, and Manuel has pledged to continue his work—and do even more." Domina slides her arm around my waist and curls into me. "No politician is perfect. Not even Cortez. But I thought..."

"I read people for a living, Domina. Or...I used to. You're right. Every politician on the planet has...issues. But Cortez is a good man. I'd bet my left eye he wasn't the one to fire you. And once he finds out who did...*Rafael* is going to be looking for a new job by morning."

The look she gives me? Gratitude and respect with maybe...a hint of love. I don't deserve it, but I'll take it for as long as she's willing to stay with me.

"We ready?" Austin asks. "I'm putting the call on speaker."

I pop the top on the club soda. With my arm around Domina's shoulders, we make our way to the table and sit side-by-side, close enough I can hold her hand.

"Are you certain he'll even take our call?" Domina asks. "It's almost 9:00 p.m."

"Perfect time to catch him unawares." Austin dials, and after the first ring, levels us with a stern gaze. "Leo, don't go off on him."

"No guarantees. He had to know what happened to me. And Domina."

"Vice President Cortez's office," a man says in lightly accented Spanish. "How can I help you?"

"This is Major General Austin Pritchard, formerly with the United States Joint Special Operations Command. I need to speak to the Vice President immediately. It's a matter of National Security."

After a pause, the man clears his throat. "The Vice President asked not to be disturbed, sir. If you'd like to leave a message—"

"Did you listen to a word I said, son?" Austin's voice gets deeper, full of the authority that only comes from leading the entire military infrastructure of the United States, and his Spanish is flawless. "I oversaw SEAL Team 6. Delta Force. And I'm telling you that Cortez is in danger and he's going to want to take my call. Or did you forget that he was nearly assassinated less than twenty-four hours ago? I can have my president call yours, but that's just going to end badly for you."

"Please...please hold, sir. One moment." The aide sounds terrified now, and when Austin jabs the mute button, I chuckle.

"You practice that speech in the mirror or something?" I ask.

I don't think I saw the man smile once in Venezuela, but now, it comes easy to him. "When you go from one of the top military commanders in the country to a civvie, you gotta get shit done somehow."

"Sir?" the aide says. "I am transferring you now."

"Once I know he's the only one on the call, it's all you, Domina." Taking the call off mute, Austin sits up a little straighter.

"Major General Pritchard?" Cortez asks. He sounds weary. No longer the confident, in control, consummate politician. Just a sixty-two-year-old man who'd rather be left alone.

"Mr. Vice President, I won't waste your time. We can speak Spanish, but I presume you are fluent in English as well?"

"I am."

"Good. Is there anyone else listening in on our conversation?" Austin launches one of Zephyr's apps, and on his laptop screen, the program analyzes the ambient noise carrying over the connection.

"Every one of my calls is recorded unless I say otherwise. I am a busy man, Major General Pritchard, and it is late. Get to the point before I lose my patience."

"Stop the recording. Right now. Unless you don't care who's behind yesterday's *incident*." While Austin's voice still carries the same authority, uncertainty flickers in his expression. If Cortez hangs up on us, we might not get another chance with him.

"You are retired, are you not?" Cortez asks. "A civilian with no government contacts or authority. Why should I believe you know anything about the attempt on my life?"

"Manuel. Listen to him." Domina squeezes my hand so tightly, even without much sensation in my fingers, I can sense how nervous she is.

"Domina? Shit. One moment." A click carries over the line, and on Austin's computer, the ambient noise level drops by half. "I stopped the recording. What happened? Rafael said you were arrested as a suspect."

"Mr. Vice President, this is Leo Basher. You and I have a lot to discuss."

CHAPTER TWENTY-TWO

Domina

"MR. BASHER? You physically assaulted my detail and waved a loaded gun at them. Give me one good reason why I should not hang up right now," Cortez snaps.

"Because I'm the only reason you didn't end up with a bullet between your eyes, Mr. Vice President. I saw the sniper and tried to warn the National Police and the IPS. I never pulled my gun. Your *detail* tackled me, beat me until I was barely conscious, and then sent me to a Ministry of Public Service black site. Do I need to tell you what happens there? Because I will. In great detail." Leo's anger bleeds through his tone, and he grips the edge of the table hard enough his knuckles turn white.

"I'm sending the video footage from the rally to your email now," Austin says. "Watch it if you don't believe him."

"The only reason I showed the agents my gun—the gun you *told me* to bring, by the way—is because those fuckwits weren't paying any attention to my warnings. I saved your goddamn life, and the only thanks I got was almost twenty-four hours of enhanced interrogation and torture."

A faint *ding* sounds from Cortez's side of the call, followed by the sound of the people cheering him on.

"Sniper! Get down! Get. Down. Now!" Leo shouts, his voice faint over that of the crowd, but still audible.

"Sniper! On the scoreboard!"

Leo's strangled cry is followed by multiple IPS agents shouting at him to get on his knees, cursing him, even calling him a terrorist. I cannot sit here and listen to this man I care so very much for be beaten, so I push back from the table and head for the patio door.

"Domina, don't," Trevor warns, and he's at my side in two steps. "It isn't safe out there."

"Please. I cannot listen to this..." As desperate as I am to escape, when I look back at Leo, I know I cannot walk away. Not with the pain twisting his expression.

"It's over, baby," Leo says, his voice rough and raspy. "Seen enough, Cortez?"

"Fuck." The single word carries so much emotion. Regret, shame...frustration. "I did not see this angle. Or any audio. Rafael showed me footage of you waving your gun at my detail and aiming at my head."

Leo, Austin, and Trevor all start talking at once. Words like deep fake, video analysis, and fucking asshole are tossed around like a soccer ball until Leo slams his fist down on the table.

"Shut up. All of you. Cortez, I never touched my gun. Well, unless you count one of your agents pulling it from my holster and slamming it into my face. You're being lied to. Probably by more than one person. Who fired Domina?"

"I did," he says quietly. "But only after Rafael showed me the video of you about to shoot me. Domina? Are you still there?"

Returning to Leo's side, I swallow hard. "Yes, Manuel."

"I am truly sorry. I should not have been so quick to believe you had anything to do with the attack."

"What about having her detained and questioned for *eight hours?*" Leo asks. "Because she didn't deserve that either."

"In my defense, I was unconscious for part of that time. The bullet only grazed my arm, but I passed out before I arrived at the hospital. The doctors said I went into shock."

The sound Leo makes is something between a groan and a growl. Angry. Feral. Protective. Something deep in my core warms, despite how worried I am that these two strong, powerful men will come to blows—even over a telephone line.

"I don't give a fuck if you were hopped up on laughing gas for twelve hours or having plastic surgery to remove a third nipple," Leo grits out. "Domina was handcuffed in front of the press. And no one from your campaign has said a single goddamn word to contradict the stories that she had something to do with the assassination attempt."

Several seconds pass. With each one, Leo's expression hardens.

"I know," Manuel says. "I have seen the reports. Domina, I am truly sorry. I will call an emergency staff meeting and find out who gave that video to Rafael. If you can forgive me, I will make this right."

"Wait." Austin straightens in his chair, a frown curving his lips. "Mr. Vice President—"

"Manuel. Please."

"Fine. Manuel, most of your information from the past twenty-four hours has come through your campaign manager?" He and Trevor exchange an intense look, and Leo swears under his breath.

"Yes. Rafael meets with several agents from the Institutional Protection Service every few hours and then briefs me."

I lean close to Leo so my lips brush his ear. "What is it?"

He takes my hand, lacing our fingers tightly. "Mr. Vice President," he says, his voice deeper and rougher than it was only moments ago. "Don't call that staff meeting. Not yet. We thought your opponent was behind all of this—and that may still be the case. But your campaign manager had a bird's eye view of what happened when I rushed the stage. If he believes that video you saw, he's either a complete and total idiot, or he's involved. Until we know which one it is...you're a hell of a lot safer if you keep playing along with the current narrative."

I choke back a sob. "What about us? Leo, the Ministry let you go, but what will stop them from changing their mind? They know where you live. How long until they come after you again? After both of us?"

My body shakes, fear turning my blood to ice in my veins.

"If they come," Trevor says, his demeanor deathly calm, "they die."

IT TAKES another hour to brief Cortez on what Zephyr found when she analyzed the rally footage. Every few minutes, he offered another apology, more regrets for his part in what happened to me and to Leo.

"Are you certain you're safe at the Presidential Palace?" Austin asks.

"I am not certain of anything," Manuel says, the weariness in his voice so much worse than at the start of the call. "But unless President Garcia is also involved—despite having nothing to gain from my death—my wife and I should be safe here until morning. Though Rafael has messaged me three times in the past hour, and I will not be able to ignore him for much longer."

Leo straightens in his chair, though he sways slightly until he braces his arm on the table. "Cortez, you're the Vice President of Panama," he growls. "If you don't want to talk to that asshole tonight, don't. Tell him your arm is killing you and you're going to bed. Or hell. Tell him you want to go fuck your wife and need some goddamn peace."

"Leo!" I gasp. Before I can get over my shock enough to say another word, Manuel starts to laugh.

"You are quite right, Mr. Basher," he says when he catches his breath. "I *am* the Vice President, and in three days, if I manage to live that long, I will run this country. I can certainly tell my campaign manager to 'fuck off' for the night."

This is a side of Manuel Cortez I have never seen. Though, perhaps, it is one he reserves only for family and very close friends. For those he trusts with his life. His anger will not serve him in the polls. But in private, I hope it will keep him alive.

"Send me a copy of that doctored video," Austin says. "My team can do things with tech that shouldn't be possible. If whoever put it together left a mark, we'll find it."

"Who is 'your team'? I agreed to trust you, Pritchard, and Mr. Basher. And by association, I suppose, the third man in the room whom you have yet to identify. But an entire 'team' of individuals I do not know? That is more than I am willing to risk."

Austin shoots Trevor a look of pure exasperation. "My 'team' is one of the best in the world. And without them, Leo would still be trapped in one of your black sites, Domina would probably be in jail, and you'd be trusting people who might be plotting a second attempt on your life as we speak. You're lucky you have *my* name. Everyone else stays anonymous. It's the only way we can do what we do."

After a heavy sigh, Manuel agrees. "Very well. We will speak at 8:00 a.m. tomorrow. But before I trust you with my life, I will look you in the eyes. Are we clear?"

"Crystal, Mr. Vice President. Good night." Austin ends the call and flops back in the wooden chair. "I used to work with guys like that every fucking day. Never thought I'd have to do it again."

"I owe you, man," Leo says, draping his arm around my shoulders. "Everything you've done for us...I'll never be able to pay you back."

Austin arches his brows, then cuts his gaze to Trevor. "You didn't tell him?"

"Of course I did. Dumbass got punched in the head one too many times. Plus, he's old as fuck. His memory's going." Trev cracks a smile, but then quickly sobers. "Family doesn't keep a ledger, Leo. We show up and do what needs to be done."

Leo

Trevor and Austin play rock, paper, scissors for the first shift on the couch. "We can move next door," I say when Domina closes herself in the bathroom to brush her teeth. "At least she has a couch that isn't ripped to shreds."

Trev angles a glance at the bathroom door. "She wanted to be here, so we're here. I've slept on worse. Or have you forgotten the five-star accommodations at La Crypta?"

"Last time I was in the field," Austin says, "I spent the

night in an abandoned shell of a building in the Mexican jungle after getting soaked to the skin in a monsoon. Your couch is like a Five Points Luxury Hotel."

Shoving my hands into my pockets, I try to figure out what to say to these two men who flew to Panama with a fucking arsenal and more support than I could ever imagine. "You need anything...?"

Trevor pauses his energetic fluffing of my mangled couch cushions to give me the side eye. "Yeah. If you and Domina are going to go at it again, put some music on first."

"Fuck you." My smile—lopsided as it is—feels foreign, but I'd forgotten what it was like to be around guys who *understand* me. My damage. My scars. My nightmares. Of all the men in the world who could have come to my rescue, Trev and Austin are the only ones still alive who were betrayed by the same man who sold me out to the Loma Collectivo—Austin's adopted brother, Gil. "Don't say a word to her, man. Not if you ever want her to look you in the eyes again."

Trevor laughs and shakes his head. "Oh, I'm pretty sure she knows. Domina isn't some delicate flower who'll wilt in the sun. She reminds me a lot of Dani. Pretty sure you were on the receiving end of at least one of her death stares last year."

I wince, then turn to Austin. "A little backup here?"

He holds up his hands. "Don't look at me. I grew up with her. Why do you think Trevor calls her Danisaur?"

"Seriously?" Before I can tell Trevor the nickname fits, the room shimmers, and I brace my hand on the wall. "I need to crash. Hard. If Zephyr calls—"

"They will wake us," Domina says, wrapping her arm around my waist and fitting herself to my side. "Come to bed, Leo. Before you pass out right here."

I won't refuse her a damn thing. Especially not a chance to fall asleep with her in my arms. "Don't trash the place," I call over my shoulder. "Though, that might be an improvement."

CHAPTER TWENTY-THREE

Leo

*T*HE SUN BEATS *down on my black baseball cap. Sunglasses hide my face, and the SR-25 sniper rifle is balanced on the roof of a three-story apartment complex. A bead of sweat rolls down my back under my t-shirt. I don't look at my phone. I've watched this asshole for a week now. He never deviates from his routine. Coffee down at Siren's from 9:00-9:30 a.m. A brief stop at a bakery for a slice of sponge cake. Then he shakes down a couple of local businesses and returns home.*

Five minutes. Or less. Checking the sights, I line up my shot. With only one good eye, my depth perception is shot, but at this range, I'm still better than most.

The man, Armando Velasquez, whistles as he ambles down the street. The moment I saw his face a week ago, I remembered everything. He was the one who took my eye. Who crushed two of the toes on my right foot. With a hammer. And then he laughed. I'll never forget his laugh.

Armando stops to fish his keys out his pocket, and I take a slow, deep breath. I don't give a fuck how wrong this is. How I should be the better man. But while the Loma Collectivo might be gone, Armando and his cronies are no innocents.

He slides the key into the lock, and I pull the trigger. Once, then twice before Armando's body has a chance to hit the ground. One down. Three to go.

"Tell us what we need to know, Basher. Who hired you? Who helped you bypass security at the rally? Was it Domina Sanchez?" Reyes aims a hard punch to my liver, and I spit bile onto the floor.

"Domina is innocent," I wheeze. "Where is she? What are you assholes doing to her?"

"None of your business, American. Tell us about the gun."

I jerk awake, unable to force the sight of Domina cuffed to another table, in another cell, in another secret facility from my eyes. But when I look down, she's in my bed, her arms wrapped around a pillow, and her long, black hair tumbling over her slim shoulders.

"Domina," I whisper, sliding back down next to her. "I need you, baby."

She blinks up at me, her eyes half-lidded with sleep. "Leo?"

Everything about her is so pure and good, I can't possibly expect her to put up with my darkness. Yet, she hasn't batted an eye. At anything.

"Let me taste you." My back and legs are locked up tight, but I don't need them to make her fly.

Shoving at the duvet, I struggle to slide down her body. "Leo, stop," she says, grabbing at my arms. "You are in pain."

"Please..." I can't explain why this is so important to me.

Why I can't go another minute without reforging our connection.

Domina gently urges me onto my back. "Lie still. Let me take care of everything."

Hooking her fingers into the waistband of my boxers, she eases them down my hips. My dick stands at attention, and if I were whole, I'd flip our positions and take control. But I never will be.

"Sometimes, you can let go." Domina straddles me, wearing only a thin, gray tank top. Her nipples pebble against the material, begging to be touched. Leaning down, her hair tumbles around my face, curtaining us from the rest of the world.

Soft kisses to my lips, my jaw, and down my neck to my shoulder. My balls ache. But from the way she moves, she's not interested in quick and dirty.

"My turn to be in control," she murmurs, pulling back with a shy smile.

"I'm yours, baby." The urge to add "forever" is almost too strong to ignore, but I swallow the word when she slants her mouth over mine.

Fuck. I have to be inside her. Now. But Domina has other ideas. She explores every inch of me—tracing the worst of my scars, touching me with something close to awe in her eyes, and swirling her tongue around my nipples. God, I never knew I could feel *this* much.

"Relax, mi amor," she whispers. My eyes, which I'd let drift close, snap open. Did she say...? But before I can ask, she wraps soft fingers around my shaft.

"God, Domina..."

She smiles, guiding me to her entrance. Her tight heat envelopes me, and I groan. How can I want her *this* much? Be this close to blowing my load like a horny teenager when this isn't our first time?

Domina starts moving her hips, her gaze locked on mine. It's her. It's all her.

Domina isn't like any other woman I've ever known. Brilliant, strong, beautiful, determined...all the things I never thought I deserved.

She braces her hands on either side of my shoulders, leaning down so her nipples brush against my chest with every thrust.

"You feel so good," she whispers. "I cannot get enough of you."

I want to tell her she's my everything, but before I can, she increases the speed of her thrusts, swiveling her hips in such a way, she's taking me even deeper.

"Oh, God...I'm so close, baby." I curl my fingers around the soft globes of her ass, holding on with such desperation, my hands shake.

Domina rests her forehead against mine. "Touch me, Leo. Make me come with you."

Fuck me. Reaching between us, I find her clit and trace circles around the small, hard nub. She shudders, her eyelids fluttering.

"Yes...yes!" she cries.

Her inner walls clench around me, and when she throws her head back and her entire body tenses like a string about to snap, I let go.

Waves of pleasure so strong, they border on pain surge through my dick. With nothing between us, everything is *more*. So much more.

I love you.

I don't say the words. I can't. They die behind the thick lump in my throat. But I know the truth. Domina is it for me. I hope to all that's holy in this world, she feels the same.

THE SCENT of bacon and eggs filters into the room. "What the hell?" I push up on an elbow, Domina tucked in the crook of my other arm. "I don't have bacon. Hell, all I have left is pizza and protein bars. We ate everything else."

Domina laughs, the sound so relaxed and *happy* I forget all about the danger surrounding us. This is the life I want. Her in my bed—our bed—every night. Making her coffee in the morning. Hell, I'll learn to cook more than spaghetti, steaks, and pressed sandwiches if that's what she needs.

"We should get up," she says, her cheeks flushing a deep crimson. "I think they know we are awake by now."

"Fuck. I should have put on some music. Trev's going to give me shit for days. But I need to loosen up first. Otherwise I'll be walking like I'm a hundred years old."

"Go on." Domina extricates herself from my arm and stretches out on her side. "I like to watch."

Tugging on my boxers, I half roll, half fall onto the floor and crawl over to the yoga mat. "Why?"

"Because you are mostly naked. Do I need another reason?" Her smile helps me ignore the pain as I slide the first therapy ball under my right hamstring.

I want to tell her she needs her eyes checked. That my body isn't worth ogling. That even without all the new bruises, I'm still almost fifty with a mangled leg, a prosthetic eye, and facial paralysis that makes me look perpetually sad, dazed, and hungover.

But she stares down at me like I'm a Greek god—or at least a man in his prime—and my protests fall away. Maybe love, lust, or being thrown together by extreme circumstances changes how you see the other person. What did Austin say? It cuts through the bullshit.

I reach for The Stick, then roll it over my quad with as much pressure as I can muster. I'm so focused on *not* screaming in pain, when Domina kneels next to me, I drop The Stick in surprise.

"Let me help?"

I hand Domina my most hated torture device. "My life is in your hands, baby." Showing her how to angle The Stick, how much pressure to use, when to stop...it's intimate in a way I didn't expect.

When my muscles are as loose as they're going to get, I wrap my arms around her. "I don't know what I did to deserve you, but whatever it was..."

Domina silences me with her kiss, and she's right. It doesn't matter. Because we're together.

Domina

Austin brings a huge plate of bacon to the table. "Pancakes are coming up next."

At my side, Leo shakes his head. "Have you two lost your minds? Going *shopping*? Spycraft 101. Don't take unnecessary risks."

"You were out of coffee," Trevor says. "Spycraft 102. Don't attempt a complicated mission without caffeine."

A stack of pancakes taller than my head lands next to the bacon and Austin joins us at the table. "And we're not in the middle of the fucking jungle. MREs are a last resort. I was careful, Leo. No tails, no obvious surveillance anywhere around the building. President Garcia might not have operational authority over the Ministry, but his orders carry weight."

"How long do you think that's going to last?" Leo shovels half a dozen slices of bacon onto his plate, then offers me the fork.

The idea of food turns my stomach, and I shake my head. "I cannot."

"Domina, you need to eat something." He rests his free hand on my shoulder, squeezing lightly. "Please. Cold pizza? A disgusting but surprisingly filling protein bar? I think there are still a couple of Huevos de Leche left unless the assholes who tossed my apartment ate them all."

I sigh, suddenly so weary, I want to curl up in a ball on the couch and never move again. "Two pancakes. Anything more and I will throw up."

He nods, then leans in and presses a kiss to my temple. "We're together, baby. Remember that. Whatever happens with Cortez today, we have each other."

Tears sting my eyes. I know he meant the words to be reassuring, but now all I can think about is how everything we have—the connection we have forged, how we are dangerously close to falling in love—could change in a heartbeat.

The conversation carries on around me and I only catch bits and pieces. How Zephyr is going to call in half an hour. How Trev and Austin passed a couple of hours running various tactical scenarios. Leo's injuries and whether he should stay in the SUV when we meet Cortez.

"No fucking way!" he snaps, slamming his right fist down on the table so hard, Austin has to grab his glass of orange juice to stop it from toppling over. "I'm staying with Domina."

"Calm your shit, man." Trevor shakes his head. "We both get it. But you were so fucked up when we found you, Austin had to carry you out of there. We had to ask the question."

Leo scrubs his hands over his face and runs his fingers through his hair. "Sorry. I spent most of my career on my own. Trusting a team is...new to me."

"As long as you understand we *are* a team," Austin replies.

"Everyone at this table, Zephyr, Ripper, Hidden Agenda, Second Sight, whatever the fuck I'm calling my group..."

"You don't have a name?" Trevor starts laughing so hard, he snorts and presses a napkin to his nose. "Shit."

Austin stares down at his plate, now mostly empty. "Zephyr said we should call ourselves 'Austin's Network of Badasses.' But there's no way I'm agreeing to that."

Everyone chuckles, and it feels so good to relax for a few moments. The conversation shifts to the most ridiculous ideas, and before long, I'm laughing so hard, my side hurts.

Maybe Leo is right. We're together, and that means everything else will be okay.

CHAPTER TWENTY-FOUR

Leo

"You look better," Zephyr says when the video call connects. "Less 'zombie apocalypse' and more 'bar fight gone bad.'"

I'd roll my eyes if I thought it would be effective. But though my prosthetic has some movement to it, the first time I tried the motion in a mirror, I decided no one ever needed to see it again. I look more like a cartoon character with a head injury than a human being.

"Arnica, ice packs, and sleep do wonders. Not as good as information we can use to put an end to this whole fucked-up situation, though. Got anything good for us?"

Domina and I sit together on the couch, her hand held in mine. Trev sits on the floor, and Austin leans against the wall, almost out of view.

"Depends on your definition of good." She splits the video screen and throws the fake video from the rally on both halves. "Whoever did this knows their shit."

The clip on the left plays, and damn. A crystal-clear shot

of my face along with the Glock 19 in my hand, aimed right at Cortez. "You know the score!" the fake me on screen shouts.

"It even sounds like you." Domina presses closer to me, and the worry in her voice is like a knife to my heart.

"That's the easy part," Zephyr explains. After a couple of clicks from her keyboard, Austin's voice pours through the speakers. "Voice editing is for amateurs."

"Shit." I glance up at Austin. "Did you know she could do that?"

"No," he says. "And I'd prefer she not do it again." He shudders like he's just seen—or heard—a ghost.

"Sorry, boss. But seriously...I can spoof anyone's voice in my sleep. Video...that's harder. Watch the clip on the right. Whoever did this is damn good, but I can show you where they spliced in footage from somewhere else."

On screen, bright red arrows point out the slight imperfections. The hand holding the gun is a little lighter than mine. When she slows the video to half speed, my lips don't sync up with the words. And behind me, the shadows are all wrong.

"So, you can prove it's a fake, but not where it came from," Trevor says. "Fuck. How are we going to convince *anyone* Leo's innocent?"

"Here's the thing." Zephyr's face appears on screen, and she tucks a thick lock of teal hair behind her ear. "The media doesn't have this footage. If they did, they'd be running it nonstop. Because this shit is news cycle *gold*."

"Not helping, Zephyr," I warn. Domina has a death grip on my fingers, and while she hasn't shut down like she did last night, she's very much on the edge.

"If you'd let me finish..." She leans forward, her stare so earnest I shut up and listen. "This was crafted for Cortez or his campaign manager. No one wants this leaked because too many people *at* the rally would call bullshit."

"So what do we do now?" Domina asks. "The election is tomorrow. If Muñoz *is* behind this, killing Manuel after the votes are counted will not do him any good. The presidency would go to Manuel's vice presidential pick, Villanova."

"He's got to try something today," Austin says. "Which means we need to get to Cortez and warn him. Zephyr, did you find anything on Rafael Perez?"

"He's a boy scout." His photo appears on screen, along with his resume. "I dug up some complaints from former coworkers on social media. He's a 'condescending jerk' and 'he thinks he's better than all of us,' but no red flags. At the rally, when Leo started shouting and the IPS converged on Cortez, Rafael looked as shocked as everyone else. Could have been an act, but if it was, he should move to Hollywood."

"Fuck. So we have nothing." Trevor pinches the bridge of his nose. "Keep digging. And see if you can get traffic camera footage from around the Presidential Palace. Cortez is holed up there for now."

"Already on it. What's the plan?" she asks.

Austin reaches for his phone. "We try to convince Cortez to stay at the palace until the votes are certified. It's the safest place for him—I hope."

CORTEZ ANSWERS QUICKLY. "We are not being recorded."

"Good. Any trouble last night?" Austin asks.

He clears his throat. "No. Other than Muñoz going on every national news broadcast to tell the people of Panama I am on my deathbed. I must show my face today and assure the voters I am fit to lead."

"Absolutely not." I can't believe he's considering leaving

the safety of the Presidential Palace until Domina squeezes my hand.

"He has to," she says. "Manuel, when are you giving the speech? And where? I can draft something for you this morning."

"At the Hotel Flores at 2:00 p.m.," he replies. "Their business center is empty this weekend and the Institutional Protection Service has already secured the second floor. Rafael contacted the press and gave them three potential locations for the speech, and we will only announce the final location fifteen minutes prior."

Austin and Trevor exchange glances, and Austin shakes his head. "It's too dangerous, Mr. Vice President. Any public appearance is a risk."

"If I were afraid of risks, Pritchard, I would still be working on my parents' potato farm. I *will* be giving a speech. It will be short, but if I do not show strength now, the entire country might pay the price."

"Hang on a minute," Austin says and jabs the mute button. "This is a bad fucking idea."

"Unless we try to draw the killers out." Even as I say the words, I hate the idea, but Cortez isn't going to listen to us. I wouldn't either in his shoes. "If we can get in there with him, maybe we can catch the assholes before they take their shot."

"We're not going in armed." Austin shakes his head. "Not after what happened at the rally. Because if we're all arrested, no one's going to be able to spring us before the election. Or before we disappear forever."

Trevor pulls up a satellite map of the area around the Hotel Flores. "Narrow streets, too many buildings. Pinch points all over the fucking place." He taps his screen a couple more times, and finds the layout of the business center. "Three ways in and out. Stairs, public elevator, and service elevator. Assuming these images are up to date."

Austin scrubs his hands over his face. "We don't have a choice. Cortez isn't going to hide away the day before the election. All we can do is try to keep him safe." Taking the call off mute, he sits up a little straighter. "Mr. Vice President, we need you to get us into the press conference."

"That will not be possible," Cortez says. "The speech will be televised, but only my staff and the camera operators are allowed in the room with me. The public will be waiting in the main foyer. I will make an appearance on the balcony to wave and show my face, but after the attack at the rally..."

"Am I on your staff?" Domina asks. Her shoulders hunch, and she shrinks back against her chair like she isn't sure she wants to hear the answer.

"Oh, Domina," Manuel says. "Yes. You never should have been fired. You have been with me from the beginning, and I would not be here without your words inspiring the people."

"Then you can get me in the room," she says. "And Leo too."

"How the hell is he supposed to get me in there?" I ask. "You saw how well that worked the last time. And we have no idea if that Rafael asshole is involved in this. Do you really expect me to let you anywhere near him without me?"

Domina's eyes blaze with heat. "I expect you to protect Manuel."

"You are my priority." Taking her by the shoulders, I touch my forehead to hers. "My *only* priority."

For several long moments, neither of us move. Finally, Cortez clears his throat. "I spoke with President Garcia last night. He has no plans to leave El Palacio de Las Garzas today, so his protective detail is now assigned to me. They are the most senior agents in the service, all with more than a decade of experience."

"Is that supposed to make me feel better?" I ask. "You had

a full detail at the rally, yet *someone* walked in with a sniper rifle."

"That is why I asked President Garcia for a whole new team," Cortez says sharply. "These agents see me every day. They could have killed me at any time over the past six months. I trust them with my life."

"So we're just supposed to sit here? The polls close in—what?—thirty-six hours? Whoever wants you dead isn't going to wait much longer." I push to my feet, stifling my groan. I need to move, despite all my bruises making themselves known. "We still don't know who's behind this."

"We have to be on site," Austin says with a small shake of his head. "We're trained for this, Manuel."

"And my security service is not?" He huffs. "What do you think you will be able to do that they cannot?"

"Observe." Austin's tone sharpens, now one hundred percent that of the man who had the entire United States military at his beck and call. "Your detail's job is to protect *you*, sir. They're trained to take a bullet. To exfil you and your family in minutes. Not to call out suspicious behavior from a hundred yards away. That's what *we're* trained for. Make sure we can get into the public areas of the hotel. It doesn't matter if we're in the room with you for the press conference. As long as we're where the crowd is, we'll find the people after you and neutralize them."

"And how will you do that?" Cortez asks.

Austin leans forward, his index finger hovering over the *End Call* button. "Plausible deniability, Mr. Vice President. It's better you don't know."

"I don't like this." In the back of the SUV, Trevor checks his rifle for the fifth time. "I can't get closer than three hundred feet. We should have called Inara. She's a better shot than I am."

Next to me, Domina fiddles with the top button on her white blouse. The dark red skirt and blazer mold to her body, and it was hard as hell to make it out the door without taking her again. Especially after securing a GPS tracker to the band of her bra. But we're on the clock now.

"The press conference in starts half an hour." I check my phone, despite having looked at it only three minutes ago. "If he didn't do his part and get us clearance, we're fucked."

Domina straightens. "Manuel will take care of our access. In six years, he has never broken a promise to me or anyone else on his staff."

"My face says otherwise," I mutter.

"He did not know we were in trouble." Taking my hands, she squeezes gently. "You don't know him as I do. When we spoke to him last night, his regret was genuine. He was convinced you pointed your gun at him."

I hold her gaze. She's so earnest, so utterly certain Manuel Cortez is exactly who he says he is, that I believe it too. For almost ninety minutes after we hung up with the man, she closed herself in my bedroom with her tablet to draft his speech. Even after everything Domina's been through this week, she's still so devoted to her job that she insisted we let her work while we went over our infil and exfil plans.

"We're reviewing everything again." From the driver's seat, Austin checks the rearview mirror. "Domina, you do *not* leave Leo's side. I'll be no more than twenty feet behind you both the whole time. You remember how the comms units work?"

"Tap once to turn it on before we go through security. If I need to turn it off, tap twice. Do not touch it unless absolutely necessary."

He nods. "Leo? Exfil route."

"Through the kitchen, into the service elevator. Down one

floor to the laundry. Follow the dryers to the fire exit. Disable the alarm, and the door leads to a back alley. You do know what I used to do for a living?"

He coasts to a stop at a light and turns. "You *do* know what *I* used to do for a living?"

"Like you'd let me forget, Stars and Bars."

"Stars and Bars?" Domina asks.

Austin shakes his head. "Ryker—he runs Hidden Agenda K&R out in Seattle—started calling me that in Venezuela. It wasn't supposed to stick."

She peers up at me, confusion in her eyes, and I lean over to plant a gentle kiss to her forehead. "Austin has more medals than...well...just about anyone alive. When he came down to Venezuela, he was a four-star general."

"And then he got shit-canned for leaving his post," Trev says.

Austin snorts. "You say that like I didn't have a damn good reason, Superman."

The back-and-forth banter makes me feel like I'm part of a team. Like I'm not the damaged has-been who can't do a damn thing but chase after cheating husbands and petty thieves. I'll never go back to the CIA. But working alone for the rest of my life? Is that really what I want?

Silence fills the SUV. Trevor checks his weapon another five times before Austin pulls into a parking space half a mile from the hotel. Domina leans against me, and I steal as much closeness as I can before we have to walk through fire.

"Stay close, baby," I say when the hotel comes into view. More than a hundred people gather outside, and even from here, I can see the lobby is packed. "Cortez should have kept this quiet, not broadcast it to the entire fucking world."

"He had to." Domina tightens her grip on my right hand. "If he did not, Muñoz would have given his own press confer-ence and called Manuel a coward. Unfit to lead. You do not understand how easily the public can be swayed in the days before an election."

"Oh, I've seen it happen." I brush my lips to her cheek. "When we're safe in bed tonight, I'll tell you all about what happened in Venezuela."

CHAPTER TWENTY-FIVE

Domina

Manuel's speech is happening in one of the hotel's many conference rooms on the second floor, but as we expected, we can go no further than the lobby.

Suited IPS agents, their gazes stern and postures ramrod straight, are stationed around the room, and the hotel brought in half a dozen TVs to broadcast his words to the throngs of people filling the space.

Leo tightens his fingers on mine. Every few minutes, we're jostled from one side or the other. Tension rolls off of him in waves. My heart races as one of the IPS agents points in our general direction.

The local news issued a retraction this morning, publicly stating that I was no longer a suspect, but more than one person has seen my face and quickly moved away from us.

I lost track of Austin not long after we passed through the metal detector, but every few minutes he calls out a clock time over the tiny comms unit in my ear, prompting Leo to steer us in one direction or another to observe.

"I have to ask you to leave," a suited agent says as he blocks us from moving through the crowd.

"For fuck's sake," Leo snaps. "This is a public event. Domina *works* for the vice president."

"She is a suspect in the attempted assassination—"

"You're working with outdated info, man. Or don't you listen to the news? She wasn't fired and she had nothing to do with the incident at the rally. Check your security briefing."

I pull my staff ID from my pocket, then show the man the text message Manuel sent me an hour ago.

Manuel Cortez: I gave your names to my security detail. If you have any trouble, show them this message and the codeword: corazón.

The agent clicks the button on his radio and speaks in rapid Spanish. "The speechwriter, Domina Sanchez, is here. With that American the Ministry detained after the rally. What do you want me to do with them?"

"Do with us?" Leo asks. "We have the damn passphrase. You're going to leave us the hell alone and get back to doing your job."

The man touches his ear, which prompts Austin to mutter, "Amateur," over comms.

On the television screens, Manuel wraps up his speech. "Those who seek to destroy us will never win because we have truth, compassion, and honor on our side! With your support, tomorrow night, I will address you as your president! For Panama! For the people! For us all!"

The IPS agent says something, but his words are lost to the thunderous applause surrounding us.

"Eight o'clock," Austin hisses. "Gustavo Bernal from the Muñoz campaign."

Leo takes my arm and turns, no longer caring about the armed and very angry man in front of us. There are too many people. Too close. I cannot see a thing other than Leo's light blue shirt as I press myself to his side.

Men and women shove at us, desperate to get closer to the balcony where Manuel will wave and pose for photos. Members of the press elbow the public out of the way, and one tries to force us apart until Leo grabs him by the knot on his tie. "Get the fuck out of my way, asshole," he grits out, and the photographer seems to deflate before my eyes.

But as soon as he fades into the sea of people, we cannot do much more than move a few steps in any direction.

"Jimmy, you better be close," Leo mutters. "We're about to be fucked here."

Over comms, Austin's smooth voice carries a harsh edge. "Stuck behind half a dozen reporters. Stick close to Diana and prepare for exfil. I've got a bad feeling about this whole circus."

Leo frames my face with his hands. For a brief moment, we are the only two people in the room. "We have five minutes until Cortez does his thing on the balcony. We'll get as close to the kitchens as we can before then. Keep your head down. Stay right behind me, and don't let go of my hand. Got it?"

I nod, the worry in Leo's tone frightening me. If anyone goes after Manuel, how will we stop them with this many people around us?

"It's a shit show out here," Trevor says. "Two, maybe three hundred people blocking the front door. Zephyr's tapped into my scope, running facial recognition. So far, no one suspicious. What I wouldn't give to be able to eavesdrop on the IPS radio frequency..."

Every step is a struggle. More than once, someone tries to force their way between us, but Leo holds on so tightly, I worry he will crush my hand. A foot slams into my toes. Teetering on my heel, I grab for Leo's belt.

My ankle buckles, pain zinging up my calf. My fingers only graze the leather.

An arm snakes around my waist. I'm jerked backward so fast, Leo cannot hold on. He spins—right into a large man in a dark gray suit. In the space of a heartbeat, we're forced apart. Half a dozen people fill the space between us.

A scream dies in my throat as something sharp jabs my ribs. "Not a sound, bitch."

I know that voice. "Pinzon," I whisper. "No..."

In my ear, Leo's frantic voice calls, "Diana! Diana! Fuck it. Domina, answer me! Jimmy, do you have eyes on her?"

A hand wraps around the back of my neck, squeezing hard enough I cry out. Dark spots swim in front of my eyes. Everything around me fades to a dull roar. Faces pass in a blur. My left ankle throbs, but are my feet even touching the ground?

Leo...where are you?

I try to call out, but my voice fails. Sunlight blinds me. The stench of exhaust fills my nose.

"Check her," someone says sharply.

My lids are so heavy. The pressure on my neck lifts, and then I'm falling. I land on something hard. An engine vibrates underneath me.

Do something!

I know I'm in trouble. That if I do not move, scream, fight, I will disappear. Or worse.

Hands rove up and down my body. Squeezing. Pulling at my blouse. My skirt. In my ear, Austin, Trevor, and Leo shout, but I cannot make out their words.

The haze muddling my thoughts starts to fade. "Outside!" I scream. The slap sends my head whipping to the side. Rough fingers yank the tiny comms device from my ear.

"She's wired!" Pinzon. I will never forget his voice. I blink hard, and his angry face swims over me. He tosses the little earbud to someone, and a door slides shut. A van. I'm in a van. But it does not matter now. No one can hear me. "Go, go, go!"

Pinzon flips me onto my stomach. I flail my arms, but he captures my wrists and pins them behind my back. The zip tie digs into my skin. I scream and kick, but Daniel isn't the only one back here with me. Another man binds my ankles. "That was very advanced technology," he says. "Leo Basher is not careless. Check her again. *Everywhere*. I will disable her phone."

Unlike Pinzon, this man's accent is lighter. More refined. I struggle to see his face until his words sink in. *Everywhere*. Pinzon's hands slide over my calves, between my legs, all the way to my panties.

"Get off me!" I cry. "Stop! Please!"

My tears soak into the rough, gray carpet on the van's floor. Pinzon chuckles as he squeezes both of my ass cheeks. He stops short of violating me, but this...this is so close, I want to throw up. His fingers dig under the waistband of my skirt, then move to my back.

The GPS tracker. He will find it. How long has it been? Only minutes. They had a plan. They knew we would be at the hotel. Knew we would be together. Knew exactly how to separate us. The van was waiting outside, the engine running.

Pinzon pulls up my blouse, and I squeeze my eyes shut. "What is this?" His hot breath over my cheek makes me gag. Digging under the band of my bra, right against the side of my breast, he finds the small GPS tracker. "Thought we would miss this, *Domina*?"

He drops the tracker right in front of my face, and the other man—he's familiar, but fear clouds my memories— slams the butt of his gun down on the small device.

"Please," I whimper. "Stop the van and let me go."

"We can't do that," the other man says. "Your lover and his *friends* ruined our best chance to kill Cortez. So we are going to make him do it for us."

"Leo will *never* kill Manuel. He is too good of a man."

Pinzon flips me onto my back. Half a dozen slices from my cactus mar his cheeks and forehead. A bloody stain covers half the white of his left eye. But it is his smile that terrifies me the most.

"He will. Or he will watch you die."

CHAPTER TWENTY-SIX

Leo

SOMEONE PUSHES ME SO HARD, I stumble several steps back. If it weren't for the crowd, I'd be on my ass. Bodies close in around me. Who the hell let all these goddamn people in here?

"Diana? Diana! Fuck it. Domina, answer me! Jimmy, do you have eyes on her?" The memory of her fingers in mine is still so fresh. Where the hell is she?

"No! Why?" Austin asks.

"Domina!" Frantic, I spin around, but catch only a glimpse of her dark curls. "She's at the back door. And I don't think she's alone!"

After a beat, Austin switches to Spanish to shout, "Get out of the way before I shove that camera up your ass!"

"I'm too far away to get there." Trevor's out of breath, and a door slams. "Still four floors to go."

Shit. He was seven stories up on a roof across the street. I can't see her anymore. Austin bursts through a wall of reporters, ignoring their rude gestures and vague threats of cutting off his balls.

"What happened? Where is she?" he asks. The bone conduction mics are more advanced than anything on the market today and filter out almost all ambient noise. Right now, I'd give anything to hear what's going on around her.

Together, we fight our way through the crowds. Austin leads, shoving, pushing, and using his entire body to part the sea of supporters desperate to see their candidate.

"Outside!" Domina screams.

I grab Austin's arm, our gazes locking for a split second. She's terrified. Which means she's not alone. Someone took her.

"Go east, Superman," Austin snaps. "We'll take the west. Meet behind the building."

What I wouldn't give for a weapon. Austin has a ceramic knife strapped to his forearm under his jacket, but he'd have to slit every throat in our path. The IPS would have us in custody in a heartbeat.

"Domina! Tell me where you are! I'm coming, baby! Just give me *something*!" Only silence answers me, and I follow Austin as he slams into a group of people all wearing "Cortez for President" t-shirts.

"Move your asses. Now!" he snarls. They're so shocked, they part like the Sea of Galilee.

We burst out into a back alley, and it's empty. The faint scent of exhaust lingers, but I don't see Domina anywhere. I run to the north, check both sides of the street, and turn south.

Austin crouches down, his fingers brushing the pavement. "Fuck!" I skid to a stop. In his outstretched hand? Domina's comms unit. She'd never remove it. She promised. And the damn things fit so well, there's no way it would have fallen out.

Trevor races around the corner, his rifle in a long, black bag slung over his shoulder. "Where is she?"

"Gone." My voice sounds strange with how loud my heartbeat pounds in my ears. "Someone took her."

"Zephyr, get us a location on Domina's tracker," Austin says, his phone pressed to his ear. "Now!"

My comms unit beeps once as she breaks into our frequency. "It stopped transmitting less than a minute ago. A mile south of your current location. Before that, it was moving at approximately forty miles per hour. Sending coordinates to your phones now. What happened?"

"Get on the traffic cameras. Someone grabbed her. They came out the back door. Her earbud was in the alley. Whoever took her was *inside* the hotel and we didn't mark them as hostiles. I need names and faces. Now!"

I run to the south end of the alley. "Leo!" Trevor calls. "She's too far away. If they got to Domina, they could have gotten to Cortez too. We need to find out if any of them are still inside."

"I don't give a fuck! Whoever's behind this *took* her, and God only knows what they'll do to her!" My right ankle sends shooting pains up my calf, and I can only manage an uneven jog back. But I use my momentum and shove Trevor—hard. He hits a dumpster and goes down. The rifle bag clatters against the thick metal. I advance on him, but Austin grabs my arms and spins me around.

"*Think*, Leo. Whoever has Domina planned this. They had a vehicle. They found her comms unit. And her tracker. Which means they know about me. Maybe Trevor too. How many people does that leave? Ten? Fifteen? Cortez, Garcia, the assholes at the Ministry. We *will* find her, but if Cortez dies, the entire country is fucked, and you *know* she wouldn't want that."

I struggle, a feral growl rumbling in my chest. Until I hear Domina's words in my head.

"Manuel is an honorable man."

"He will be good for Panama. Muñoz would take us back to the tyranny of Noriega."

"This job...it changed my entire life, Leo. My words matter. Not only to Cortez, but to the people. I make a difference."

The pain in my heart makes it hard to breathe. But I shake off Austin's hold and slump against the building's wall. "I love her."

"No shit, Captain Obvious," Trev says, rubbing his shoulder. "Next time, punch me instead." He gets to his feet and brushes dirt from his black pants. "I don't know what the fuck that puddle is, but I only missed it by two inches and it smells—"

Screams from the front of the hotel drown out his words, and we all tense. Racing back to the corner of the building, we stick close, Austin in the lead and Trev bringing up the rear.

Men and women pour from the building, their faces stricken, terrified, and panicked. A young boy falls, but no one helps him.

"Leo!" Austin shouts, but I'm already moving. The kid tries to get to his feet, but the crowd doesn't see him—or doesn't care—and he curls into a ball with his hands over his head.

I can get there. Another few seconds, and I can get there. "Fucking *move!*" A man stops less than a foot away from the boy. He's big—football player big—and the brief moment it takes him to decide how to get as far away from me as he can gives me the opening I need.

Grabbing the boy's arm, I haul him up. He can't be more than twelve, and I let him hold onto my neck while I shoulder through the panicked crowd. "Where are your parents?"

"I don't know!" he cries. Shit. I have to find Domina, but what the hell am I supposed to do with this terrified kid in my arms?

"Paulo! My God. Paulo!" a woman calls. The kid straightens, and I turn toward the sound. White hair, a cane...his grandmother? Thank fuck we're at the edge of the throngs of people.

The woman reaches for him, but before I let him go, I ask, "This you, kid?"

He's crying now. Sobbing, really, but manages to nod, so I set him on his feet. "Here you go, ma'am. What happened in there?"

"I do not know." The older woman dabs at her cheeks with a handkerchief. "Vice President Cortez came out onto the balcony and waved to all of us. But then there was a bright flash and smoke and people started screaming. The doors...we could not all fit through..."

Shit, shit, shit.

The boy wraps his arms around his grandmother's waist, and I limp as quickly as I can back to Austin and Trevor.

"Flash bang—or some sort of explosive—inside. We have to get to Cortez. Now!" If he dies, will the assholes who took Domina have any reason to keep her alive?

Trev shoves his rifle bag at Austin and double-times it back to the dumpster.

"What the fuck are you doing? We need to get back in—"

Trevor vaults onto the corrugated metal lid and peers down at me. "There's no way we're going through the front door. You know a faster way to get in? Because I don't. Get up here and give me a boost. I didn't bring a grappling hook."

Austin climbs up next to him while I stand there, gaping. He's right, but I should have known...

Bracing himself against the wall, Austin cups his hands on his thigh. "On three."

By the time I haul my ass onto the dumpster, Trev is wedging his tactical knife under the sash of one of the narrow, second-floor windows. They're barely wide enough, but after a string of curses, Trevor gets his shoulders through.

Austin passes him the rifle case, then nods at me. "You're next."

Shit. I'm in no shape to scale walls. But for Domina, I'll do anything. Even push my body to its limits. And beyond.

Austin gets me close enough to curl my fingers over the sill, but my shoulder pops, and shooting pains run down my back. I scramble for purchase, scuffing my shoes against the brick wall. "I'm slipping!"

Trev grabs my wrists, and Austin shoves at my feet. It's just enough to get my torso through the window. I tumble onto the hard tile floor, and Trev holds out his hand. "Get up, brother. There's rope in my bag. Toss it down for Stars and Bars. I'll check the hallway. Make sure we're clear."

I let him help me up. We lock gazes for the briefest of moments. He'll kick my ass later for tackling him—and I deserve it—as long as we get Domina back. But for now, we're solid.

I tie the rope around my waist and toss the other end out the window. The sudden weight almost sends me crashing into the wall when Austin grabs on, but less than a minute later, he pulls himself up and lands on the floor in a crouch.

"You weigh a fucking ton," I mutter.

Trev signals for us to follow him down the hall. It's almost quiet here, though the screams and shouts from downstairs provide a low-level background hum.

We're sneaking around the business center of a goddamn hotel while Domina's out there somewhere. Probably scared out of her mind. Hurt. Alone.

And I'm free with two men who would die for me at my side.

"Base? Any idea which room the target's in?" Trev asks.

"Checking." Zephyr's reply comes only a few seconds later, but each one feels like an hour. "From the broadcast, he entered the Rosa room from the back left. Check out Tulipán. Ahead on the right. Third door."

We only make it a few steps before she breaks in again. "Got Charlie on the breaking news situation. I'm staying on traffic cameras. Will let you know what he finds."

"Charlie?" I hiss at Austin.

He mouths, *"Ripper."* I'm fucking sick of code names. Especially for people I've never met.

Moving as one, we head for the Tulipán room. Trevor tosses the black bag at Austin and pulls a small Sig Sauer from his ankle holster. "This is gonna get messy. Cover me."

"With a fucking sniper rifle?" After a muffled curse, Austin pulls out the SRS A2 and flips off the safety.

I've never felt so helpless in my entire life. No gun. No body armor. No idea where the woman I love is now. Or if she's even still alive.

"Leo. Door," Trev snaps. I trade places with him, my hand on the lever knob. "On my mark." He blows out a breath, counts down, and I shove the door open. "Nobody move!" Trevor shouts as he breaches the small room. "Hands in the air. All of you. Right fucking now!"

Austin and I follow, though without a weapon, I'm less than useless.

Shit. Omar, Isobel, and that pissant, Rafael, are the only ones in the room. They huddle together behind a table laid out with a full spread of coffee, donuts, and pastries. Another table a few feet away is turned on its side, and broken china litters the floor.

"Where's Cortez?" I grit out.

No one says a word. Fuck this. I grab Rafael by the lapels of his preppy, over-starched jacket. "Where is your goddamn vice president? Someone *took* Domina, and until we find her, I'm holding *you* personally responsible, you traitorous piece of shit!"

When he gapes at me, I slam him down onto the table. Delicate china cups crash to the floor. Coffee seeps into white linen and splatters Rafael's tie.

"Answer me! Now, asshole!"

Austin's saying something to Omar and Isobel, but I only care about the man shaking under my grip. Trev jams the pistol against Rafael's temple. "We know you're involved. Sending Cortez that doctored video? That was dumb as fuck."

"I...please! There was so much noise! And smoke. Manuel's security detail surrounded him and told the rest of us to hide in here. They took him to a secure location. But we don't know where and no one came back for us. Why haven't they come back for us?" He takes a shuddering breath.

Before he can start vomiting even more drivel, I lean close, getting right in his face. "Domina. Is. Gone. Do you understand me?"

His eyes widen. "What? How?"

"If I knew that, do you think I'd be here right now?" I lift him two inches, then slam him back down. "Tell me who you're working with and *maybe* I'll let you live. Otherwise..."

"Leo. Let me have a go," Trev says. The lethality in his voice would make the most hardened soldier piss his pants, and I step back. Yep. A dark stain spreads across Rafael's crotch. "If you think you're scared now, fuckwit, just wait..."

"I'm not working with anyone!" Rafael slides to the floor. Tears spill from his eyes. He fumbles with his jacket, but Trev slaps his hand away.

"Next time you move, I'm taking out one of your kneecaps. Then the other."

"M-my phone," he stammers. "In my pocket. The video

from the rally… The National Police sent it to me. I…I did not see Leo with a gun. I didn't see him at all. I was focused on Manuel. When the agents surrounded him, I hid behind the chairs until they told us to move."

I haven't taken my eyes off the asshole since we came into the room, and dammit. He's panicked as fuck, but I'd know if he were lying. "He's telling the truth." Reaching into his pocket, I find his phone. "Unlock code."

"Eight-seven-three-one-five-two."

It only takes me a minute to find the email.

"Mr. Perez, this video is from moments before the Vice President was shot. The man waving the gun is Leo Basher. He is an American who used to work for the CIA. The Ministry of Public Service has him in custody. Make sure the Vice President sees this footage, but do not share it with the media. It will hamper the investigation."

"It's not signed," I add. "From some generic 'investigations' mailbox."

"Base can clone the device and work her magic," Austin says from across the room. The rifle hangs at his side, and the other two staffers hold onto one another next to him.

For a beat, no one says a word. The silence is too much. Domina's gone. We don't have a single fucking lead. She could be anywhere by now. Or…nowhere. If they've killed her…

No. They took her for a reason. They'll keep her alive.

The single thought is the only reason I'm still standing. They want her for something. But whatever it is? It can't be good.

I stagger over to one of the chairs. If I don't sit down, I'll fall. Every bruise, scrape, cut, and scar screams at me. It's all too much. If I never see her again…I'll never get to tell her I love her. And my life? Without her, it's not worth a damn thing.

CHAPTER TWENTY-SEVEN

Domina

WITH NOTHING TO do but squirm under the stares of the two men who stole me away from Leo, I have no idea how long we've been in this van. The driver turns every few minutes.

Are we still in the city? Or are they taking me somewhere far away where no one can get to me?

"Leo will never kill Manuel."

"He will, or he will watch you die."

Would Leo really kill to save me? Tears burn my eyes. Yes. He would. To save me—or to avenge me.

Shame floods me, choking my throat. I have never wished death on another person, but if I die...I hope these men die too.

Pinzon stares at my breasts with a hunger that frightens me. The other man mostly ignores me. Where have I seen him before? He is young. Thirty? His brown eyes flick to mine. No warmth. No sympathy. Only icy detachment.

They *will* kill me. I can identify them.

Leo, please...find me.

The van slows, and the driver—I have not been able to see his face—calls out, "Two minutes."

The man with cold eyes reaches behind him for a roll of duct tape. The sound as he tears a strip makes me choke back a sob.

"No!" I scream when he approaches, but Pinzon grabs a fistful of my hair and slams my head against the floor of the van. Dazed, I fall silent. The tape seals my lips. The harsh scent of glue burns my nose.

Pinzon removes his tie, and I watch helplessly until he fastens the dark gray silk over my eyes. Unable to see, I scream again, though it's so muffled, would anyone hear me?

A hand wraps around my throat, cutting off my air. "Last warning, bitch. Or I will make you bleed."

My body convulses, desperate to breathe. I try to nod. He releases me, and I suck air through my nose.

The blindfold soaks with my tears. I have never felt so alone. So helpless.

Papa's slurred voice runs on a loop through my mind. *"You are worthless, Domina. If you cannot bring me a beer, get out of my sight!"*

The van jerks to a stop. A moment later, sunlight warms my feet. Wherever we are, they aren't worried about anyone seeing a bound, gagged, and blindfolded woman. But they don't want me to scream. There must be people close by.

Focus. Leo will not do anything without knowing you are still alive. If you can talk to him...

Rough hands grab my legs and drag me toward the back of the van. I smell flowers. Gardenias. A gentle breeze kisses my cheeks as someone—Pinzon, I think—throws me over his shoulder.

I cannot fight. My wrists are bound so tightly, my fingers are numb.

A door opens and shuts. Then another. And another. Upside down, unable to see, I'm so disoriented.

How many times can they hit me before I get a concussion? Do I have one already? I cannot hold a thought in my head for more than a minute.

Stairs. Down. My head bounces against Pinzon's back. Nausea crawls up my throat. If I vomit, I will choke and die. Swallowing hard, I try to stifle my whimper.

A slap to my ass shuts me up *and* quells the nausea. I never thought I would be grateful for someone hitting me.

Until I fall. A fresh scream wells up inside me. I thrash, desperate to use my hands, but the zip tie digs into my wrists.

Landing knocks the air from my lungs. My head cracks against hard tile. Every muscle in my body strains, desperate for air. Before I understand what is happening, fingers dig into my cheek, then tear the duct tape from my skin.

Burning pain jars me enough to draw in a wheezing breath. "Help me!" I scream. "Help!"

I do not care if they hurt me. I have to escape. Find a way back to Leo.

"Make all the noise you want," Pinzon snaps. "No one will hear you." He rips the blindfold away, and I blink up at him.

He looms over me, mouth open, that same, lecherous gleam in his eyes.

"You will die for this," I rasp.

His laugh sends terror wrapping around my heart, squeezing so hard, I gasp for air. "We are the ones in charge now, bitch. Be good, and we'll let you live. Otherwise..."

I have to find a way out of here. My head pounds as I scan the room. It's small. Not much bigger than a closet. A dim bulb shines from a fancy, stained glass light fixture on the ceiling. Tile floors. Dark wood walls. No windows.

I start to wheeze when I find the door. It's closed. No

knob. Only a shiny, metal plate. No way out. Even if I weren't bound, even if Pinzon weren't here...I couldn't escape.

The zip ties are too tight. I should stop struggling, but I cannot help myself. "Where am I?" I gasp. "How long...are you...going to keep me here?"

Pinzon smiles down at me again. I *hate* his smile. Leo should have blinded him.

"Overnight. Tomorrow, you will watch your precious candidate die. Then your lover. After that..." He pulls a switchblade from his pocket. I flinch at the snap. "Maybe we will have some fun together when Muñoz is declared the winner."

"Stay away from me, asshole!" I wriggle back, but there's nowhere to go. His idea of *fun* is my worst nightmare. Kicking out, I catch him in the shin.

"Fucking bitch!" He grabs my swollen ankle. This is it. He will hurt me now. "You are lucky we need you to look... presentable tomorrow. But once your *boyfriend* kills Cortez..."

The blade slides under the zip tie and snaps it in two. Before I can react, Pinzon spins me around and frees my hands.

I try to get to my knees, but he shoves me back down. "You want to spend the next eighteen hours hogtied? Try that again!"

My stomach twists into a knot. I start to shake. Pins and needles prick at my fingers. Bright red welts mar my wrists.

The door bangs open, and I yelp, throwing my hands up in front of me. The other man—the one I recognized from the van—looms in the open space.

"Get the fuck out of here," he snaps. "She isn't to be touched until tomorrow, and I don't trust you to keep your hands to yourself."

"I almost lost an eye!" Pinzon says. "I deserve—"

"You'll get what you deserve when Cortez is dead. Until then, stay away from her." The man grabs Pinzon by the arm and practically shoves him out the door.

All I can see is a short hallway, but after a string of muttered curses, Pinzon's footsteps echo on the stairs.

If I can get out... Except I don't know what lies beyond those steps.

The man leans against the doorjamb, blocking any hope of escape. His stance is casual, but he rests a hand on the butt of a gun strapped to his hip.

"Ms. Sanchez. Domina. Do you know who I am?"

"No. Please, let me go. Leo will never kill Manuel. Not even to save me. Your plan—whatever it is—will fail, and I do not want to die."

"Oh, I think Mr. Basher will do exactly what we say." The man pulls out his phone, taps the screen, and shows it to me.

The video is grainy, but Leo has Rafael pinned to a table. "Where is your goddamn vice president? Someone *took* Domina, and until we find her, I'm holding *you* personally responsible, you traitorous piece of shit!"

Oh, God. They had cameras in the hotel. If they could do that... Did they hear our conversation with Manuel this morning? Or last night? Are they watching the apartment building?

The man tucks his phone back into his pocket. "We have eyes everywhere, Domina. And right now, your lover wants to burn down the entire world. Do you really think he won't kill *one* man to save you?"

Lifting my chin, I stare up at him. Showing fear will not help me now. I need information. Anything that might help me live through this.

"If he'd killed Rafael, you would have shown me that. So yes. I do believe in Leo."

He chuckles. "We are going to have a little talk, and you

will tell me everything about the men Mr. Basher is with. Everything I do not already know, that is."

Dragging a chair partway into the room, he sits, pulls the gun from its holster, and rests it across his thigh.

"You need me...presentable. So you cannot shoot me. Or break bones. Why do you expect me to tell you anything?" Challenging this man could be a terrible mistake, but none of this makes any sense.

"Have you ever heard of stress positions, Domina?" he asks. "They are designed to inflict the maximum amount of pain while leaving very few marks on the body. At the moment, you are...comfortable. Yes?"

Fear sours my stomach, but I cannot let him see how very frightened I am. "I was kidnapped and thrown in the back of a van. Punched, slapped, *dropped*."

"But you are not currently screaming. That can change very quickly." With a casual wave of the gun, he sighs. "I should introduce myself. My name is Sergio Muñoz. Eduardo Muñoz is my father."

I am too shocked to find any kind of retort. Sergio smiles, but unlike Pinzon, there is nothing in his eyes when he does so. No desire. No joy. No hatred or anger.

I did not know the lack of emotion could be so terrifying.

"My father is very sorry for all of this," Sergio says, shrugging his shoulders. "If you had not been home when Daniel broke into your apartment...all of this could have been avoided. But once Mr. Basher interfered..."

"Daniel attacked me! Leo was only trying to protect me," I scream.

Sergio levels a stern gaze at me. "We are in a basement, Domina. There are two solid wood doors between the stairs and the main floor of the house. Make as much noise as you want. No one will hear you."

I slump back against the wall. Right now, I need information. And to conserve my strength.

"Leo Basher stopped us from killing Cortez at the rally. His warnings ensured we could not get to him today at the hotel either. So now, he will do it for us. And you, Domina, are the key to our success. Tomorrow, after Cortez is dead, my father will be declared the winner. If you do not cause trouble and do what you are told, once that happens, we will let you go."

"I have seen your faces, Sergio. I know you have to kill me too. I am not a fool."

He leans forward in the chair, the gun still firmly in his hand. "When my father runs this country, we will own you. As well as the National Police, the Institutional Protection Service, and the rest of the agents at the Ministry of Public Service. So we do not have to kill you. If you tell *anyone* we orchestrated this entire thing, you will disappear. Along with every person you have *ever* cared about."

His words sink in, and I want to cry. Scream. Force his hand so he shoots me and I do not have to be a pawn in this ugly, terrible game.

"Your father is a tyrant. Under his rule, the people of Panama will be worse off than we were fifty years ago!"

"Watch your tone, Domina," Sergio says. "My father is a true patriot. You will see. He will return Panama to its former glory. Now, tell me what you know about Major General Austin Pritchard and the other man who flew to Panama with him."

My mind races. Sergio knows Austin's name. That means he has contacts at the Ministry, or there is a traitor in the Presidential Palace. My only hope—Leo's only hope—is if sometime before tomorrow, they let me talk to him.

"You can do whatever you want to me." I stagger to my feet, using the wall for support. My ankle buckles, but I refuse to let myself fall. "Since you seem to have so much information on Leo already, you must know there is no way he will do what you want unless he is *very* sure I am alive and unharmed."

Sergio rises and advances on me. I sidestep him—or try to. My heel catches on an uneven tile, and my knees slam into the ground. He presses the barrel of the gun to my temple.

This is the end. He's going to kill me, and I'll never see Leo again.

But after a full minute where I do not dare move, Sergio swears under his breath. "Fucking bitch." He shoves the gun back into the holster and kicks the chair into the hall. The door slams, the sound so loud, it hurts my ears.

But it's the *thunk* of the lock that breaks me.

CHAPTER TWENTY-EIGHT

Leo

Five hours. Domina was taken five hours ago. We questioned Omar and Isobel, Zephyr cloned Rafael's phone, and Trevor and Austin haven't stopped making calls since we returned to my apartment. Even with the non-stop activity, all I can do is sit on my ruined couch and stare out the patio doors.

I've called her phone a dozen times. Zephyr can't ping it, so whoever has her turned it off or destroyed it.

"Leo!" Trevor shakes my shoulder, and training takes over. My fist flies toward his face, but with no depth perception, I miss. By a lot. "You're on my last nerve. We're trying to help you."

"You should have left me in that goddamn black site!" I shout. "Domina might have been in police custody then, but at least she was *safe!*"

Trevor snorts. "The hell she was. The National Police took her phone, refused to let her call a lawyer, and probably would have held her for weeks without charges. I know things look like shit right now, but we *will* get her back. Assuming you pull your head out of your ass and help us."

I stare at him in disbelief. "How the fuck do you think this is going to work? Zephyr lost the van less than two minutes after the tracker went dead. The traffic cameras over half the city went out. Clearly we're not dealing with amateurs here. Domina could be anywhere right now. We don't even know if she's still alive."

Austin shoves his chair so hard, it tips over and slams against the tile floor. I've never seen him this mad—not even when I was a complete jerk to him and Dani in Venezuela.

"Think, Leo. If these fuckwits wanted her dead, they would have killed her at the hotel. My guess? She knows something about Cortez, his security, or his movements that Muñoz thinks will give them a better chance to kill the Vice President before the polls close."

"Is that supposed to make me feel better? They'll torture her, Austin. Until there's nothing of *her* left. And then they'll kill her." I jerk to my feet, desperate for a minute of fresh air, but before I take two steps, my phone rings. The name on the screen stops me in my tracks.

Domina.

I lock eyes with Austin. He doesn't hesitate. Before the next ring, he tosses me a cable so I can plug my mobile into his computer. "Keep them talking as long as you can."

Them.

He knows this isn't Domina. So do I, but for a split second, hope flared white hot. Now, my heart is nothing but ice.

"Where is she?" I ask when I jab the button on screen. "If you've hurt her, I'm going to cut out your tongue and feed it to you before I kill you."

"You are in no position to make demands, Mr. Basher," a man says. His voice is refined, a thick, Panamanian accent lending an almost musical quality to his words. "Listen carefully. Manuel Cortez will vote tomorrow sometime between 1:00 p.m. and 3:00 p.m. at the Church of the Holy Trinity."

"So will a hell of a lot of other people. The polls close at five, and after that, Muñoz will be shit out of luck."

"That is why you are going to kill Cortez before then."

Suddenly, everything makes sense. The man who broke into Domina's apartment. Being detained and tortured after the rally. All of it. I feel sick. But I have to play along.

"In what universe, shithead?"

I know the answer. I know exactly what this coward is going to say next, but I need to keep him talking. And get proof of life. I have to tell Domina I love her. That I'm coming for her no matter where she is or how many people I need to kill to get to her.

"We have Domina Sanchez. If you do not assassinate Vice President Cortez by 3:01 p.m. tomorrow, she will die. Painfully."

It doesn't matter that I knew it was coming. The words still shake me to my core. "I'm not a killer. Even if I were, what makes you think I can get anywhere near the Vice President? After today, he's in fucking lockdown. No one—not even his staff—knows where he is or how to get in touch with him. Believe me, I've tried."

The man laughs—the kind of laugh you hear from deranged murderers in horror movies—and it raises the hair on the back of my neck. "You are very much a killer, Mr. Basher. Or do I need to remind you—and the men you are with—of the former Loma Collectivo members you shot in cold blood less than six months ago?"

Trevor and Austin turn to me, and I sink down onto the

sofa. There's no way anyone could know what I did. I was alone and I never told a soul.

"I will keep your secret, Leo. I promise."

Except Domina. Betrayal and fear battle for control in my head. Did she volunteer the information willingly? Or did they torture her until she had no choice?

"Leo," Austin hisses. "Say something!"

"I don't know where you're getting your intel, fuckwit, but you're wrong. I'm a disabled, retired has-been who hasn't been able to shoot straight in years. Even if I were physically able to get to Cortez, why would I believe you'd let Domina go?"

Another chuckle, and Mr. Smooth Talker is getting on my last nerve. "Once the Vice President is dead, we will have no reason to kill Domina. Our *network* has people everywhere. If she keeps quiet, she will be allowed to live the rest of her life in peace. If, however, she makes trouble for us, she will disappear."

Muñoz is behind all of this. I'd bet my one good eye on it. But that knowledge does us no good if we can't find Domina before tomorrow. I lock eyes with Trevor, and he mouths, *"Proof of life."*

"I want to talk to Domina. Now. Or this conversation is over."

"I am afraid that is not possible, Mr. Basher. We cannot have your *friends* learning where she is. But I did record a short video of her not long ago."

My phone vibrates with a new message. I tap the screen, and my world grinds to a halt.

Domina sits in a wooden chair, her hands resting on her thighs. A dark red mark on her cheek sends my rage boiling over, but I keep quiet. I have to. Her blazer is gone, and her white silk blouse is dirty and untucked. But there's no blood, and she isn't bound that I can see.

A guy dressed all in black and wearing a full face mask stands behind her, his gloved hands on her shoulders. "Say hello to your lover," he says. His accent is different than the asshole on the phone. And where do I know that voice from?

"Leo?" She's terrified and trembling as she darts a quick glance at the man behind her.

"Tell him how we are treating you."

Domina squeezes her eyes shut for a long moment, then stares directly at the camera. "They haven't…hurt me. But, I'm scared, Leo. I want to go home. The first night we spent together—"

The man grabs her hair and wrenches her head back. "Enough, bitch!"

"Don't do it, Leo!" Domina shouts. The asshole clamps his hand over her mouth, hauls her out of the chair, and shoves her against the wall. She crumples to the floor, cowering.

"Another word, and you'll be sorry," he snarls. "Stop the video."

In the second before the feed cuts out, Domina looks back at the camera, and thank fuck, the light hasn't left her eyes completely.

"You still there, shithead?" I ask.

Smooth Talker sighs. "You do not have to be so vulgar, Mr. Basher."

"How do I know you didn't kill her two minutes after that recording? You want me to assassinate the man who's about to become the President of Panama, you'd better give me some goddamned proof of life."

"I cannot let you speak with her," the man says. "But you may ask her a question. One I could not possibly know the answer to. I will record her answer and send you the video in a few hours."

I get to my feet, desperate to pace, but with my phone

tethered to Austin's computer, all I can do is ball my hands into fists hard enough my knuckles crack.

Think! What could she say that might let us know where she is?

"I am waiting, Mr. Basher."

Shit. I don't have time to come up with the perfect question. "Tell her I'm sorry for failing her. That I'll do what you want because it's the only way to save her."

"And the question? I am losing my patience, Mr. Basher."

He's not the only one. "The night we met...what did I tell her to hang on her chair?"

The call disconnects, taking my last shred of sanity with it.

TREVOR SETS a mug of coffee in front of me. "Talk."

"I'm done talking, *Superman*. Leave me alone." I've played the video a dozen times. I told myself I was looking for anything that would let us know where she was being held. But really, I just wanted to see her face again. Hear her voice.

I tap the screen again, but he snatches the phone from my hands. "Zephyr's analyzing the video six ways from Sunday. If there's something on it, she'll find it."

"And what if she doesn't? In less than twenty-four hours, I'm supposed to kill the Vice President of Panama. Austin can't reach Garcia *or* Cortez, and we have no leads." I drop my head into my hands. "They've hurt her, Trevor."

"You don't know that. She looked...okay on the video," he says. "Scared, but not injured."

"Only one person in this world knew about the men I killed before I left Venezuela," I whisper. "She told them."

Betrayal tugs at my heart. Domina would have never willingly broken her promise to me. But she did, all the same.

Trevor sits back, rubbing his hands up and down his thighs. For a long moment, he doesn't say a word, and I lift my head.

Shit. From the look in his eyes, Trevor isn't here in Panama anymore. He's back in La Crypta wondering if anyone would ever find him. "When I was arrested in Boston," he says quietly, "the cops told me it was all because of an article in the Washington Post. An article *Dani* wrote that identified me as a former intelligence officer."

"She didn't…"

"Of course she didn't," Austin snaps. "Her editor published a draft story with notes she never intended to see the light of day. When she found out…" He shakes his head. "If we hadn't gotten Trev out of there, I think it would have killed her."

Trevor wanders over to the window. The sun paints the sky in orange, pink, and purple, and I wonder if Domina can see it where she is now.

No. *They* wouldn't allow it. If she could see out, someone else could see in. Memories of that dirty warehouse in Caracas make my palms sweat and my whole body ache.

"Leo?" he asks. He's backlit, but his frown is evident in his voice. "What if it *wasn't* Domina?"

"No one else knew. I got an anonymous email a few weeks before I turned in my retirement paperwork. I figured it was from Luis or Franco Rojas. In the years Luis was on the run, Franco had done a lot of research on the Loma Collectivo. He knew they were responsible for what happened to me."

I take a sip of coffee, needing something to do with my hands. As much as I want to believe Domina didn't talk—that they didn't *make* her talk—there's no other explanation.

"Wait." Trev crosses the room and braces his hands on the table, staring down at me. "When did you turn in your retirement paperwork?

"The day after I killed the last of them. I told Balin I'd seen too much—sacrificed too much."

Signing those papers felt like freedom. The rest of my life ahead of me. Whatever that was worth. Teddy Balin—my SSO—tried to convince me to stay, but...

"Shit!" I throw the coffee mug against the wall. Austin and Trevor stare at me like I've lost my mind. Maybe I have. "Balin showed up in Venezuela the morning after I sent in my paperwork. At my fucking house!"

"Don't tell me you used your GPS to find those assholes?" Trev asks.

"I'm not a goddamn idiot." I sink back down. "Or...I didn't think I was. I used a paper map. And when Balin showed up, I hadn't burned it yet. I was in the middle of that shit when he knocked. Fucker asked for a cup of coffee. He was alone in the room with my files for at least five minutes."

Everything makes sense now.

"Leo Francis Basher."

"When I met Cortez, he called someone to vet me. He had my entire dossier in under ten minutes," I say. "He wouldn't tell me who he called, but said my reputation was of an 'incorruptible intelligence officer whose powers of observation were unmatched.' And that I had no sense of self-preservation."

Trevor laughs so hard, he has to brace his hand on the wall to catch his breath. "Well, he got that right."

"There's more." I can't believe I didn't put all this together earlier. "He called me 'Leo Francis Basher.'"

"It's your name. What else was he supposed to call you? Bugs Bunny?" Austin asks.

I shoot him a look I hope says, "Dumbass," before I continue. "The CIA is the *only* agency with my full name. My driver's license, P.I. license, my apartment lease? All the records from my civilian cover identity? No middle name. And those fucksticks who tortured me in Venezuela knew it too. Along with the assholes from the Ministry."

Trev drops into a seat across from me and runs a hand through his hair. "The CIA is in on this. We're fucked."

CHAPTER TWENTY-NINE

Leo

"I'D GIVE my left nut to get Sampson here right now," Trevor says, staring at a sheet of butcher paper tacked up on my living room wall. "Never seen anyone with his tactical skills."

Austin scrubs his hands over his face. "He's going to call in thirty."

"Yeah, but he won't be at the church tomorrow."

I look up from my laptop. The blueprints Zephyr sent me are starting to blur with how hard I've been staring at them. "It's an eight-hour flight from Seattle, and since we have no idea who's watching us..."

"The day West can't figure out how to hide his entry into a foreign country is the day he tattoos his middle name on his forehead," Trevor mutters.

"What the hell are you talking about?" I cut my gaze to Austin, but he's just as confused as I am.

"Filbert," Trev says. "Westley Filbert Sampson."

For a full minute, the three of us laugh so hard, everything else falls away. Until I stop to catch my breath. Then the weight of what we're trying to do slams back down on my shoulders.

"He can do his thing from Seattle." Though Austin and Trevor argued with me for an hour, it was my call to keep the three members of Hidden Agenda—a K&R firm that partners with Trevor's employer, Second Sight— from flying to Panama City to join us. "All we can control is what happens inside these walls. Zephyr's monitoring the cameras you installed around the building, but we have no fucking clue who's watching us from across the street. Down the block. A rooftop two kilometers away."

After muttering something about me being right—I should have asked him to repeat it so I could get it "on tape" —Trev goes back to sketching the layout of the streets around the church.

Zephyr's face pops up on my screen. "Tracing the call from Domina's phone was…difficult."

"But not impossible?" I ask.

She frowns, taps her keyboard, and shows me a map of North, South, and Central America. Red dots flash all the way from Canada to Zimbabwe. "They routed the call through a dozen different countries. I had to hack into Domina's mobile carrier, but once I did that, I managed to trace the signal. But they're not taking any chances. The call pinged off five different towers in a ten-mile radius around *your* apartment complex. Best guess? They drove in circles the whole time."

"If she's close—"

Zephyr stares at me, and even over a video call from Boston, her expression is crystal clear. "These guys are pros, Leo. I'd bet all the tea in this city they purposely drove around your building to distract you—us—so we wouldn't look for her anywhere else."

I sit up straighter, rolling my head around until my neck cracks. "Any luck on the video analysis?"

"It's a room," she says with a shrug. "The walls are cherry wood. The tile looks expensive. Only thing I can say for sure? It's small. The way the voices echo, it's less than a hundred square feet. Only a little bigger than a closet. But there was one thing that seemed...*off* to me."

The video pops up on screen. "Look at her face in this last short clip. She might be trying to say something."

The few seconds as she crumples to the floor loops, and I stare at the screen until my eyes water. "What I wouldn't give to be able to read lips."

"What did you just say?" Austin asks. He rounds the table, his gaze pinging between me and Zephyr's face in the little window on my screen.

"Domina's saying—mouthing—something. Look." I nod, and Zephyr starts the clip playing again.

"Fuck me. Send this to Griff. Right now."

"Who the hell is Griff?" I push to my feet, squaring off with Austin. "I don't want *anyone* else involved in this."

Zephyr mutes her mic, but she's clearly talking to someone. And ignoring me.

"Griff is one of my guys," Austin says. "And he's deaf. We're not *involving* him. But if anyone can tell us what she's trying to say, it's him. You want to get her back? This is how we do it. By using all the resources we have—carefully."

"Guys?" Zephyr is practically bouncing in her chair, her voice half an octave higher. "He said he can't be a hundred percent positive, but his best guess is 'Moon Ohs.' Or..."

"Muñoz." I brace my hand on the back of the chair. It's nothing we didn't already suspect, and it doesn't do us much good. But knowing Domina had the presence of mind to send us a message—that they haven't broken her—gives me the smallest shred of hope.

"You're sure that's the only thing she said?" Austin asks. "Play the whole thing again."

Zephyr arches her brows, her lids fluttering like she can't believe Austin doubts her. "I've been over every single second of the vid a hundred times. But sure. Check it again, boss."

I can't watch. If I do, this sliver of light I've found amid the darkness will vanish entirely. Wandering into the kitchen for a glass of water, I can't help but hear her voice—and that of the man with her.

"Enough, bitch!" he snaps.

"*Stupid bitch.*"

"Stop!" I drop the glass onto the counter, and it's a miracle it doesn't shatter into a thousand pieces. "Go back. Two seconds."

"Enough, bitch!"

"I missed it." Back in front of my laptop, I lean down and stare at the man behind Domina. "That's Daniel Pinzon. The asshole who broke into Domina's apartment."

Zephyr's eyes light up, and she smiles. "I can get a list of all of Pinzon's known associates and search for *anything* that ties him to Eduardo Muñoz. Back in a bit, boys. Now, we're getting somewhere."

Domina

Sitting against the wall, hugging my knees to my chest, I close my eyes. Sleeping is out of the question. After they forced me to record a video for Leo, Sergio and Daniel left, but it's been hours—I think—and they could come back any time.

Did Leo understand the one-word message I tried to send him? That Muñoz is the one planning this whole thing? I had no warning before Sergio and Pinzon burst in with a chair and a phone, both wearing black balaclavas and gloves.

If I get another chance, I can say more. I hope. But what? More than a single word, and they'll be able to tell. Pinzon? That will not help.

Tears sting my swollen eyes as I realize just how little I know. Eduardo and Sergio are behind it all. Daniel is the one who took me from the hotel. Gustavo Bernal from Muñoz's campaign is involved somehow. But I do not know where I am. Or if they are going to take me somewhere else before the vote tomorrow. How will they kill me if Leo fails?

Quiet sobs shake my entire body. I drop my head onto my knees. "Stop," I mutter when I have no more tears to cry. "You have been on your own your entire life. You can get through this."

My stomach twists into a knot. My throat is parched. Why didn't I ask Sergio what time it was when he came to make the video? The election will be certified by 8:00 p.m. tomorrow night. Or...is it tonight now?

I use the wall for support and get to my feet. With my swollen ankle, I cannot stand to keep my heels on, so I limp, barefoot, to the door.

Pounding on the dark wood, I shout, "You cannot keep me here with no food and water! Sergio? You need me alive. Please!"

The last thing I want is for Pinzon or Sergio to come back. They could still hurt me—even if they do need me to look... presentable. But I need information, and there is only one way I will get it.

I must bang on the door for a full ten minutes. My arm aches, along with my throat. Maybe using the last of my strength was not a good idea. When I cannot stand any longer, I limp back over to the corner and slide down the wall.

My eyelids are so heavy. Every blink hurts. Maybe sleeping would not be so terrible. Curling into a ball, I try to remember the comfort of Leo's arms around me. His scent. His deep voice. I can almost feel his body pressed to mine.

Until someone kicks me in the ass. "Wake up, Domina," Sergio says sharply. "Time for another video."

I jerk up, and the room starts to spin. "Please," I croak. "I need water. Food. A bathroom."

Sergio pulls out his phone and checks the screen, then turns to Pinzon, who's standing right behind him. "You did not check on her? At all?"

A vein at the thug's temple throbs. "I almost lost an eye because of her."

So quickly, he is only a blur, Sergio punches Pinzon in the stomach. "Fucking idiot. We need her coherent for this."

Pinzon straightens with a groan. "Sorry, boss."

Holding out his hand, Sergio gives me a curt nod. "There is a bathroom right outside the door. I will have a bottle of water brought down after we are done."

I do not want to trust him. But I am too weak to get up on my own, so I place my hand in his.

The bathroom is small. Only a toilet and sink, with no window. Sergio refuses to close the door, but he does turn his back so I can relieve myself with some dignity.

I stick my head under the faucet and manage a couple of sips before he wraps strong fingers around my arm and drags me back to my small prison. Like before, he instructs me to sit in the chair and look only at him.

Pinzon pulls the balaclava over his head, stands behind me, and presses his hands down on my shoulders. I want to squirm, but I force myself to remain as still as possible.

"If you tell him anything about us, we will hurt you before we let you go," Sergio warns. "Badly and for many hours. Do as you are told, and you will go free with nothing but the unpleasant memories of a night spent on this hard floor."

"And you kidnapping me. Feeling me up, hitting me," I mutter. Pinzon squeezes the soft muscles of my shoulders so hard, tears spring to my eyes. "I am sorry! Please..."

With a snap of his fingers, Sergio warns the other man to stop. It takes me several seconds to get my breathing under control again.

"Starting to record...now. Domina, we have a message from Mr. Basher. To prove to him you are still alive, we also allowed him to ask you a question. One you will answer."

I take a shuddering breath as Leo's voice fills the room. "Tell her I'm sorry for failing her. That I'll do what you want because it's the only way to save her."

"And the question? I am losing my patience, Mr. Basher," Sergio says, his voice rough on the recording.

"The night we met...what did I tell her to hang on her chair?"

My tears spill over, and I swipe at my cheeks, wishing I had even another minute to find a way to give him more than a simple answer. But from Sergio's expression, he is already losing patience with me.

"Bells," I whisper. After a hard swallow, I clear my throat. "You told me to put bells on my chair, and it made me feel safe. *You* made me feel safe, Leo. I...I lo—"

Sergio tucks the phone back into his pocket. "That is enough. Daniel, take the chair and retrieve the bottle of water at the top of the stairs for our guest."

I rush to stand before Pinzon yanks the chair out from under me. "Please don't do this. You can still let me go. I...I will leave Panama. With Leo. We will move somewhere far away and you will never see us again."

"Even if I believed *you* would do this," Sergio says, clearly amused, "you have made it very clear that Mr. Basher will kill me for touching you. In fifteen hours, Cortez will die, along with your precious Leo, and there is nothing you can do to stop it."

Pinzon hands Sergio a bottle of water, and the younger man tosses it to me. It is ice cold, and I crack the seal, downing half of it before I realize it tastes...off.

Sergio watches me intently, an emotionless smile curving his lips.

"What did you do?" Fear steals the strength from my voice. I tremble, shrinking into the corner of the room.

"Only a sedative. Tomorrow is a big day for all of us, Domina," he says. "We must be well rested to do our parts. I'm told you will feel the effects in a few minutes, so I suggest you get comfortable."

The door slams shut, and I throw the bottle at it with a scream. I was already dizzy, and my heart races, thudding so hard, I wonder if I will pass out from that alone.

It's hard to keep my eyes open. Hard to think. What did Leo say to me? Did I tell him I love him? I wanted to.

Lying on my side, I try to picture him. His face as he slept. His hand on mine. His lopsided smile.

I hope I see him again. I hope...

CHAPTER THIRTY

Leo

A TINY MOTH clings to the ceiling, opening and closing its wings like it's breathing. Do moths have lungs? Do they breathe? Why don't I know this?

With a groan, I pull Domina's pillow closer to my chest and roll onto my side. The clock on my phone reads 4:03 a.m., and I've only slept in short, fifteen or twenty minute bursts since yesterday morning.

We spent three hours with West on a secure video call going over dozens of ways the plan could go pear-shaped. The former SEAL practically told us we were fools for even *attempting* to do this on our own. Until we shared our theory that my former SSO—a man who still supervises every CIA officer in Venezuela, Panama, Colombia, Ecuador, and Peru —is a piece of shit traitor working for Muñoz.

Before Austin and Trevor ordered me to get some shuteye, we took bets on whether Sampson would ignore orders and show up anyway.

If only I could sleep. I pull my phone off the charger and

bring up the second video of Domina that showed up a little after midnight.

She looks so scared sitting in that plain, wooden chair, Pinzon's hands on her shoulders, tears in her eyes.

My own voice spills from the speaker. "The night we met...what did I tell her to hang on her chair?"

"Bells," she says, so quietly, I have to strain to hear. After a beat, she stares directly at the camera. "You told me to put bells on my chair, and it made me feel safe. *You* made me feel safe, Leo."

Safe, my ass. I couldn't protect her. I was holding her fucking hand when she was ripped away from me.

I watch it another six times, wishing I could talk to her for even a minute. I need her to know I love her, but there's no way in hell I'll pass that information along to the bastards who took her. And even if today *doesn't* end with Manuel Cortez's dead body all over the news, it would take a fucking miracle for me to survive long enough to have Domina in my arms again.

No amount of tossing and turning is going to bring me peace, so I shuffle back out to the living room.

Austin's stretched out on the sofa, his arm flung over his eyes while Trevor uses Street View to "drive" all around the church for the hundredth time.

"Take the bed," I say, dropping into the chair next to him. "I'm not sleeping anyway."

"If we can't get a lock on Domina's location, you're the one who has to get Cortez into Kevlar, fit him with a squib pack, *and* shoot him in the space of thirty seconds." Trev sits back and looks me up and down. "And then run before his security detail puts a bullet in your brain."

"If I have to do all of that, we're fucked and you know it."

His denial rings hollow, and I pull up the new app Zephyr sent to my phone. "You think this thing is going to work?"

"If Zephyr says it's solid, then it's solid. The whole team has been working on a way to speed up traces for a year."

The whole team.

Every few hours, another person logged into the ZEO app and introduced themselves to me. West's wife Cam, who runs one of the leading companies in business security systems, explained how Muñoz's team could hack into the Presidential Palace's security feeds to spy on Garcia and Cortez.

Royce—the guy who designed the GPS trackers—walked Austin through the operation of the state-of-the-art drones he and Trev brought with them. The head of Hidden Agenda K&R, Ryker McCabe, called in a shit ton of favors to get three extra-large Palermo's pizzas delivered a little after 7:00 p.m. Inside the boxes? Two hundred feet of det cord, jammers that won't touch *our* comms units but should disable all other radio and cell signals in a quarter-mile radius, and fifty thousand dollars in cash. Along with enough pizza for ten people.

"Dax called," Trev says on a yawn. "He got in touch with his contacts."

"Can they do it?" Trevor's boss lost his sight at the hands of the Taliban, but in addition to running a private security firm in Boston, he's spent the last seven years building a network of the most influential—and deadly—military vets around the world.

Frowning, Trevor laces his fingers together over his head and stretches from side to side until his back pops. "If you'd asked me that eleven months ago, I'd have said no way in hell. But then Dax and Ry—and you—broke me out of La Crypta. I should be dead. Not coming up on a year with the woman I've loved since I was a teenager."

"Trevor..." I can't ask him to do this. Either of them. Austin's engaged. Trev and Dani might as well be.

"Don't," he says. "We're here, and tonight, we're all leaving this fucking country together. With Domina."

He says something about catching an hour or two and heads down the hall.

That's the plan. Find Domina. Save Cortez. Expose Muñoz. And run.

"Leo? It's time." Austin raps on my bedroom door. By the time the sun came up, I was so exhausted, I fell asleep the moment my head hit the pillow. But now, we only have ninety minutes to get to the church.

"Anything from...*them*?" The last video of Domina came in more than ten hours ago, and I need to see her face one more time before everything goes to shit.

"No." He tosses me an earbud. "Zephyr and Rip are monitoring the cameras all around the church. If they catch *anything*, we'll know in seconds. Get dressed. Wheels up in twenty minutes."

"I need to loosen up," I say, gesturing to the PT equipment along the wall. "Give me ten, and I'll be ready to go."

Grabbing my phone, I lower myself down to the yoga mat. I haven't prayed in two decades, but as I shove one of the studded therapy balls under my right ass cheek, I close my eyes. The words I learned in grade school come back to me, and I hold onto them like they're my last hope.

Once I'm dressed, I join Trevor and Austin in the living room. Six large bags are stacked by the front door, and Trevor passes me a glass filled with a thick, green liquid. "What the hell is this?"

"Energy drink. Bottoms up."

I choke down three sips before I dump the rest down the drain. "I'd rather drink battery acid than that shit."

My phone vibrates, and Austin taps his earbud. "Z? Start a trace."

"Morning, shithead," I say when I answer the call. "Nice of you to finally return my messages."

"I have more important things to do today, Mr. Basher. But since you were so insistent…"

Slamming my fist down on the counter, I let my anger boil over. For the first time since I lost Domina, it serves a purpose.

"Listen, shithead. I'm going to die. You think anyone's going to let me murder Cortez and then just…walk away? I'll either be shot on sight or locked away in one of those Ministry hell holes where I'll be tortured until I don't know my own name. You ever have someone you cared for? Maybe someone you even…loved? Two minutes. Just give me two minutes to talk to her on a live video call. After that, I'll do it. I know how it'll happen, and it'll be a goddamn spectacle. No one in Panama will *ever* forget the day Manuel Cortez died."

The man sighs. "Americans love their profanity, don't they?"

"Give me something to call you besides shithead, and maybe I'll be a little nicer."

"You can call me Jefe."

"Fuck that. Shithead fits you much better. I'll be at the church in half an hour. Have Domina call me before 1:00 p.m. or not only will I walk away, but I'll find you and set your balls on fire before I shove those crispy little fuckers down your throat."

I hang up, and Zephyr's voice in my ears is the sweetest thing I've ever heard. "Got him. Domina's phone is on the Avenida Israel heading into the heart of the city. Time to get the drones in the air. "

Domina

"Get her ready for transport."

Lying on the floor of the van, my wrists bound behind my back, blindfolded, and gagged, I struggle to focus. I remember nothing after Sergio and Pinzon left me alone.

When they woke me—it could not have been more than an hour ago—Sergio dragged me to the bathroom. I was so dizzy, I could barely walk. *"Wash your face and do something with your hair. You are a mess."*

I vaguely remember telling him to go to hell. And his reply.

"Cause any trouble today, and you will get there long before I do."

Turn after turn after turn, I struggle to control my nausea. When they shoved me into the van, the blindfold slipped— only a fraction—enough for me to see a tall, ornate iron fence with large gardenia bushes covering the bars five feet up. Multi-colored flagstones formed a beautiful driveway under my feet. A rich neighborhood. No wonder they gagged me. And did not care if anyone saw them.

I wish I could talk to Leo. Or at least see him. Not knowing what Sergio has planned for me is the worst kind of fear.

Pinzon sits so close, I can smell the detergent he uses. He felt me up again when he bound my wrists. At least my ankles are free. But I do not dare kick or struggle. A third man joined us in the back of the van. I cannot escape. All I can do is listen. And hope I learn *something* that might save Leo before the end.

THE VAN JERKS TO A STOP. Sergio pulls off the blindfold, and I blink hard until his face comes into focus. "Listen very carefully. Cortez is due to cast his vote in the next two hours. Daniel, Charles, and Gustavo will escort you to the ninth floor and stay with you until the Vice President is dead. Screaming will do you no good. You will not be *rescued* by anyone. If Mr. Basher's friends attempt to breach the building, we will know, and you will die. Do exactly what you are told, and we will let you go by the end of the day. Do you understand?"

I nod—what else can I do?—and Sergio rips the duct tape from my lips. "That *hurts!*"

"I am sorry, Domina." He cups my cheek and drags his thumb gently over my mouth. "You are a beautiful woman. Smart. And brave. Perhaps one day, you will see that my father is the leader Panama needs."

"Never." The word escapes on a whisper, and I cringe as Sergio's expression hardens. For a moment, I think he might hit me, but he merely drops his hand and smiles.

"Take her up," he says, and opens the van's back door. Sunlight blinds me, making my eyes water.

Pinzon grabs my arm and drags me to the edge. "Stand, bitch."

I try, but my swollen ankle wobbles, and I pitch forward. Right into Pinzon's chest. He grabs my ass, squeezing hard enough to leave bruises. I swallow my scream.

We're parked in an alley, a large SUV behind us. I can hear cheering—from the church where Manuel will cast his vote? They would want me close, I think. Close enough for Leo to see me die if he refuses to do what they ask.

Pinzon and another man—light skin and distinctly American features—each take one of my arms. We move quickly to a plain door at the back of the building.

It smells like new construction inside. Fresh paint,

sawdust, plastic. My ankle throbs with every step. Why did I insist on wearing heels yesterday? If I had not, perhaps…

Stop. Focus. You have to find a way out of here.

But with three men surrounding me, there is no hope of escape. A bright inspection sticker on the elevator door proclaims it safe—dated only three days ago. No wonder they picked this place. It's empty.

The ride to the ninth floor takes seconds. Down a long hallway, apartment doors on both sides, until we come to Unit 928.

"Bring her to the window," Gustavo says. He locks the apartment door from the inside and wedges a large piece of plywood under the knob. Unzipping a large duffel bag, he removes a rifle, unfolds the stock, and shoves a magazine into the gun.

The American—Charles—grips my arm hard enough to leave a bruise as he and Pinzon drag me across the room.

I look around, praying for my head to clear. It is still so hard to think, but the dizziness has mostly passed. The kitchen is unfinished, wiring exposed on one wall, and the tall window…

Oh, God. No.

It's open, letting a stiff breeze into the room. There is no balcony. No railing. Just a plain, wooden sill that cannot be deeper than ten centimeters in front of a window large enough for even Leo to stand in.

"Up," Pinzon snaps.

I jerk my head up to meet his hungry gaze. "It is too narrow. I will fall!"

"That's the idea." He and Charles lift me.

Kicking at them, I scream. "No! Stop! Please!"

"Fuck this," Pinzon mutters when I catch him in the chest. I collapse onto the dusty tile, jarring my shoulder.

Charles pulls a zip tie from his pocket and binds my

ankles. I am going to die. I know it now. They will shove me out the window and I will fall to my death without ever seeing Leo again.

There is no reason to fight. When they lift me, I let them. Charles positions me on the left side of the open window. My heels slip, and Pinzon wrenches my feet so they form a wide *v*.

My legs shake, even after only a minute. All I can do is lean against the sill and pray for strength.

Two blocks away, hundreds of people line up at the church's meeting space to cast their votes. I am so high up, the building so new, that no one will think to look for me here. But the men who took me will tell Leo. I am certain of it. So he can see how much danger I am in. And see me fall.

"If you move," Pinzon says, positioning a large, rolling tool cart next to the window then sitting in a chair behind it, "you will fall. If Charles lets go, you will fall. And if you try to get down? Try to jump back into the room? Once Cortez dies, we will make you wish you had died too."

CHAPTER THIRTY-ONE

Leo

THE STREETS around the Church of the Holy Trinity are packed with people. Only a few thousand are actual voters. The rest are here to see Manuel Cortez cast his vote.

"Base to Alpha Team," Zephyr says in my ear. "Cameras just caught a caravan of six black SUVs leaving Cortez's home."

"I thought he wasn't there. The thermal scans—"

"Those SUVs are a decoy. If he's where we think he was all night," she says, "another group of vehicles will join up with the caravan in five minutes."

"And then?" Austin asks. He and Trevor dropped me off six blocks from the church. By now, they should be in position. Trev in the bell tower—with the best ear protection money can buy—and Austin at the other end of the street.

"They'll be at the church in fifteen minutes. Max."

I pull out my phone and launch one of the half-dozen apps Zephyr and the rest of the team sent us overnight. The wheel on screen spins for a full thirty seconds, and then turns green. No one's listening in on us. Yet.

Standing at the fringes of the crowd, I pull a large Bluetooth earbud and hook it over my ear before pulling up my text app.

Leo: Hey, shithead. If I don't talk to Domina in the next ten minutes, I walk.

I pat my jacket pocket, then my hip. I have enough weapons strapped to my body to take down a small army, but none of them will do me a damn bit of good if I can't get to Domina in time.

Carefully, I make my way closer to the large, squat building the church uses for bible study and community events. Dozens of National Police in full riot gear patrol the area. If the tinted glasses and the fake cast on my arm don't disguise me enough, shit could go sideways in a hurry.

My phone rings, sending my heart shooting into my throat.

Incoming video call.

It's not from Domina's phone. That would be too simple. Tapping a button on my watch—launching the app that Zephyr and Royce developed to speed up cellular triangulation—I answer.

"Domina!" Fuck, fuck, fuck. She's terrified. Wind whips her hair, and she's pressed against a thin expanse of unfinished wood. A man grips her right arm, but to her left... there's nothing but sky behind her.

"Leo?" Her voice trembles. Tears spill onto her cheeks, glistening in the sun. "Please...don't do this."

The asshole at her side gives her arm a hard shake, and she yelps until he pushes her back against the wood. Oh, God. He's not wearing a mask. She's seen his face. She's seen *all* their faces.

"I have to. If there's a *chance* they'll let you go, I'll do anything."

"No, no, no," she cries. "Not this. You said you wanted something real. You can still have that. Just...not with me. Walk away and—"

"Domina, look at me." I hold the phone closer, moving back to the edge of the crowd so it's quieter. "When this is all over, I want you to go somewhere to see the stars. Can you do that for me, baby? Try that bar we found the other day. Remember the one?"

"The...bar?" She's so confused, and I squint at the phone. Her eyes are cloudy, almost unfocused. Shit. I'm going to lose her if I can't make her understand.

"Yes, baby. The bar where we saw all those stars. You can find that, can't you?"

Please, Domina. Put it together. Stars and Bars. Austin.

"Y-yes. I...I think so. The one...with Superman on the wall..."

Thank fuck. She remembered Trev's code name.

"Good." In my ear, Zephyr tells me Cortez's motorcade is less than ten minutes out. "Domina? Fuck. I have to go soon."

It doesn't matter that we have a plan. That Zephyr's tracing the call. That we have five people in Seattle trying to match the view behind Domina to a location if the trace fails. That Dax worked a goddamn miracle with his contacts. Or that there's no fucking way I'm going to murder the future President of Panama when I know I could lose Domina anyway.

The lump in my throat is the size of the moon, and tears burn my eyes. "This isn't how I wanted it to go. I'd do anything to be able to hold you right now, but I can't."

On screen, she sobs so hard I'm terrified she's going to fall. If it weren't for that asshole holding her, she'd already be dead.

"I love you, Domina. What we had...it was real. It was everything."

"L-love...you...too." Someone yanks the phone away, and she screams, "Leo!"

A second later, a man snaps, "Shut up before I let you go." *The idiot holding her is American.*

Daniel Pinzon's face fills the screen, and I want to punch all his teeth out for his gleeful smile. "If you or your friends even *try* to get to her, she dies." He turns the camera to show me the street below. They're so high, she'd never survive a fall. Panning back up, he focuses on Domina's feet. Her scuffed heels. The narrow window ledge. The zip tie around her ankles. How much she's shaking.

"This building is empty. We will know if anyone tries to break in. And then she will fall."

"Listen, shithead—I know that's your boss's name, but it fits you too—if she dies, you better run as far and as fast as you can, because I have friends. Friends who will *never* stop looking for you. And when they find you, they'll have a contest to see which one of them can carve you into the smallest pieces possible, and how long they can keep you alive while they do it."

"Watch it," Austin warns. "Don't give that idiot an excuse to drop her."

Pinzon just laughs. "Better work fast. Time is running out." He flips the camera once more to show a full body shot of Domina on the ledge. The American hides behind the wall, forcing Domina a few inches from the side of the window. Her entire body shakes. A zip tie binds her wrists. She's completely helpless up there. Nowhere she can go but down.

Before I can say "I love you" one last time, the call drops.

"Shithead gave us everything," I hiss. "Tell me you have her location." Dropping the Bluetooth on the ground, I crush it with my boot. The less tech on me that *didn't* come from my team, the better.

"Two blocks south, one block east," Trev answers. "Got eyes on her from the bell tower. The door's blocked. There's a third man in the room with an AR-15 trained on her. But he's in my sights. The other two…"

Ryker McCabe cuts in to our comms channel. "Pinzon—fucking coward— is hiding behind a tool chest, and the other one—some former CIA pissant named Charles Thomas—is pressed so tight against the wall, the only part of him exposed is his arm. Not even Inara could guarantee kills with how they're positioned."

And if we try, Domina could fall. Will fall.

He doesn't have to say the words. We all know the deal.

"Plan A or Plan B?" Austin asks.

I turn in a slow circle, scanning the crowds, clocking each member of the National Police, the IPS agents standing just inside the open double doors of the meeting space, and Domina. She's only a flash of dark hair over a white blouse and crimson skirt from this far away, but I know she's there. And she can see everything.

My watch buzzes. On the screen, a pulsing blue blip hovers over a map of the city. Moving south at a fast clip.

"Plan C. We're going rogue."

Zephyr activates the signal jammers as I push my way through the crowd. If Austin doesn't move his ass, we're all in deep shit. But thirty seconds later, I hear, "On my way to the roof."

Running my fingers over the det cord in my pocket, I pray to all that's holy in this world he can get there in time. We only have one shot at this, and if we're off by even a few seconds, Domina will pay the price.

Four black SUVs pull up next to the church's meeting space. I pass my fake ID to a poll worker, and he scans a thick stack of printouts to match my name and address to this district. "Enter to the left, Mr. Cameron," he says, exhaustion evident in his voice. "Keep the line moving."

"Cortez is being escorted into the building now," Zephyr says. "Through the back. And you've got a tail. Sergio Munoz. The candidate's son. Eight o'clock."

Perfect. Mr. Smooth Talker had to come see the spectacle firsthand.

"I can't wait to knock that little shit on his ass and tell him daddy lost because he couldn't keep his mouth shut," I mutter.

In the voting booth, I pull the det cord from my pocket and drape it along the edges of the table. Leaving the timer under the ballot, I finger the switch.

Cortez waves to the crowd with both hands, his fingers forming twin *Vs* in the air. The IPS agent at his side leads him to a booth twenty feet away.

I scan the room, pen poised over the ballot.

"Sergio is directly on your six now," Zephyr says.

"Jimmy? Tell me you're in position." I can't make a move until I know there's at least a chance Domina will live through this.

"Waiting for your signal," Austin says. "Superman?"

"Third man in the room is an idiot. He's begging for two between the eyes."

This is it. In under three minutes, I'll know if Dax is as good as Trevor claims he is. And whether I have a future with the woman I love.

The lights in the building flicker—Zephyr's doing—but no one seems to notice. Except for the suited IPS agent next to Cortez's booth. His gaze swings from one end of the room to the other until it lands on me.

My watch counts down, and when it hits sixty seconds, I

flick the switch on the timer, then reach into my jacket pocket for the small flash-bang grenade.

Shuffling slowly from the booth, I wait until my watch starts buzzing for the last ten seconds of the countdown before I pick up the pace.

Shit. An older woman halfway across the room makes a beeline for the vacant space. Now or never.

The flash-bang sails all the way to the back wall. My lenses turn opaque, and I jam my palms over my ears. The percussive blast disorients me for a split second, but I whip off the glasses, then grab the elderly woman and shield her with my body before the explosion turns the booth into nothing but splinters and burning paperboard.

Cortez is flat on the ground, three agents lying on top of him, shielding him with their bodies. The fourth—the one watching me—draws his weapon. His eyes blaze, and he takes aim.

"Jimmy!" I hiss. "Go. Go now!"

"Three seconds, Superman," Austin says. "Get ready to burn the whole fucking thing to the ground."

Domina

My thighs shake, the muscles ready to give out. Until several loud bangs—so much louder than I thought they would be— echo through the streets. "No!" I scream.

Charles tightens his grip on my arm. Behind the toolbox, Pinzon jabs his phone screen. "I can't reach Sergio. The call won't go through." I do not dare turn my head to look at him. If I move, I will fall. But the anger in his voice... "Something's wrong. Gustavo. Toss me your phone."

A strange sound pierces the air. Not a whistle. Almost a whisper. Then another.

Screams come from the church. Leo...I will never see him again. My sobs turn into a wail.

I'm flying. Unable to draw a breath. The impact drives the air from my lungs. Twisting, rolling. I squeeze my eyes shut, not wanting to see the ground rushing up to meet me.

A heavy weight presses down on me. Is this what death is?

Four quick shots—so close they hurt my ears—shock me enough to risk opening my eyes. I'm on the floor of the unfinished apartment. Under...

"Austin?" I gasp. "How...?"

He smiles, still shielding me with his body. "Target secure. Hostiles neutralized."

It's only then I notice the rope stretching out the window and up. I must be hallucinating. Am I dying? If this were real, Leo would be here. Wouldn't he?

"You're going to be okay now," he says as he rolls off of me. "Let's get you out of here."

I start to shake—or maybe I never stopped—and black spots float in front of my eyes. I blink hard, and he's still here. Helping me sit up. Cutting the ties from my wrists.

Pinzon and Charles are dead. Blood pools under their bodies. I twist, desperate to see the third man.

"Hey," Austin says, his voice gentle. "Don't look. It's not pretty. He's dead, and none of these assholes will ever hurt you again."

I want to hug him. I would, if my arms weren't numb. "But," I manage through my shock, "you're...Stars and Bars. Not Superman."

He laughs, snaps the plastic around my ankles, and nods toward the window. "Maybe just for today, Superman won't mind sharing the secret identity."

CHAPTER THIRTY-TWO

Leo

No matter how many times you've done it, staring down the barrel of a gun is enough to make a man's balls crawl back inside his body. For a split second, I wonder if everything is about to go to shit.

The shot should be louder. I almost laugh at the thought. But I did just set off six feet of det cord *and* a flash-bang grenade. My hearing might be fucked.

"Take him!" Agent Balboa shouts, and I watch as a swarm of National Police converge on Sergio Munoz. Blood stains his side. One of the officers leans down and grabs the pistol Sergio dropped when he was shot, and tucks it into his pocket.

"Mr. Basher." Agent Balboa holsters his weapon and offers me his hand. "I don't know how you pulled this off, but the Vice President is in your debt."

Cortez tries to get the rest of his detail to let him up, but they ignore his orders.

"The *President-Elect* can thank me later. I have somewhere I have to be."

Balboa could still have me detained. Vandalizing a polling place is a serious crime, but he merely nods and ushers me to the side door. "Expect a call this evening, Mr. Basher. And stay available."

We'll see about that.

"Target location," I demand as I toss the fake cast in the gutter and take off at a run. Every step sends shooting pains down my right leg, but I don't care how much it hurts. Austin confirmed she was safe, but I won't believe it until she's in my arms.

"Atrium," Austin says. "Front door's wide open and we're waiting for you."

The sidewalks are too crowded. People running from the explosion, locals pouring from buildings to see what all the commotion is about.

I give up fighting my way through and veer into the street. Dodging cars is a dangerous game, but there are fewer of them.

The apartment building comes into view, the first story nothing but glass walls from floor to ceiling.

And then I see her.

Domina sits on a stack of pallets, shoulders hunched, arms wrapped tightly around herself. Austin stands next to her, one hand on her shoulder, the other at his side—holding his Sig Sauer.

I skid to a stop in the doorway, suddenly afraid to touch her. I don't know a damn thing about what she's been through the past twenty-four hours. But her gaze locks onto mine, and the desperate need churning in her red-rimmed eyes...I can't wait another second to have her in my arms.

"Leo," she whimpers and tries to get to her feet. But she wobbles, and I catch her when she falls. "I thought...I heard the shots. Austin said you were okay, but..." Sobs wrack her body. Domina buries her face against the curve of my neck, and her tears soak into the collar of my shirt.

"I know, baby. But I'm here now. You're safe. It's over."

She stiffens. "It's not. Muñoz is behind all of this." Trembling fingers skim the back of my neck, but she doesn't raise her head. "His son...he's the one who took me. He and the man who broke into my apartment."

"Shhh. I know. Sergio is in custody. And..." I glance over her shoulder at my watch, "his father is about to find out how much pain a Navy SEAL can cause with just his thumbs."

* * *

Domina

Nothing seems real. Not Leo's arm around me. Not the plush, smooth ride of the SUV, not the banter coming from the front seat. Trevor and Austin relive the past few hours like they were some sort of video game, and all I want is to sleep.

The car rolls to a gentle stop, and I lift my head from Leo's shoulder. "Where are we?" Even that simple question takes more energy than I have, but I don't recognize the area. We're nowhere near our apartment building.

"The Five Points Hotel," Leo says and presses a kiss to the top of my head. "We're going in the service entrance, then straight up to the penthouse suite."

"The penthouse? Why can't we go home?"

"Still too many moving pieces to risk it. We'll be safe here until we hear from Cortez—and the rest of the team."

Rest. I need to rest. But not as much as I need a shower. Clean clothes. Food. And to understand how Leo and I are both alive—and together.

"Put your arms around my neck," he says. "I've got you."

He's solid and strong, his skin warm under my touch. Every part of my body hurts, but when Leo carries me, I feel like I'm floating. Like my feet will never touch the ground again.

My eyes flutter closed. He'll take care of everything. I know he will.

The elevator hums for several long moments, then jerks to a stop. Leo's uneven gait almost lulls me to sleep until Trevor says something about checking the suite before we enter.

"Clear," he calls.

I smell flowers. Lilies, I think. Forcing my head up, I blink hard. Plush, beige carpeting, a dramatic living space with sweeping views of the ocean, overstuffed couches, and through an open door, there's even a kitchen.

"You and Domina are on the left," Austin says to Leo. "I'm on the right, and Trev's got one of the rooms downstairs. Head to the back of the kitchen to get there."

One of the rooms?

Before I can ask just how big this suite is, Leo's headed for "our" room.

As exhausted as I am, the strange surroundings have me on edge. Until Leo kicks the door closed and sinks down onto a love seat with me in his lap.

He tucks a lock of hair behind my ear and holds my gaze. "I thought I'd lost you," he says, his deep voice rough.

"I thought you had too." Fresh tears spill onto my cheeks. I don't have to be strong anymore. I'm with Leo, and though I have so many questions—how they found me, what's going to happen to the men Austin and Trevor killed in that apartment, how Cortez is alive when I heard all those shots and explosions, what's going to happen now—I do know one thing.

I love this man. I can shatter into a million pieces in Leo's arms, because he'll be here to help put me back together.

Leo

Domina jerks awake with a whimper.

"Easy, baby. You're safe." I pull her against my chest, tangling my fingers in her hair. "Breathe for me."

She shudders. Under the light-as-air duvet, she finally started to warm up an hour ago, but after what she went through, the adrenaline crash hit her hard. I need to get some food into her, but after a hot bath—where she sobbed in my arms until she had nothing left—she was so tired, she fell asleep the second I wrapped her in one of the hotel's fluffy robes.

"We're really safe?" she asks.

I nod. "Austin and Trev are in the next room. Along with a retired Navy SEAL who—in his spare time—teaches Krav Maga to some of the deadliest men in the world. No one's ever going to hurt you again. I promise."

"What am I wearing?" Domina wriggles out of my arms and pushes up on an elbow.

"The Five Points has really nice robes."

"Then why are you naked?" The barest hint of a smile curves her lips, and pieces of my shattered heart start to mend.

"Because holding you was a hell of a lot more important than putting on a pair of boxers." I drag a knuckle along her jaw and she leans in. We haven't talked. Haven't kissed. I don't know what happened to her in the twenty-four hours we were apart, but if her half-lidded eyes and parted lips are any indication, she needs this as much as I do.

Domina straddles me, plundering my mouth until I'm rock hard for her. "I need you, Leo," she whispers, kissing her way down my neck to my shoulder.

"Wait." I wrap my arms around her and roll onto my side. "We have all the time in the world. Austin texted half an hour ago and said he was ordering takeaway. Thai, I think. Did..." Fuck. I don't know how to ask, but I have to. "Did they feed you at all?"

She shakes her head. "N-no. But..." The desperation in her voice breaks me. "I need to know...this is real."

"I'm real, baby. *We* are real." Cupping the back of her neck, I hold her gaze for a long moment. How did I not see it when I first got her back? The uncertainty in her eyes? "I want you like I want my next breath, but...we should join the others. You'll feel better once you eat something—and we explain everything that happened after they took you."

Domina flinches.

Fuck. Be sensitive, asshole.

"Okay," she says quietly. "But you will stay with me?"

I touch my lips to hers. "Always. I love you, Domina. If you aren't sure about anything else, be sure of one thing. You're it for me. For as long as you'll have me, I'm yours."

BEFORE WE LEFT my apartment this morning, I packed a bag for both of us, and Domina lets me help her into a pair of yoga pants and a crimson t-shirt. Her ankle is still swollen, her wrists rubbed raw, and she stood on that fucking window ledge for at least two hours. So I keep my arm around her waist to steady her until we reach one of the sofas in the suite's main room.

She tenses when she sees Sampson. SEALs—even retired ones—have this look about them. One that says they could make you disappear without a trace and not even break a sweat. But he stands the moment we exit our bedroom, his hands clasped behind his back.

"Domina. I'm West. I've worked with Trevor a time or two." His slight Southern twang helps put her at ease—or maybe that has more to do with the dozen takeaway containers on the large, circular coffee table and the scent of Pad Thai.

She nods, but presses closer to me.

"West landed just before Pinzon let me talk to you. He went directly to Muñoz's house. We knew Sergio was at the church, but Eduardo...we had to neutralize him at the same time as everyone else."

"Neutralize?" Domina's voice cracks, and I rub circles over her back.

"He's alive," West says. "Killing him would have been too easy. And turned him into a martyr. Panama's new president can put him on trial and show the people who they *could* have elected. Cortez will be a hero, and Muñoz won't breathe free air for the rest of his natural life.

Over plates of pad thai, bowls of tom yum soup, and double helpings of mango sticky rice, the four of us explain how we managed to keep Cortez alive long enough to get to her.

"Dax—he's Trev's boss—spent half the night working his contacts. He and Ryker were Special Forces, so he knows *everyone.* Including Agent Ricardo Balboa of the Institutional Protection Service."

Austin cracks the seal on a bottle of Perrier and passes it to Domina. "Balboa joined Cortez's detail before the press conference at the hotel. He saw Pinzon and Sergio take you. Figured out Muñoz was behind it all. We couldn't get in touch with Cortez directly because Balboa insisted he go completely dark until the vote. But Dax was able to get a message through."

"And...how did you find me?" she asks.

I shake my head, still in awe of the men and women who put everything on the line for us. "Zephyr and Royce—he used to work with Cam, West's wife—developed a way to speed up mobile phone traces. We were hoping it would help us find you last night, but Sergio only called me when he was driving around the city and he had some high-level tech on his side. Pinzon—the dumbass—decided to show off and let us see everything around you.

Domina shrinks back against the cushions, cradling the green glass bottle to her chest. "I don't know where I was before the apartment. Except...in a basement."

After a quick glance at me, asking for approval, I think, West clears his throat. "You were in a storage closet at Muñoz's house. We found your jacket and the broken zip ties."

"Sergio and Pinzon blindfolded me," she whispers. The bottle of water shakes in her grip. I need her to tell me *everything* she went through, but I can't ask. Not yet.

"They're gone," Austin says as I steady her hand. "You were pretty out of it when I got to you, but Trev shot the guy behind you, and I took out Pinzon and Chuck Thomas, a former CIA field officer."

"And Sergio?" she asks.

West snorts. "From what Ry said, Sergio sweet-talked a nurse and got out of his restraints, but then he tackled one of the National Police officers guarding his hospital room."

"So he's..." Domina looks from me to West and back again.

The former SEAL leans forward, elbows on his knees. His voice gentles, but the look in his eyes is deadly serious. "Three officers tried to get him to listen to reason before they opened fire. Sergio knew he was going to prison. Probably knew it wouldn't be one of the good ones. He made his choice."

Austin's tablet beeps, and he taps the screen. "It's Zephyr."

"Put her on speaker," I say. As fragile as Domina's control is right now, I won't keep secrets from her. She needs to know everything.

"Got an update on that CIA piece of shit, Balin," Zephyr says, then swears under her breath. "Shit. Domina. Are you okay?"

"Y-yes?" She looks to me, and I drape my arm around her shoulders. "What...CIA piece of shit? The man from the apartment?"

"No, baby. God, there's so much I still need to tell you. Remember when we talked to Cortez at your office? And he knew everything about me?" After she nods, I blow out a breath. "He'd talked to my former SSO. Senior service officer. The guy I reported to for my last six years in Venezuela."

Confusion furrows her brows. "And that makes him a 'piece of shit'?"

"No, but him working with Muñoz does. And handing my dossier over to the Ministry of Public Service." I flex my free hand, trying to banish the memory of that long, painful night shackled to a table in the Ministry's custody.

"He confessed to everything," Zephyr says with a grin. "Tank and Ford—they work for Dax—paid him a visit. He's going to prison for a very long time."

THE LIGHTS of the city twinkle against an inky black sky by the time Domina stops asking questions. She's calmer now— not quite steady, but no longer shaking—and I'm about to suggest we call it a night when there's a knock at the door.

In under five seconds, Austin, Trev, and West have taken up defensive positions around the room, and I scoop Domina into my arms and crouch with her behind the bar.

"Identify yourself," Austin calls, his Sig Sauer aimed right at the peep hole.

"Manuel Cortez. May I come in?"

My phone vibrates, and I check the screen. The camera Trev installed above the suite's door shows the Vice President standing alone, hands at his sides.

"It's him. Stand down," I call and help Domina to her feet. "You okay with a visitor?"

She's exhausted. Every time she moves, small lines of pain tighten around her eyes. But she nods and links her fingers with mine. "I want to see him."

Manuel moves with all the speed of a man who's run a marathon. Or four. But he's relaxed in a way I haven't seen since I met him.

West and Trevor stand guard at the door, keeping all the IPS agents outside except for Balboa.

"Domina," he says, approaching like he's about to hug her, "I am so sorry." She looks vaguely uncomfortable with him so close, so I drape my arm around her shoulders and he stops. "Can you forgive me?"

For a long moment, the two stare at one another. And then Domina nods. "You did not hurt me, Manuel. There is nothing to forgive."

I want to argue with her. To yell at both Cortez and Balboa and ask them why they refused to take our calls the previous night. To remind them the only reason the Vice President is alive right now is because a man I've never met called in a favor the size of the Chrysler Building to reach Balboa so we could coordinate a fake assassination if we couldn't find Domina in time.

But the President-Elect carries enough guilt in his eyes.

"I owe you an apology as well, Leo. I should have known the video from the rally was fake. I should have demanded the Ministry release you. I made many mistakes this week. Mistakes that could have ended many lives."

He's telling the truth, so I nod. "We're square, sir. As long as no one minds that I blew up a polling place this afternoon."

He laughs, and much of the tension in the room fades. "I made a rather generous donation to the Church of the Holy Trinity. They will build a new recreational center after the holidays. You are, however, lucky you did not destroy any ballot boxes. That...might have been more difficult to overlook. Though I won with close to sixty percent of the votes. So..." With a smile, he turns and heads for the door. "Thanks to you, my opponent will be in jail for a *very* long time." Pausing with his hand on the knob, he meets my gaze. "You will always have a friend in the Presidential Palace, Leo. But... try to stay out of trouble from now on."

"I plan on it, sir. Thank you."

EPILOGUE

Domina

THREE TIMES, I woke in the middle of the night. Once, my scream brought Trevor, Austin, *and* West bursting into the room. All of them shirtless.

I gaped at the sight of all those muscles, until I realized I was only wearing a thin tank top and panties. Then I hid behind Leo until we were alone again.

The bedside clock reads 8:14 a.m. West is flying back to Seattle this morning, but Austin and Trevor are staying for at least another day or two—long enough they can work with the National Police and find anyone else who might have been working with Muñoz. I feel better knowing they will be close—even once we return to Leo's apartment. Or mine.

"Morning," Leo mumbles and drapes his arm around my waist.

I could get used to this. Waking up with this man. But though we said the words more than once yesterday, I need to know it was real. That he did not tell me he loved me because we came so close to losing one another, but because he truly means it.

"What happens now?" I ask. Unable to look at him, I pin my gaze to the silver and glass light fixture on the ceiling.

Leo sits up, shoves a pillow behind his back, and gathers me in his arms. "Now? Austin is going back to the apartment to make sure it's safe. But we can stay here as long as you want." He shakes his head gently. "West's wife designs security and alarm systems for big businesses. The Five Points uses her for all of their hotels worldwide. This room isn't costing us a damn thing."

"Nothing?" Shock temporarily distracts me from the real question. The one he did *not* answer.

"Not a cent. She made a call, and lucky for us, the suite was empty. They texted us the door codes, and that was it." He runs a rough palm down my arm. "You're cold."

I pull the duvet up to my shoulders, though the temperature in the room has little to do with the goosebumps covering my skin. It takes me several minutes to work up the courage to meet his gaze.

I'm struck by the difference in his eyes. How bloodshot the left is, and the perfectness of his prosthetic. I haven't noticed—or cared—about his injuries or scars since he showed up at my office after the break-in. But now, a pang of guilt hits me. I never asked if *he* was okay. If he'd been injured. If he was in pain.

"Leo—" I cup his cheek, and he stares at my wrist. At the bright red welt from the zip ties. "Don't," I say and nudge his chin up.

"I should have protected you," he whispers.

Before I can protest, he eases me against the pillows and stumbles toward the bathroom. He almost makes it, but his right leg gives out two steps from the door.

"Dios mio." I get to my feet, ignoring the pain in my ankle, and grab his arm. "Get on the bed. Lie on your stomach."

He opens his mouth to argue with me, but I level a stern gaze at him until his shoulders slump and he half crawls, half limps back to bed.

Kneeling next to him, I start massaging his right calf. The hard, tight muscles—along with the man—turn to putty under my fingers, and by the time I reach his ass, I am brave enough to confess my fears.

"Turn over?" Stretching out next to him, I stroke my hand over his torso. His chest hair tickles my palm. After I press a kiss to his shoulder, I take a deep breath. "What happens with *us* now?"

"Us?" Fear roughens his tone. He slides his fingers into my hair, twisting them so I cannot pull away. The control soothes me in a way I never expected I would want, but now, desperately crave. "I love you, Domina. I'll spend every day for the rest of my life telling you—showing you—if you'll let me."

"After everything," I manage over the lump in my throat, "do you even want to stay in Panama?"

"This is your home, baby. If you want to stay, then so do I." A lopsided smile curves his lips. "Might need to get Cortez to smooth things over with the CIA's Chief of Station, but that should be easy enough. Hard to ignore a call from the President of Panama."

"What if I don't know?" With a sigh, I lay my head on his chest. "I love my job, Leo. But maybe it's time for me to move on. To do something that lets me relax. See my friends. Travel. With you."

His firm lips press to my forehead. "I'm yours," he says. "As long as we're together, wherever we go, whatever we do... I'm yours."

"I don't have to decide now, do I?" Hooking my leg over

his, I savor the way my core clenches and the thin silk of his boxers strains against his hard length.

Leo grins and frames my face with his hands. "The only decision we need to make right now is who gets to be on top."

AFTERWORD

Thank you for reading Rogue Defender. Leo and Domina's story was such a joy to tell, and I hope you enjoyed it as much as I enjoyed getting to know the two of them.

If you're curious about the other members of Leo's team (family, really), you can find their books below. All of my Away from Keyboard and Gone Rogue books are standalones, but family is so important to all of them, that past characters always show up again eventually.

Austin and Mik - Rogue Protector

Griff and Sloane - Rogue Officer

Trevor and Dani - Call Sign: Redemption

Ronan and Zephyr - Protecting His Target

West and Cam - Breaking His Code

Ryker and Wren - On His Six

Royce and Inara - In Her Sights

You can find a complete list of all the Gone Rogue and Away From Keyboard books (and couples and reading order) on my website at https://patriciadeddy.com.

Stay tuned for the next book in the Gone Rogue Series, Rogue Operator!

And for all the latest news, I hope you'll consider joining my newsletter list (sign up on my website) and my Unstoppable Forces Facebook group!

Thank you so much for reading!

ACKNOWLEDGMENTS

This book would not be what it is today without the help of some very special people.

Lauren: You are always a force for good and positivity and light in my writing, and I am so very thankful for all of your help and cheerleading.

Sam: There are days you keep me sane. Thank you for identifying the one thing I was missing in a crucial chapter. It turned my entire day around. Your friendship and tireless support mean the world to me.

Aarti: Our friendship brings me so much joy. We met at the perfect time, and I am so very thankful to have you in my life.

And finally, my bestie.

Jill: I know our lives have been so busy of late, we haven't had the time to just...talk. But that's the best part of being besties—picking up right where we left off when life lets us breathe again. Love you!

ABOUT THE AUTHOR

Patricia D. Eddy writes romance for the beautifully broken. Fueled by coffee, wine, and Doctor Who episodes on repeat, she brings damaged heroes and heroines together to find their happy ever afters in many different worlds. From military to paranormal to BDSM, her characters are unstoppable forces colliding with such heat, sparks always fly.

Patricia makes her home in Seattle with her husband and very spoiled cats, and when she's not writing, she loves working on home improvement projects, especially if they involve power tools.

Her award-winning *Away From Keyboard* series will always be her first love, because that's where she realized the characters in her head were telling their own stories—and she was just writing them down.

You can reach Patricia all over the web...
patriciadeddy.com
patricia@patriciadeddy.com

facebook.com/patriciadeddyauthor

twitter.com/patriciadeddy

instagram.com/patriciadeddy

bookbub.com/profile/patricia-d-eddy

tiktok.com/@patriciadeddyauthor

ALSO BY PATRICIA D. EDDY

Away From Keyboard

Dive into a steamy mix of geekery and military prowess with the men and women of Hidden Agenda and Second Sight.

Breaking His Code

In Her Sights

On His Six

Second Sight

By Lethal Force

Fighting For Valor

Finding Their Forevers (a holiday short story)

Call Sign: Redemption

Braving His Past

Protecting His Target

Defending His Hope

Gone Rogue (an Away From Keyboard spinoff series)

Rogue Protector

Rogue Officer

Rogue Survivor

Rogue Defender

Dark PNR

These novellas will take you into the darker side of the paranormal with vampires, witches, angels, demons, and more.

Forever Kept

Immortal Hunter

Wicked Omens

Storm of Sin

By the Fates

Check out the COMPLETE By the Fates series if you love dark and steamy tales of witches, devils, and an epic battle between good and evil.

By the Fates, Freed

Destined: A By the Fates Story

By the Fates, Fought

By the Fates, Fulfilled

In Blood

If you love hot Italian vampires and and a human who can hold her own against beings far stronger, then the In Blood series is for you.

Secrets in Blood

Revelations in Blood

Holidays and Heroes

Beauty isn't only skin deep and not all scars heal. Come swoon over sexy vets and the men and women who love them.

Mistletoe and Mochas

Love and Libations

Restrained

Do you like to be tied up? Or read about characters who do? Enjoy a fresh COMPLETE BDSM series that will leave you begging for more.

In His Silks

Christmas Silks

All Tied Up For New Year's

In His Collar